Two Graves Dug

Two Graves Dug

Penny Mickelbury

Five Star • Waterville, Maine

First Edition, Second Printing.

Published in 2005 in conjunction with Tekno Books and Ed Gorman.

Set in 11 pt. Plantin by Minnie B. Raven.

Printed in the United States on permanent paper.

Library of Congress Cataloging-in-Publication Data

Mickelbury, Penny, 1948–
    Two graves dug / by Penny Mickelbury.—1st ed.
      p. cm.
    ISBN 1-59414-301-3 (hc : alk. paper)
    1. Private investigators—New York (State)—
New York—Fiction.   2. Lower East Side (New York, N.Y.)—Fiction.   3. Serial rape investigation—Fiction. 4. Girls—Crimes against—Fiction.   5. Puerto Ricans—Fiction.   I. Title.
PS3563.I3517T94 2005
813′.54—dc22   2005006641

Two Graves Dug

Chapter One

Carmine Aiello is a lowlife. I know this because not only do I know Carmine personally, I'd also heard about him years before I met him, like you do when you grow up in a neighborhood where everybody knows everybody else, or knows enough about them to think they know them, and what I know about Carmine is this: he's a whiner and a complainer and a coward, and he'd be dead if he wasn't connected. He's a low-level player in one of the low-level crime families—the kind of jerks who brag about their proximity to John Gotti so long and hard, you know Gotti wouldn't recognize them if he tripped over them; the kind of creeps who walk around calling people spics and niggers. The only reason one of us hasn't popped him is because it would be a waste of good ammunition.

A few years back, a couple of East Village skinheads caught him in an alley between Grant Park and Avenue B and beat the shit out of him, helping themselves in the process to his jewelry, his wallet, his snakeskin Tony Lamas, and his leather jacket. Carmine screeched like a damsel tied to the railroad tracks and tried to convince the world that his assailants were "a gang of spics and niggers," even though everybody knew it was the skins, and so much did nobody give a shit that the white punks weren't even challenged for doing a job off turf. Not even Carmine's own crew cared.

So. All that to say I wasn't any too pleased to hear three times in one morning that Carmine Aiello was looking to talk to me. I live exactly eight blocks—five long crosstown blocks and three short uptown blocks—from my office. I wasn't two blocks from home before the first message came my way, courtesy of Willie One Eye at the newsstand where I buy my papers every morning—the *Times*, the *Daily News*, the *Wall Street Journal*, and *El Diario*. At the next corner, where I flirt with Mrs. Campos and buy fresh orange and carrot juice, I got the evil eye instead of a wicked wink, and the instructions, grudgingly shoved through clenched lips, that I was to call "that Carmine asshole" as soon as I got to my office. By the time I made the uptown turn and my third and final stop—a respect call at Itchy Johnson's shoeshine parlor and barber shop—I was so pissed off that I barely heard his growled, "What the hell does that ugly piece of shit want with you?" I was thinking two things: that I needed to alter my morning routine, and that I'd have to pay a visit to Carmine Aiello. Soon.

That's what I was thinking when I stopped in front of my building and surveyed it with pride, as I did every morning, never tiring of the habit. Then, I thought, why the hell shouldn't I have a routine? It's how people—*my* people—know me; know who and what and how I am. Not to mention where. It's important that they believe they know and understand me, and screw Carmine Aiello! Damned if I should change years of carefully-crafted habit to thwart a whiney lowlife like him.

I'm a private investigator, licensed by the city and state of New York for the last six years. What I really am, though, is a channel. Not the spiritual kind, the worldly kind. I bridge situations. And people. And I fix things—problems, hassles, disputes; and I find things—people, mostly, some of whom really are lost and some of whom know exactly where they are. Mostly I practice my trade in my neighborhood: the Lower East Side of New York City, the East Village, Alphabet City. The places that border Little Italy and Chinatown and the Village and SoHo and TriBeCa. Places where rich and famous private investigators, the kind in best-selling novels and blockbuster movies, wouldn't be caught dead. Or maybe that's the only way they'd be caught in my neighborhood. But when asked, and if I'm interested, I'll take a job anywhere, even in Queens, which I've done on more than one occasion.

I decided what I wanted to do and be when I read my first Robert Parker book at the age of thirteen, almost twenty years ago. *God Save the Child* was the name of the book, and I wanted to be Hawk *and* Spenser. Tough *and* smart. So I got a Sociology degree from City College and survived the police academy and four years as a New York City police officer, walking a beat on the eastern edge of Central Park. All the while growing and grooming my reputation in my neighborhood as a tough guy, but a smart one. Too smart to use drugs or get caught stealing or fighting, and too tough to take an ass-whipping from anybody.

I always knew that people in my neighborhood needed a good private cop. God knows the public ones never did much for us. Besides, there's a lot of life being lived in this part of Manhattan. Just because it's being lived on slim budgets in narrow tenements doesn't make it cheap life, or narrow life. I also always knew that I was just the right guy for the job: second-generation New Yorican, product of a black Puerto Rican mother and a brown Puerto Rican father, fluent in English, Spanish, and Spanglish; light-skinned enough not to threaten the cultural racists and yet not so light as to engender the distrust of the blacks of African descent.

I stood in front of my building, looking at it for a moment; looked at the buzzer box with its three names, always feeling a little puffed-up at the sight of my own in the third position, because I'm on the ground floor: *Phillip Rodriquez Investigations.* There are two other names on the buzzer box: the Dharma Yoga Studio in the middle, and Y. M. Aguierre at the top.

Yolanda Maria is my partner and she lives on the top floor of the building, because it was her idea to buy it. If we were going into business for ourselves, she said, we should own our own building. When you pay rent to somebody, she said, you're working for that guy and not for yourself. She also contributed the most money, since my dedication to being smart *and* tough had included no components of being thrifty. Yo, on the other hand, had determined to be wealthy with the same degree of intensity and commitment that I fashioned my Spenser/Hawk mutation. She'd begun saving money when she was ten, and by the time we met during our junior year at City College, she had a five-figure bank account.

I thought Yolanda Maria was marvelous the moment I met her, even before she began sharing her financial philosophies with me. But before my respect and admiration for her had a chance to flower into something more, shall we say, intense, Yolanda informed me that, one: she was a lesbian and proud of it; two: she did not lend money to friends, no matter how broke they were; and three: she thought I had potential, primarily because our grandmothers had been best friends when they lived next door to each other in Spanish Harlem a zillion years ago. I discovered her potential when she laughed and hugged me when I asked her to marry me anyway, and we've been best friends ever since.

I love this building almost as much as I love Yolanda

Maria. It's a small structure, and narrow, like the East Village itself, and interesting only given its history: it began life as a meeting/rooming house for immigrants seventy years ago. The huge one-room ground floor we left open, like a living room with desks and phones, carving out, at the rear of the room, a kitchen and a bathroom and a storage closet. We use Shoji screens to section off private work space for Yolanda. The top two floors once were sleeping warrens for newly-arrived Italians, Germans, Irish, Poles: dingy, ugly little spaces which we transformed into a mirrored studio for yoga and an airy loft for Yo, as elegant as any in SoHo, with its own rooftop deck. All this I think about every morning upon arrival at my building. I can't help it. It makes me proud.

"Peace, Brother Man, and *Buenos Dias,*" Yo sang out as I walked in the door.

All the blinds were up and weak, struggling sunlight spread out over the office, the shiny hardwood floor surrounding the muted gray carpet in the center of the room bouncing the light back toward the ceiling, adding to the sense of warmth and well-being created by Yolanda's presence. She is, and I can say this without the slightest trace of machismo, an excruciatingly gorgeous woman. She's a black Puerto Rican with a dancer's body, a model's face, Einstein's brain, and Celia Cruz's personality. The thousand-watt smile of greeting she offered, which outshone the thin stream of sunlight, made me grin like a fourteen-year-old. The mug of steaming coffee on a purple napkin in the center of my desk merely served to enhance the warm, fuzzy feeling.

"Back at you, my Sister," I said, tossing her the bottle of carrot juice, still dripping water and ice chips. Our greeting

11

was as habitual as anything else we did—the carrot juice I brought her and the coffee she fixed for me—and the doubt resurfaced. "Do you think we're too much creatures of habit?" I asked.

She froze in the act of turning a huge, healthy palm toward the light and fixed me in a stare that unnerved me, and I hastened to explain myself.

"You would let a piece of *caca* like Carmine Aiello disturb your psyche to such a degree?" She asked the question as if to a being unfamiliar with any of the basic principles of self-worth. In addition to being the most beautiful woman I know, and one of the smartest, Yolanda also is my best friend, and her opinion of me is as important as that of my mother or grandmother. So, it hurts like a kick in the nuts when she looks at me or talks to me like I'm mentally deficient.

"How the hell would you feel hearing all over the 'hood that Carmine was looking to talk to you?" I didn't try to conceal the injury to my feelings her failure to commiserate had produced. Instead, I took too big a gulp of coffee and burned my mouth. I stifled the curse because there was nobody to blame but myself, and glared at Yolanda.

"Probably like taking a shower," she said, "but certainly not like changing my life." She crossed mocha arms over a bosom she'd taught me years ago not to drool over and tilted her head to one side. "I'd also be real interested in knowing what he wanted to talk to me about. *¿Mi entiendes?*"

I certainly was beginning to understand. Now that the pique was wearing off, the pieces were falling into place. Carmine knows the rules, and he wouldn't violate my space and my privacy without good reason. And he certainly wouldn't deliver a message in person, unless there was real urgency attached. I still was pissed at him, but there was a little edge of concern lurking in the corner, next to the fledgling interest. I sipped a little more coffee that still was too hot to drink, blew Yo a kiss, did an about-face, and walked out of the office, out of the building, and back down Avenue C. I zigged and zagged west, toward the Bowery, guzzling the orange juice and missing the coffee. As I'd done on my walk earlier, I let my tan suede jacket flap open in the breeze, refusing to acknowledge the chill it contained. It was the third week of October and, this close to the East River, definitely the beginning of a new season. But for me, the memory of summer's heat remained too close to bundle myself against fall's arrival. My mother liked to tease me that I was too many generations removed from my Puerto Rican roots, because I preferred cold weather to hot. I loved winter in New York: the skinny island where an icy, slicing wind could find you no matter where you walked, and if you were walking crosstown into the wind—well, God help you, it was enough to send even an Eskimo scurrying for cover down into the nearest subway station. This was my island by choice, if not by heritage.

Carmine lived on one of those creepy, crowded blocks off the Bowery. I'd know which one when I got there. I knew where he lived because everybody knew where he lived. Because we hated his sleazy guts didn't mean we didn't have to acknowledge him. Everybody, in every part of New York City, acknowledges, in some way, the crime bosses who control things. That's the way it is, the way it's always been, like rich people live uptown and poor people live downtown. And while it's possible these days not to have to play ball on some hoodlum's team—like it's now possible that rich people live downtown and vice-versa—it still is not possible to pretend that the hoodlums don't exist and that they don't control a healthy share of the balls and bats and gloves, not to mention playing fields.

Finally forced to concede that my black Hanes thick cotton tee shirt wasn't keeping my chest warm enough, I was zipping my jacket when I turned the corner into Kenmare Street. I was looking at the zipper instead of at the world, when I made my turn and smacked into Carmine.

"What the fuck . . ." He stopped short when he saw it was me. "Hey, Rodriquez. How's it hangin'?"

"I hear you want to talk to me, Carmine. What about?" I knew I sounded snarly, but just looking at him returned me to my riled and piqued state.

"Lemme buy you a coffee. I know you ain't had yours yet."

Without a word, I followed him three storefronts down the block and into a little bakery I'd never noticed before, working hard to control the variety of negative feelings inside. *Damn him for knowing so much about my life and habits!*

The coffee shop was a warm hug. It smelled of cinnamon and chocolate and rising yeast, and my caffeine addiction reared its ugly head and dared me to be rude to Carmine until it was satiated. So I sat across from my host in a back booth and watched him arrange himself. Literally. He unbuttoned his coat but didn't remove it. Instead, he draped it off his shoulders so that his shiny black shirt was revealed. He smoothed the shirt front and stood the collar up, then pulled the cuffs down over his wrists. His face wore the concentrated look of a surgeon. I wondered what the hell he was doing, until I remembered that he claimed familial ties to an actor of the same name. I studied Carmine: short, fat, nearly bald, with beady eyes and a nose like a pickle and acne-scarred skin. And the man had the nerve to envision

14

himself resembling a movie actor? If I were Danny Aiello, I'd kick Carmine's tubby ass all the way across Brooklyn, back to the Canarsie section of Queens where he'd begun his low life.

"What do you want, Carmine?" I asked after the first hit of cafe con leche was spreading caffeine through me. I was looking sideways at the tray of pastries the fat man had ordered, my desire for a Napoleon dueling with my bruised pride. Did he know about my sweet tooth, too?

"You know Jill Mason, right? The shrink?" he asked, chewing a cannoli and making it look delicious.

I nodded. I knew who she was, actually had met her several months ago at some community affair, had found her polite and pleasant. And, as I recalled, quite a bit more than pleasant to the eyes. "What about her?"

"Somebody beat her up." Carmine shoved the remains of the cannoli into his mouth and wiped his lips daintily with a napkin.

I sat up straight and wiped my mouth, too, hurrying to chew and swallow the Napoleon so I could talk. "When? And where?" I couldn't believe that somebody as important as Jill Mason had been assaulted on my turf and I didn't know about it. "And what's it to you?" I almost snarled at him. "Since when does your heart bleed for spics and niggers?"

He had the good grace to blush and lower his eyes briefly. "Doc Mason is a stand-up lady." His pudgy hand slapped the table when he said it, as if to add strength to his pronouncement.

"Even if she is a nigger?" No need for me to make it easy on Carmine. He deserved the payback for linking his name to mine on my turf, first thing in the morning before I'd even had coffee.

"Look, ass wipe, I'm tryin' to hire you. You still work for a livin' or what?"

"For you, Carmine? I don't think so." I drained the mug and stood up.

"Jill Mason gets whacked, I'll put it out all over the neighborhood that it's on your head, I swear to God I will."

I sat back down and looked hard at Carmine. He wasn't bullshitting. I studied the plate of pastries, contemplated, snagged another Napoleon, and ate it slowly while my host explained the soft spot in his heart for Jill Mason: she'd saved his daughter's life. I hadn't known Carmine had a daughter. But a lot of hoodlums had kids they professed to adore, often tucked away someplace where they couldn't discover what a lowlife daddy was. No reason Carmine should be an exception, though I had trouble picturing what kind of woman would suffer his mean, ugly ass. I nodded thanks to the waitress and sipped my refreshed coffee, and wished this place weren't a Carmine Aiello hangout, so I could pay a return visit and bring Yolanda. She's the one who had hooked me on Napoleons when we were students.

I was wondering how Carmine knew so much about Jill Mason. I knew what I knew because it's my job to know things, and what I knew about the good doctor I'd only recently learned—that she was born in the 'hood and had, like lots of intellectually-gifted blacks and 'Ricans, scholarshipped out—in Mason's case to Hunter College and Columbia University for med school. That she had married a rich white guy—a banker—from uptown and had been a partner in one of those fancy East Side psychiatric clinics where people are rich enough not to be called crazy. That she had earned high six figures for enough years to be considered rich herself. That her husband and kids had been killed two years ago in a car crash on the Long Island Thruway that she had walked away from with scratches. And after that, she'd walked away from the Upper East Side and taken the Number 6 Train back home to the East Village, where she opened a clinic and where she worked long and hard and virtually for free. She didn't need the money, and that fit the needs of people who didn't have much of it but who had plenty of neuroses and psychoses and could be convinced to dump them in the lap of a sister from the 'hood.

"How'd she save your daughter's life?" I wanted to smack myself. Here I was, actually interested in something Carmine Aiello had to say. I hoped I'd managed to sound bored and pissed.

Carmine blushed again. "That part's none of your business. The part that concerns you is who's terrorizing the lady."

"How'd we get from her getting beat up to her being terrorized?"

Carmine inhaled deeply and dramatically and exhaled an impressive display of exasperation. "Ain't you been listening? The beating's just the last thing. Her office was broken into and trashed and she's been getting threatening phone calls—"

I interrupted. "What kind of threatening phone calls? From a male or a female? And what did the caller say? What time of day? And when was her office trashed?"

"I don't . . . what . . . why . . ." The fat man sputtered and choked like an almost-out-of-gas pimpmobile. Then he collected himself and his thoughts. That was interesting to observe. Carmine collecting his thoughts. "I can't answer any of that. You gotta talk to the lady herself. I'm just tellin' you what I know happened, you know what I'm sayin'? I don't know all the particulars."

"How do you know about any of it? Why would she tell you?"

He flushed again. "I happened to be there when she got one of the calls. I'd just picked up my daughter. She was the last patient that night and we were just standing there, making small talk, and the phone rings and she excuses herself and picks it up. Then she starts shaking, like all of a sudden it was twenty below zero and she was freezing. She drops the phone and backs up from the desk and starts grabbing at her chest. So I rush over to the desk and grab up the phone and listen and I hear, '. . . they're dead and you got all that money but you won't live to spend it.' And then a click and a dial tone."

"So was it a male or a female? And did it sound like one of our people from the 'hood or like somebody from the Upper East Side? And did it sound like a joke, Carmine? Like whoever it *was* was just after fun and games?"

He gave me a funny look and his face folded over on itself for a second, then re-opened. "A whisper. It was a whisper, like somebody with a bad cold, ya know what I mean? And there wasn't nothin' fun and games about how it sounded. And there sure as fuck wasn't nothin' fun and games about how Doc Mason was actin' after that call. I'm tellin' you, she was scared white." Then he blushed again and I thought I'd work this case if for no other reason than to cure Carmine of some of the more blatant manifestations of his racism.

"When did all this happen, Carmine?"

"That phone call thing, the one I heard, about a month ago, on a Tuesday night. The break-in, before that; and the beating, two nights ago."

I drained my cup and shook my head at the waitress before she could make it all the way to the table. Then Carmine and I sat in silence for a while, me pushing every thought from my mind except one: whether I'd really accept money from him. He'd said he wanted to hire me. After hearing why, I very much wanted to know why someone was scaring the shit out of the only shrink crazy enough to hang out a shingle in Alphabet City. And I wanted to beat that someone into the pavement. That part I'd do for free. I was damn tired of every time something good happened in the 'hood, some asshole looked to find a way to maim or kill it. Poor people in the East Village had as much right to Doctor Jill Mason as rich people on the Upper East Side.

"If I take this job, Carmine, this is strictly between you and me, *capiche?*"

His incongruously dainty mouth curled into a slight snarl. "You people hate me that much you can't take my money above the table, Rodriquez?"

"Only about as much as you hate us, Carmine, but with better reason," I answered him, holding his eyes with mine. I wanted to be sure he understood my words and all the meaning they held, and when I saw that he did—he uncurled his mouth, raised his hands palms up and out, facing me, and then placed them flat on the table—I told him to come by the office at six thirty and sign the contract.

"You won't say nothin' about my kid, will ya, Rodriquez?" Carmine spoke softly and there was no edge to his voice, no hint of the menace he usually worked to convey.

I stood up and slid into my jacket, zipped it, and looked down at Carmine. "When you buy my services, Carmine, you buy the client confidentiality that comes with the package. If you hadn't run your mouth all over the neighborhood, nobody would even know you were lookin' to talk to me."

Before I reached the corner, the wind had sliced into all the warmth I'd garnered in the cozy little pastry shop. No longer chilly, it was flat-out cold. I needed to go back home and dress more appropriately. I also needed to chat with Itchy Johnson, which was closer to home than where I was now, so I darted out into traffic and snagged a taxi, not normal behavior for me, but necessary. I was too far from home to take the time to walk and in too much of a hurry to pick Itchy's brain.

Not just the proprietor of a tonsorial parlor, as the gilt-edged sign above the mirror proclaimed, Itchy was legendary in the neighborhood. He was an old man now, probably pushing eighty, but still tall, lean, and trim, and still a flashy dresser, though minus the long, conked hair style so apparent in photos of his past: now he was bald as a billiard ball. In his youth, before migrating downtown from Harlem, he'd been a small-time player—a numbers runner and, later, a bookie operating in the back room of his barber shop on 146th Street. I'd heard him spin the tale so many times I knew all the pertinent details. Now he sold Dick Gregory's Bahamian Diet and something called Noni Juice from a small desk in the back corner of his shop and leafed through books of photographs from Harlem's glory days. He no longer cut hair and only rarely shined shoes, since the kind of people who still wore the kinds of shoes that needed waxing and buffing didn't frequent Itchy's establishment, and he only rarely talked with the customers, since most of them were young men and women sporting *au courant* hairstyles and attitudes. But throughout the day people like myself, who'd known Itchy forever, or wished they had, stopped in to exchange greetings, to listen to music no longer played in public places, to listen to stories no longer told or remembered.

I nodded to the barbers and customers en route to Itchy's corner and, even before I sat, he was growling at me. I could hear his raspy voice over the only music he allowed to be played in his place—vintage rock and roll and classic jazz and, at my urging, Tito Puente, Celia Cruz, Mongo Santamaria, and Carlos Santana. Today it was Smokey Robinson and the Miracles.

"And what the hell did he want?" Itchy crossed his long legs at the knee. Today he wore deep cranberry-colored sharkskin slacks, with silk ribbed socks and alligator shoes in the same color, and a long-sleeved cream silk shirt.

"I'm the one doing the wanting, Itchy," I said quietly. "You feel like talking about the old days?" I didn't know if Itchy was unusual or not, not being able to count many people his age among my acquaintances; but, like my eighty-something *Abuelita,* he seemed to vacillate between being driven to remember the past and flat-out refusing to admit that there was such a thing. Sometimes I thought it was because his memory was fading, while other times it seemed that remembering hurt him, saddened him. Now he narrowed his watery eyes, lowered his bald, shiny head, and looked up at me over the tops of his gold-rimmed glasses. Nothing but Smokey's smooth falsetto crooning for a few very long seconds. I didn't mind the wait.

"Depends," he said.

I waited but he didn't say any more. He'd closed up the way old people of color often close up in the presence of the enemy, usually white people in positions of authority, and he sat there giving the wall-eyed stare that accompanied the silence. But, dammit, I wasn't white or the enemy! And Itchy wasn't budging. Shit. "He hired me to find out who beat up Jill Mason." I'd have told the old critter how many Napoleons I'd eaten, if he'd asked. No way I was going to risk banishment from Itchy's good graces, client confidentiality be damned.

"I knew her grandparents," Itchy said in his voice from the past. "Both sets. Her mama's people came from down South somewhere. Georgia, I believe. But her daddy's people been here in New York since slavery. Elijah and Sarah Mason. Lemuel and Eula Graves. Nice people, all of 'em. That oldest Mason boy used to work for me. The second oldest was Jill's daddy. And her mama was the last born to Lem and Eula Graves. Can't recall her name, though I can see her face. Pretty brown girl, and smart as a whip. Lot of talk 'bout her goin' to City College. Then she met that Mason boy—Robert, I think his name was, or Richard—and that was the end of that."

His eyes watered some more, and clouded, and I didn't know whether to speak or keep quiet. The noisy arrival of two boisterous young men on a blast of cold air decided for me. Itchy rose quickly, eyes now snapping, gait long and loose like that of a young gangster, and strode to the front of his shop with a sense of purpose. He tolerated no rowdiness in his establishment. By the time he got back to me, his face was set and his eyes were flicking like they were looking to get a bead on something alive.

"How come Carmine came to you with this? She don't even want her own parents to know about it."

The question surprised me. It also annoyed me a little, though I wasn't exactly sure why. "You know what Jill Mason wants and doesn't want?"

"Oh, yeah," he said, like I'd asked him if he knew how to sharpen a straight razor on a leather strop. "I'm still connected up on the old neighborhood, still go to the same church as I used to, big Baptist church up St. Nicholas Avenue and 135th. Some of those folks been going to that church for sixty years or more. Older than me, a lot of 'em . . ."

I couldn't take it any longer. "Itchy." I said it quietly and, I hoped, respectfully enough to conceal my mounting exasperation. "What do you know about Jill Mason, about her family? Anything that might give a reason for somebody to want to hurt her?"

"They had to leave from Uptown. Middle of the night. Didn't take nothin' but what they were wearin'. Left the car, too, though it wasn't worth much. But, of course, that didn't satisfy 'em. Didn't do nothin' but make 'em madder." He shook his head and pursed his lips and said "umh" the way old people do, and then looked up at me, waiting.

"Maybe if you told me what you were talking about, Itchy?"

He grinned at me then, and slapped his thigh, and talked about a time more than fifty years ago as if it were last week. A time when the mob controlled life at all levels in New York City, and when it could be as dangerous to be Colored here as in any part of the South. Back then, most blacks and Puerto Ricans lived well north of the East Village—up in Harlem and in Spanish Harlem. Didn't even think about getting off the subway until it got north of Central Park. It was up in that Harlem, in those days, that Itchy had his first tonsorial parlor and was a bookmaker and a numbers runner—I knew all this because he'd told me enough times, but he'd never before mentioned the names of friends or associates, except that of his cousin, Bumpy Johnson. Now he said it was in that Harlem that he was friends with the Masons and the Graveses. It was in that Harlem that the oldest Mason boy defied the mob and set up an independent numbers operation. And died for it.

Itchy, on the other hand, was a cousin of the legendary Bumpy Johnson, who ran the largest and most well-organized numbers operation in Harlem and who defied the mob to do it and lived to tell the tale. The Mason boy was a hot-head, not satisfied to work for Itchy, who worked for Bumpy, who worked for the even more legendary Queen of Harlem, Stephanie St. Clair. One day, young Mason stood on the corner of 134th Street and Lenox Avenue and told Lucky Luciano's goons to take their wop asses back downtown where they belonged. Then he fired on them with a machine gun he'd stolen from one of those same goons a month or so earlier. His family moved away from Harlem that very night, as did all their close relatives and friends, the Graves family included. That was in the middle 1940s, as Itchy "recollected."

"Next time I saw Elijah Mason, he walked through that front door there and sat in my chair. Cut, shave, and shine, and not a word about what had happened." That was in 1955, Itchy recalled. Elijah was driving a produce wagon, from which he also sold half-pints of whiskey. His wife took in sewing. And his second boy had just married the Graves girl. Their first child, Jill, was born that next spring. "I remember because Elijah got killed just before the baby was born—maybe a couple of months—and Sarah passed on just after." He got quiet and his gaze lengthened as he looked into the past.

I looked around the shop while I waited for him to swing back to the present, and tried to imagine how it would have looked in 1955. Some of it I could see: the aged cordovan leather chairs and the silver-capped, swirling barber pole and the gilt-edged mirror. But the floor was a shiny new hardwood; the sinks behind each of the four chairs were modern pedestals; vibrant, healthy ferns hung suspended from the ceiling; and a huge television was mounted on the wall, permanently tuned to ESPN. The place looked and felt modern, like the chairs and the pole and the sign had been carefully-selected purchases from an antique store. Only the elevated shoeshine chair and pedestal and Itchy himself looked as if they belonged in the past.

"They moved into Elijah and Sarah's place right around the corner there on Avenue B . . . Robert and Leola! That's it! Robert and Leola Graves Mason, and they still live right around the corner. That's why Jill came back downtown, to keep an eye on them. They're pretty old now."

I couldn't stop the look I gave him. Calling somebody old, of all the nerve. He caught the look, chuckled, and flexed his muscles in a weightlifter's pose. Impressive still.

"How'd they die, Itchy?" I sensed he didn't want to answer that one, and I prepared myself to push him if necessary.

"Sarah had a heart attack and was gone like that!" He snapped his fingers. "And they say Elijah's horse stomped him to death."

Something about the way he said, "they say." I raised my eyebrows and my open palms at him and he shrugged.

"Come on, Itchy," I said, patience all but gone. "Either the horse killed him or it didn't. You could tell, you know, if a horse stomped somebody to death." I hoped I sounded dry.

"Oh, the horse killed him all right, no doubt about that. It's just that nobody never could figure how Elijah got himself under the horse's feet."

Chapter Two

Warmer now, with a turtleneck sweater, heavy corduroy slacks, and a scarf hugging my chest beneath a leather bomber jacket, my feet happily and cozily encased in their Doc Martens, I hurried back to the office. What I'd planned to be a leisurely morning of paperwork had just become a push to prepare for an early-afternoon meeting with one of our half-dozen on-retainer corporate clients. At Yolanda's insistence, we catered to them unabashedly when the time came—in this case, quarterly for New York University, for which we performed a series of elaborate security checks and balances at sensitive locations, like the admissions office and laboratories and the computer center.

Because we'd once intercepted a deliberately-planted virus at the main computer in the admissions office—actually Yolanda had intercepted it; I'm barely computer literate—we were beloved at NYU. They knew how much we'd saved them in time, money, and destroyed records, and groveled at our feet almost as much as we groveled at theirs. Not only did we detect the virus before it was able to spread and do real damage, we also were able to identify the cretin who introduced it, and I'll claim that honor, since Yo despises jerks, bad guys, hoodlums, and lowlifes in all forms. He was a former student, dismissed for stalking three female classmates.

So, we busied ourselves preparing for our meeting with NYU's administrative vice president and its security chief, Jeffrey Dahl. But all either of us wanted to talk about was

Jill Mason and the tale Itchy Johnson had spun, which is rare for Yo. She's much more interested in the corporate world, but she had listened with ever-widening eyes while I related the details of my meeting with Carmine and later with Itchy, and she had reached the same conclusion that I had: surely the mob wouldn't be busting Jill Mason's chops because of something her dead uncle did before she was born! At least we hoped not, but we didn't have time to knock it around, either before or after the NYU meeting; because afterward, while Yo drafted a contract for Carmine, I had to rush to the home of a couple on Avenue A whose nine-year-old daughter didn't come home from school as usual. And then I had to help the cops tell them that she never would.

I was late for my meeting with Carmine but he was so busy leering at Yo that he didn't care. He signed the contract without reading it and wrote out a check for double the retainer. "So I don't have to keep comin' back here," he growled, though we both knew he was just showing off for Yolanda.

"I had a chat with Itchy Johnson," I said to Carmine while Yo poured him a beer and he ogled her sideways.

He nodded thanks when she gave him the beer, swallowed half of it in one gulp, sighed, and wiped his mouth on the back of his hand. Yo gave him a napkin, and he placed his glass on top of it and wiped his mouth with his hand again. "That's a good thing, Rodriquez. Itchy knows a lotta stuff."

"He doesn't know how long your people hold a grudge. Maybe you could enlighten me?"

He was truly puzzled. When, after several seconds, he hadn't even attempted a response, I supplied the bare-bones facts of my conversation with Itchy and Carmine looked even more puzzled. Then the anger crept in.

"You think I would do somethin' to that lady and then hire you to . . ."

Oh shit. "No, Carmine!" I stood up quickly, raised my palms upward, and walked over to where he was seated on the couch. "I truly do not think that. I'm only looking to understand all the possibilities. I have to do that, you know. I have to rule out stuff, no matter how crazy it may sound. I have to rule out the possibility that a grudge could be held for so long. *Capiche?*"

Carmine had been watching me closely, looking to see, I knew, whether I was shitting him, and finally I could see the satisfaction on his face and I let him see the relief on mine. We both relaxed and drank some more beer. Yolanda looked at us as if we were a rare museum exhibit or some extinct species. I could hear her calling men and our behavior prehistoric. Pre-Neanderthal is what she always said.

"What happened to him?" Carmine asked, apparently apropos of nothing I could fathom. "The punk who fired on Luciano. What happened to him?"

I'd asked Itchy the same question, and gave Carmine the same answer I'd received: burial in the Harlem River the same day, body neither searched for nor found. Carmine slapped his hands together in an up and down motion, signifying that the matter had been resolved with the Mason boy's execution those long years ago. Whoever was after Jill Mason, it was because of something she'd done herself, not because of who she was related to. And I was truly relieved by that, because I had no intention of injecting myself in mob business. Not ever.

"I think I'll take a walk over to Doctor Mason's, then, and introduce myself," I said, standing.

Carmine looked at his watch. "She ain't there," he said,

looking wistfully at his empty glass. "Her last patient leaves at seven fifteen and she leaves at eight. She walks over to East 7th Street and checks on her parents, then she walks over to 2nd Avenue for a taxi home. Every day but Saturday. She quits at two on Saturdays."

Carmine smiled almost charmingly when Yolanda poured him another beer, and his bonhomie extended to me. Without my having to ask, he told me that he knew Jill Mason's routine because, as a new patient, his daughter was the last patient and Carmine, as a gesture of kindness and gratitude, often waited and walked Doctor Mason to her parents' and then waited downstairs for the fifteen or twenty minutes she was with them, before hailing a taxi for her and seeing her safely into it. "She tries to act like she's not scared but I know she is, 'cause if she didn't want me to wait and help her, she wouldn't let me."

I thought about that for a moment. Jill Mason had a routine, just like I did, that anybody paying attention could figure out in a week's time. I had three additional questions for Carmine. I asked them, he answered them, and he left. Yolanda and I sat quietly for a long time. She broke the silence.

"I don't like it," she said.

I shrugged. "What's not to like? Carmine paid us double 'cause he was drooling over your chest." But her solemn look and feeling didn't flinch or fade. I knew to pay attention. "What are you feeling?"

"Bad news. Bad energy. Bad vibes."

"Well, yeah. Carmine can have that effect—"

"Not Carmine!" She snapped the words out of her mouth like she was breaking a twig between her fingers, and her eyes flashed black. Yolanda was my business partner, emphasis on both *business* and *partner*. She knew and understood and was fascinated by everything about business and computers and organization and planning and goals. She was so lukewarm to the concept of private investigations that, even after so many years, she still rolled her eyes when forced to confront the true nature of her livelihood. She also possessed a sixth sense that made my Grandma genuflect and cross herself. Whether it involved a potential stock investment or a potential client, if Yolanda had a "sense" about it, I listened and heeded. And waited for her to share. She took her time.

"What would be a good reason to hurt a shrink?" she finally asked.

I gave serious consideration to the question and couldn't think of a good reason to hurt a shrink and said so. Shrinks help people. Save people's lives, just like surgeons. After all, if you save a person's sanity, isn't that the same as saving a person's life?

Yolanda's look told me she agreed with only part of my assessment. "Shrinks know secrets," she said. "Shrinks know things nobody else knows. People tell shrinks things they don't tell another soul. And, just like priests and lawyers, shrinks go to the grave with those secrets."

Well shit. That certainly cast things in a different mettle. I was starting to feel a little bad vibe-ish about this job, too. It had seemed simple enough: find out who's terrorizing Jill Mason, who just happened to be a shrink. I'd thought drugs; doctors, including psychiatrists, keep drugs in their offices. And I'd thought money; even people who didn't know Jill Mason knew she was loaded. I even thought some kind of racial thing was possible. The world hadn't changed so much that there wouldn't be people who harbored resentment toward a black female professional, especially a rich one. But I hadn't thought of Jill Mason as being a keeper of secrets. I was about to say that to Yolanda when she got up and started to do stuff: close the blinds and put the empty beer bottles and glasses on a tray and turn on the desk lamps. Then she went across the room, behind the partition to the computer corner, leaving me to my thoughts.

I looked across my desk at Carmine's check, being surprised, now, after the fact, that he'd written a check and not paid in cash. *Carmine and Theresa Aiello* it said, along with the address and telephone number. So ordinary. So like every other normal citizen. Except that it was Carmine, who, not twelve hours ago, I had thought of as slime. Now he was a client. Now I knew stuff about him: he had a joint checking account at a credit union with a wife named Theresa and a daughter he cared enough about to take to a therapist several times a week. And because he cared about his daughter, he cared about his daughter's therapist. Enough to pay me way too much money, even considering he was trying to make a good showing for Yolanda.

I looked around my office, half-expecting that it, too, had changed at some point during the day. The blinds on the windows that were high enough up the wall to hug the ceiling were closed, and no light reflected through the wall of glass blocks at the front of the building. The nubby gray carpet that covered the center of the floor beneath the desks looked darker, but it always did at night, I told myself, just as the surrounding hardwood didn't seem so shiny. The modern, brushed chrome gooseneck lamps, designed to look like they were from another era, were bowed low on all three desks, as if trying to be incongruous. I wanted to imitate them. I felt vulnerable, suddenly, and I didn't know why. I wished Mike or Eddie were around. They were re- tired cops who worked for me part-time—loud, rowdy, irreverent, funny guys, unloved by Yolanda because they were loud and rowdy and irreverent—but damn good investigators and a guaranteed foil against feelings of vulnerability. They were handling a skip-trace way out on the Island and wouldn't be in the office until next week. I sure didn't want to feel vulnerable until next week.

The lights from the computer monitors behind the Shoji screens on the far wall reflected gently. There were three of them and only Yolanda understood why. I understood only that I appreciated the results they produced at her command. Tonight, their presence was comforting, as was Yo's insistent tapping at the keyboards. But all the plants looked spooky, not alive and vibrant as I knew them to be. The door at the end of the room that led to the bathroom and the kitchen and the storeroom stood ajar, only darkness visible beyond it, and looked sinister. And whatever the hell was wrong with me needed to quit!

I raised the hinged neck of the lamp, pressed a button on its base and increased the wattage, and looked down at the piece of notepaper next to Carmine's check. On it he'd written Jill Mason's office and home addresses, and her parents' address. She lived in Chelsea, in a loft. I knew the building. The cheapest loft in it went for half a million. Her office was in a building I knew, too. When I was growing up in that neighborhood, sociologists called buildings like it tenements. In it, on the upper floors, lived people who almost certainly had secrets. At ground level are the shopkeepers— sellers of old meat and older vegetables, cheap wine, stale bread, expired milk, fresh cigarettes and cold beer, fifty-dollar blue jeans and hundred-dollar sneakers. The people upstairs buy the stuff downstairs with angry resignation, as if walking ten blocks or riding the subway two stops to better goods and services was prohibited by law. Same thing was true for the people who lived in Jill Mason's parents' building. I looked again at the piece of notepaper, at the address of Robert and Leola Mason. I knew that building, too. Full of more people who could—who most likely did—have secrets. Including Robert and Leola Graves Mason?

I took a spiral notebook from my desk and wrote down everything that I had done that day, including the ugly business involving the little girl on Avenue A. I also made a note not to charge the parents, Bert and Angie Calle. Carmine paying double would take care of their fee. I wrote down not just what I'd done but what I'd thought and felt about what I was doing, who I'd seen and spoken with, no matter how casually. Very often, in fact, almost always, I revisit these first-day notes during a case, and I always find something helpful. Even though I make case notes at the end of each day, those first-day notes and impressions and feelings have a unique perspective that can't be duplicated.

When I was finished, I stood, stretched, and gathered the tray of bottles and glasses and carted it back to the kitchen. I rinsed the bottles and put them in the recycling bin and the glasses into the dishwasher. Because I hadn't eaten lunch at the office today, the kitchen was clean. Demonstrating that it had a mind of its own, my stomach rumbled like Mount St. Helens and reminded me that I hadn't had lunch anywhere today. And it was almost nine-thirty at night.

"Yo!" I bellowed, leaving the kitchen and meeting her scurrying from the warm glow of the computer corner toward me.

"What?" She wore her computer glasses low on her nose and looked at me over their rims with a wrinkle of concern creasing her brow.

"Let's eat. And take a walk past Jill Mason's office."

★ ★ ★ ★ ★

Nightfall had brought winter. A slicing wind, bearing semi-frozen droplets, cut through my leather bomber jacket like it was tissue paper. I wrapped my scarf around my head and ears—my hair hadn't grown back all the way yet—and buried my hands deep in my pockets. Yolanda was similarly bundled, the difference being her long overcoat, which no doubt prevented her lower extremities from feeling like ice bars. It was time to move the long underwear to the front of the closet. And find my hats! I shave my head for spring and summer, Hawk-like, and wear it full and long in the winter, like Spenser. Having winter arrive before my hair did was unplanned. And unappreciated.

As usual, foot and vehicular traffic was plentiful in our 'hood, and we didn't talk much en route to Jill Mason's office because we weren't able to walk side-by-side on the narrow, crowded sidewalks long enough for conversation. We wove in and out between people and cars, in the street for half a block, back on the sidewalk for a block, back in the street for a block. Heads down, shoulders hunched, eyes narrowed slits staring into the mean wind and watering. A month from now, those tears would freeze before they reached chin level.

At the corner of 1st Avenue and East 2nd Street, Yo and I reunited and we locked arms, running across the Avenue against the traffic. It was too cold to wait for the light to change and the mayor's crusade against jaywalking in the city had never taken firm hold in our part of town. We stopped directly in front of the building where I'd spent the first seven years of my life. It looked worn and sad and more than a little shabby, but not lifeless. A lot like New Yorkers of a certain age: you can tell life has been hard on them, but you can also tell there's still lots of life left in them.

All of the ground-level stores on this side were still open and doing good business: a bodega, a pawn shop, a newsstand, and a Chinese take-out. We rounded the corner, putting the wind at our backs. The bank was closed but the cash machine in the lighted lobby was doing a good business. Next door, the video store was busy, too. The nail salon next door to it was dark and empty. The iron gate pulled securely across the next doorway and padlocked was illuminated by an overhead spotlight that shone on a black and silver plaque. *JILL MASON, M.D.* it said, and in English and Spanish it listed office hours for every day except Sunday. Everything just like Carmine described it.

"I don't know how they do it," Yo said in an almost whisper. "Listen to people's problems all day. Look at that: the woman works six days a week, listening to other people's shit, when she's got enough shit in her own life."

"She does more than listen," I said, stepping closer and examining the metal gate and its lock. "I mean, she must talk some, if people like Carmine's kid get better, right? Otherwise what would be the point?" I grabbed the gate and shook it. It didn't even wiggle. I walked next door to the coffee shop, with its steamed windows. I held the door open for Yo and followed her inside. It was a grungy little place, but the smell of brewing coffee and the sizzle of burgers on the grill were proving a comfort to a dozen trusting souls in from the elements this night. So comforting that, except for the guy on duty behind the counter, not a single one of them looked up as we entered.

"Wonderful ambiance," Yolanda breathed. "Why don't we eat here?"

I was so hungry I couldn't even joke about it. I cut her a look and approached the counterman, an already old thirty-something with the look of drugs and the joint about him, before he could move toward us. I wanted to talk to him without being overheard. Yolanda followed at a near distance.

"*¿Que paso?*" I extended my hand and he looked at it, then wiped his hand on a towel stuck in the waistband of his khakis and shook. When I had my hand back, I gave him my card and waited for him to read it before I said, low enough so only he heard, "Somebody's been giving Doctor Mason some trouble, and I'm looking to find out who."

Nothing moved but the man's eyes, from the card, to me, back to the card, to Yo, back to me, back to the card, which he finally slipped into his shirt pocket. "You know my uncle," he said. "Willie One Eye." Meaning, maybe he talks to me, maybe he doesn't. But he at least considers it.

I nodded. "For a long time." Which means, it's okay to talk to me, Bro. Check with Willie. He'll stand up for me.

He patted the pocket where he'd put my card and looked out of the corner of his eye down the counter where a guy had raised his coffee cup into the air, signaling the need for a refill. "I heard there was some shit happened over there, but I don't know nothin' about it. I hear anything, I'll tell Willie." And he moved off down the counter to refill the coffee cup. I watched him closely. His khakis and white shirt were clean and starched, his black hair long but recently cut. He'd been clean long enough to have a steady gait, and straight long enough to have a steady gig that included responsibility for the cash drawer. If this guy ever told me anything, I could trust it.

I surveyed the crowd and briefly wondered whether it would do any good to ask if anybody knew or had heard anything about Jill Mason's troubles. I shrugged off the thought. No point to it. I followed Yolanda out into the cold night and up the street. She was moving with a sense of purpose, so she'd apparently decided on a place for dinner, and I was so hungry I didn't care if she tried to convince me to eat something that was good for me. I could always make detour and grab a slab of ribs from that Southern food joint on 10th Avenue before heading home; something to keep the vegetables company. But she surprised me by running down a taxi stopped at the light, hauling us both inside, and directing the driver to a Chelsea corner that was home to my favorite burger joint.

My imagination was already chewing when Yo removed a sheaf of papers from her purse and dropped them in my lap.

"Jill Mason, her dead uncle, Itchy and Bumpy Johnson, a brief history of race relations between Harlem blacks and the mob. Jill was driving the car when her husband and children were killed two years ago. His family made a stink, but then they'd been bitchin' about her since her black self married their white son fifteen years earlier, so I don't think there's much fire in that smoke bomb, even though she did collect several mil in insurance." Yo reached over and pulled one paper-clipped set of papers from the others. "Read this one carefully."

I was sifting through the stack of papers, holding them up and trying to decipher a few words here and there from the headlights of the traffic. "Why this one?" I asked, squinting at a sentence that revealed Itchy Johnson's first name to be Malachi. "What's in it?"

"Secrets," Yolanda said, and I could tell by the way she said it that asking her questions would do me no good. And since I couldn't read in the dark, I kept quiet, watched the traffic, and thought about Yolanda.

Something about this case had gotten to her and I didn't know whether to be grateful, annoyed, or worried. Yo didn't like the nature of investigating, though she was able to appreciate the process and the results. She was happy doing the business end—billing people on time and making sure the money was paid; the part I didn't like or do well. And because she understood computers much better than people, and because she believed in preparation, I always had access to every piece or hint of information that could be useful to me in any given investigation. But Yolanda didn't like the ugliness of a world that caused so much pain and made so much of that pain profitable to people like us.

I massaged the stack of papers in my lap as if they were Braille and I could read them with my fingers. What I had here was information, yes. But also something more. Something here bothered Yolanda. Secrets. I should be happy that she was interested, engrossed even, in a case, even if I was slightly annoyed that she didn't show this level of interest in all our cases. But I was mostly feeling uneasy.

We were in the restaurant, warm and cozy and halfway through a brew, before Yo spoke to me. She had let me read the Itchy Johnson stuff first, had watched me read it a second time, before she said anything.

"What do you make of it?" she asked.

"It was a long time ago, Yo, and he's an old man." Like any normal person about to be caught in a bind, I tried equivocating to buy myself some time. Since I didn't know what she was after, better not to take a position on anything.

"He's a liar," Yo said dryly.

"Understandably so," I said quickly. "Think about what life was like back then, Yo. About what it's like now, for that matter. Why wouldn't a guy like Itchy claim kinship to a powerful figure like Bumpy Johnson? He probably escaped many an ass-whipping because some punk thought he was Bumpy's cousin."

Yo watched her meal arrive—a turkey burger with all the trimmings—and got busy spreading mayo and mustard and adding lettuce and tomato to build a very respectable-looking sandwich. I busied myself in like manner, building my hundred-percent beef burger which was six more ounces of meat than Yo's paltry poultry thing. I was hungry enough and filled with enough anticipation of the first bite that Yolanda's aura was ineffective. Almost. I took the first bite, chewed, and waited.

Yolanda frowned at her sandwich. "People who lie about small things, Phil, will lie about large things," she said to her burger, then picked it up and took a serious bite.

We both chewed, me masticating her words as well as my food. She was right, of course, only it didn't seem like such a big deal to me. Most people would, if they could, claim a closeness to a powerful figure. Just like Carmine Aiello claimed to work for John Gotti and to be the cousin of Danny Aiello. Everybody knew Carmine was lying and nobody took him any more—or less—seriously for it. And maybe that was the difference: everybody knew Carmine was full of shit. And everybody believed Itchy really was related to a renowned figure of the underworld, even if it was the Black Harlem underworld of more than half a century ago. Hollywood had made a movie about the guy starring Lawrence Fishburne, legitimizing Bumpy Johnson for posterity, and, by extension, Itchy.

Question was, did I care? Did that mean everything the old dude had told me about Doctor Jill Mason was a lie? Yo read my mind. As usual.

"The stuff about Jill Mason is all on the money, who her parents and grandparents were and where they were from . . . And maybe Itchy told only one lie in his life. And maybe it was even a good lie. But I don't think so, Phil. Nobody tells just one lie."

There was nothing stupid about what Yolanda had just said, but the stupid commercial jingled like loose change in my memory: *"Betcha can't eat just one."* Shit. "You going home," I asked, "or to Brooklyn?" Yolanda's long-time lover, Sandra Gillespie, lived in the Fort Green section of Brooklyn. A former dancer with the Alvin Ailey Company, Sandra now taught dance to awkward little girls in awe of her celebrity, and to professional dancers looking to keep their edge, also in awe of her celebrity. She and Yolanda spent every night together but refused to live together, which puzzled me. But since I'd been told on more than one occasion that it was none of my business, I left it alone.

Instead of answering, however, she said, "You might want to pay a visit to the Schomburg Library. It's up in Harlem, on 134th Street. Anything that happened involving blacks, it's on a piece of paper or film in that library." Then she added, "And I'm going to Brooklyn. Walk with me to the subway."

I stifled my protest. That also was none of my business, that she chose to ride the damn subway at all times of the night. But we both knew what a drag it was trying to get a taxi across the river to Brooklyn, and she knew better than I, she being a darker shade of brown. Taxi drivers, most of them some shade of brown themselves, had a bad attitude about driving black people to Brooklyn at night. Yolanda had an even worse attitude about being treated like shit, so she kept her money in her pocket and her temper in check and rode the train. I walked her to the station and down the stairs and, satisfied that there were enough people on the platform to generate a feeling of safety, I kissed her goodbye and braced myself for the long walk home. The solitude would do me good, give me time to think. I could also work off the second order of fries and the chocolate cake. I was full and feeling mellow—the feeling enhanced by the smell of wood smoke in the air. People had their fireplaces going tonight. Then the wind did its sandwich thing. That's what I call it when frigid, razor-sharp winds whip simultaneously off the East River and the Hudson River and meet somewhere in the middle of the lower part of Manhattan, sandwiching helpless, hapless pedestrians in the middle.

"Shit!" The exclamation was involuntary. I may as well have been naked for all the good my clothes were doing. I stepped into the street and hailed a taxi. I could think just as effectively riding home, and sitting in front of my own fireplace. And wondering why Yo thought I should pay a visit to the Schomburg Library. I wished I'd asked her.

Chapter Three

I was at Jill Mason's office the next morning before she was. That was intentional. I wanted to observe her arrival, and I wanted to see if anyone else was observing her arrival. But if anybody was, I couldn't tell. It was too cold to do anything but shake and shiver. I was bundled and hunched inside my coat and hat and scarves and praying that the good doctor would arrive on time. According to the plaque, she opened for business at eight fifteen. I was counting on her arriving half an hour before that. She did.

I saw her from a block away and knew immediately who she was, even though the wind was in my face making my eyes water. The wind was behind her, and because she was so tiny, she was propelled forward by the force of it. Even from a distance, it was clear that she was a lovely woman. That was the appropriate word to describe women who looked like Jill Mason. Pretty was too trite, and beautiful didn't contain enough of the unspoken elements.

Jill Mason also looked rich. Not the flashy, tacky rich of the mob or drug dealers or musicians or others who just got rich and want the world to know they have bunches of money. Jill Mason looked rich, as if it were as natural a part of her as having brown skin the color of dark Godiva chocolate. But I knew that Jill Mason had been born around the corner from me, her family as poor as mine, and that thought made me stand straighter, stretching to my full five-foot-eleven. I knew I didn't look rich, but it suddenly was necessary for me to look . . . dignified. She certainly

did. Her fur coat and hat were worth many thousands of
dollars, but it was clear that she wore them because it was
cold, not to make a statement of any kind.

She walked briskly, aided by the wind, head up, eyes forward, and hands swinging gently at her side, a purse in the
right one and a briefcase in the left. When she got closer, I
could see apprehension in her eyes, and that made me
angry. This woman shouldn't have to live in fear. No
woman should have to live in fear, and certainly no little
girl should have to live in fear. "Doctor Mason," I said as
she approached, and immediately regretted it. She jumped
and backed up, fear widening her eyes. Even terrified, she
was lovely. No wonder they said people always fell in love
with their shrinks. I was in love with Jill Mason and she
wasn't my shrink.

We spoke simultaneously. "I'm sorry," I was saying, as
she was asking, "What do you want?" I answered quickly,
telling her my name and why I was there. She smiled
slightly at the mention of Carmine's name and reached her
hand out toward the padlock on the gate. I realized that
she'd had her keys in her hand all along, in readiness. I
nodded an internal approval.

"Can I give you a hand?" I asked, and allowed her a brief
but thorough scrutiny.

She gave me the key and stood aside while I opened the
lock and pulled the gates apart, re-locking the heavy, expensive lock and approving of it. She pointed to the key that
opened the wooden-looking steel door to the office, and
once again I nodded an internal approval and wondered
how in the hell anybody had ever broken into this place.
Now I stepped aside, let her enter, and then followed,
closing the door, which I heard click and lock. She quickly
turned on lights and looked around. It was barely notice-

able, but she released the breath she'd been holding. This woman really was afraid.

I followed her through the well-appointed waiting room—nicer, I knew, than any other doctor's waiting room in this part of town; some kind of Persian or Oriental rug covered the floor and who cared if it was fake, though I suspected that it wasn't. It had a deep, royal blue background and lots of claret and gold in it and it was very pretty. Half a dozen armchairs, upholstered in the claret and gold of the rug, were spaced throughout the room, and a beige, upholstered sofa was on the wall opposite the receptionist's window. There were tables throughout the room, and on them magazines, little vases of flowers, and little bowls of peppermints.

I made my hands into fists and clenched my teeth tightly together. "This is a beautiful room," I said, pushing the words through my teeth. What I didn't say was that I'd kill before I'd let anyone hurt this woman. Just walking into her office probably cured a lot of problems for a lot of people.

"Thank you," she said, putting her coat on a hanger and hanging it on a wooden wall-mounted rack in her office. She placed her hat, scarf, and gloves neatly on top of the rack and turned to face me. "I thought you were just part of Mr. Aiello's bombast." She gestured to a Mission chair and an African print sofa. "Please have a seat. Wherever you're comfortable. Mr. Rodriquez, is it?"

Her voice was low and mellow, and I definitely was in love. I removed my overcoat, grateful that I'd added a suede sport jacket to my black wool turtleneck and black wool slacks, grateful that I hadn't made today a jeans and sweatshirt day. Jill Mason was the kind of woman you wanted to look nice for, though I honestly don't think it would have mattered to her what I wore. She gracefully ex-

changed her fur-lined boots for a pair of black flats that went quite nicely with her black knit pantsuit and white silk blouse. The entire ensemble was some designer's idea of what a woman of class would wear to a job, without intimidating those whose paychecks were smaller by several zeroes.

She lowered herself—tenderly, I thought—into a Mission-style rocking chair, the mate to the chair I was in, and faced me. Her hair was copper-colored and it was shoulder-length and framed her face like parentheses. Her jewelry was gold: flat clip-on earrings, a Rolex watch on the left arm, a cuff bracelet on the right, and a simple gold band on her left hand, the only ring. I knew from Yolanda's report that Jill Mason was fifty years old and had, just two years ago, buried her husband and two children, both girls. She looked sad and tired and fearful. But she did not look beat-up.

"I confess that Carmine had to convince me, Doctor Mason. What usually comes out of Carmine we don't call 'bombast' though it also begins with a 'b.' " I allowed a moment for her smile, then, "He told me you'd been beaten up."

She sighed and closed her eyes briefly. "More of a roughing up than a beating. Pushing, shoving, threatening. I was—am—frightened." She was about to say more, when a tiny chime-like sound stopped her. "My receptionist," she said, excusing herself and going into the outer room. I stood when she left and kept standing so that I could explore her office.

It was as comfortable as the waiting room, but in a different style: a well-done blend of modern and Mission. Lots of natural wood and bold, African colors and patterns on the walls and sofa cushions. The Berber rug was warm and

neutral and made all the furniture feel right at home. Except for the doctor's desk, which was at an angle in the far corner of the room, out of sight and out of mind. Unless, like me, one were looking for it, and I was. Here was the phone on which Carmine had heard the back end of a threat. Here was the desk he said had been trashed. All was in order, now. Scrupulously so. I leaned over and around in one of my contortionist's positions and studied the photographs in simple gold frames, knowing who I would see: Doctor Mason and her husband and their children. They looked happy. Their smiles included their eyes, not just their mouths. Doctor Jill Mason's smile no longer reached her eyes, I thought, as I resumed my place in the Mission chair. Just in time.

"I apologize . . ." she began. I cut her off.

"The need for apology belongs to me, Doctor Mason. I'm the one who's here unannounced and without an appointment, which I'm sure you do have in a matter of moments. So may I schedule one? So that we can talk—"

Her turn to cut me off. "Do you really think you're necessary, Mr. Rodriquez?" she asked, then blushed at the recognition of how I could interpret that question, if I were a thinner-skinned individual. "I mean do you really think . . . Mr. Aiello isn't overreacting just a bit?" She frowned a little, as if in thought, trying, it seemed, to answer that for herself.

I shook my head gently and leaned forward in the chair toward her. I wanted her to take me seriously. And to be comfortable with me. "It's true that Carmine is an excitable fellow, but there was no huff and puff, no bombast in him when he talked to me about you. He was genuinely concerned. For you and for his daughter."

"For his daughter?" she said quickly, and fear invaded her eyes.

"For what would happen to his daughter without you to do whatever you're doing for her. Which, if I'm reading Carmine correctly, weighs in on the miracle scale at the loaves and fishes or walking on water level." I offered what I hoped was an assuring smile and wondered what about Carmine's daughter had frightened her.

She lowered her eyes and was silent for a long moment. "Can you return this evening, Mr. Rodriquez, after my last patient? Allowing time for me to dictate my notes, say eight fifteen?"

"I'll be here," I said, standing and reaching for my coat. "Would it be okay if I brought you some dinner?" She began a protest, but I kept talking. "How do you feel about Southern Bar-Be-Que? Ribs and chicken?"

"From that place on 10th Avenue? It's owned by a woman from somewhere down South?" she asked, with the first hint of animation I'd seen in her.

"North Carolina," I said, one hand on the doorknob. "And I'll bet you'd rather drink white wine with your meal than beer." I didn't make it a question and she didn't bother to answer it.

"Thank you, Mr. Rodriquez. I'll see you later."

I was thinking too hard about why somebody like Jill Mason should be in the kind of trouble that buys ass-whippings by the time I left to think about being cold, though I was walking double-time out of habit. I made my morning stops as usual and almost on time. I mentioned to Willie One Eye that I'd met his nephew and he nodded, without comment. I received a come-hither wink from Mrs. Campos, apparently forgiven for being sought by Carmine, and pretended to blush in shame. Itchy seemed a little distant, but I was too preoccupied to focus on it too much. Besides, Itchy was a moody guy; he'd been known not to speak to me at all on occasion. Yolanda, however, could have been the sunrise over San Juan Viejo. Only two things made her that happy: Sandra and money.

"What happened, Sandra win the lottery?"

"Almost that good," she said with even better humor. "She won a grant to officially open a dance school! No more teaching in church basements and union halls and following her students all over town, from one rented studio to another. Everybody will come to her, now."

"And who's more excited, you or Sandra?"

She pretended to ponder the question as she opened her carrot juice and poured it into a glass. "I'm pretty psyched, but she's over the moon!"

"Tell her I said, 'Break a leg.' "

"Tell her yourself. She'll be here at seven thirty."

"But I won't. I'll be picking up dinner for me and Doctor Mason," I said, and filled her in on my morning, being surprised again at the level of Yolanda's interest in this case. She sat on the edge of her chair, literally, listening to every word, asking questions, clarifying details. Her interest was intense until I announced that, following my morning meetings at NYU, I planned to spend the afternoon uptown in Jill Mason's old neighborhood.

"What do you hope to find, poking around on the Upper East Side?"

"The woman lived up there for more than twenty years, more than half her life." I couldn't help the hint of exasperation in my voice. Surely that much should be obvious, even to Yolanda. But she was shaking her head at me in that way.

"I'm telling you, Baby Boy, that whatever is after Doctor Mason is right here in the 'hood. Any trouble looking to find her uptown would have found her uptown, before she moved back downtown."

I hated it when she called me Baby Boy even more than when she shook her head at me. That was something she started when we were in college, when I'd behave in a way that she called "spoiled little macho boy." If I'm honest, I'd have to admit that lots of Latin men—and black men and Italian men and Greek men, for all I know—exhibit similar behavior. It's the grown-up version of the pout boys do when they don't get their way with or from some woman of importance: grandmother, mother, sister, lover. Since Yo was, in a way, all those things for me, I would get really injured when she wouldn't give in to something I was demanding. She'd called me a baby boy at one of those times, and it stuck. To justify its adherence, I took my coffee to my desk and began rereading last night's report on Jill Mason.

"Are we billing Bert Calle?" she asked, still full of her good humor and pointedly ignoring my pique.

Bert was the father of the little girl whose beaten and raped body was found on the roof of her apartment building over on Avenue A. Jesus! Was that just yesterday? I shook my head. "I'm sorry I forgot to talk to you about that."

"No problem. I didn't think so. Damn shame," she said and shook her head. "How're you supposed to make a kid feel safe in the world, when they're not even safe in their own homes?"

That stirred something in my memory I'd wanted to ask her opinion about. "What do you think is wrong with Carmine's kid?"

She shrugged. "Carmine."

I laughed, finished my coffee, and picked up the phone. I'd left word in a few places last night that I'd be looking to talk to a couple of my cop buddies this morning, guys I'd walked the beat with and who had access to the people who really know what's what on the Upper East Side: the doormen and porters and bellhops and maids and nannies. The invisible people. People like *mi abuelitos,* both of whom had been doormen in ritzy Upper West Side buildings for more years than I am old and who knew more about the residents of those buildings than the snobs ever could imagine.

It was arranged that I would talk to the day-shift doorman and a porter in Jill Mason's former residence, and to a porter in her former office building. Two 'Ricans and a black man, proof of our changing times. Back when my grandfathers were looking for work, Colored men were barred from opening the doors for, and tipping their hats to, the denizens of ritzy hotel and office and apartment and department store buildings on the Upper East Side, so they worked on the West Side, which made getting to work a pain in ass because they had to cross the Park. I shook off the bad memory, stood, grabbed my coat, and pulled it on, all the while muttering curses to myself, which apparently were louder than I'd intended because Yo sauntered toward me from behind the screen.

"You okay?"

"Just marvelous," I muttered. "I'm outta here." She tossed me one of the cellular phones and I dropped it into the inside pocket of my overcoat, grateful for its tinyness. One of many things I didn't miss about being a cop was all the crap you had to wear and carry.

"So what, there ain't no hoodlums on the Upper East Side?" She gave me that in her Rosie Perez voice and, without another word, I got my gun from the desk drawer and made a big production of removing my top coat and sport jacket, strapping on the holster and gun beneath my left arm, and re-clothing myself. That was one point of departure from Hawk/Spenser: I didn't like guns. Didn't like 'em as a cop, didn't like 'em now. Had shot somebody only once and didn't ever want to do it again. Give me a good old fistfight any day. Problem is, every asshole on the planet has a gun these days because the little punks are too cowardly and weak to go it *mano a mano*. Yo, on the other hand, despite her dislike of aspects of the business, was a strong advocate of my being armed—with weapon and phone—at all times.

"You satisfied now?" I asked, pique in full bloom.

Yo sniffed disdainfully at my charade and blew me a kiss as I left. So much for attitude and fits of pique.

I could have gotten off the train at 77th Street; it would have been closer to my destination. But I got off a stop earlier, at 68th Street-Hunter College, so I could wonder what it had been like for Jill Mason, getting off here more than a quarter century ago, when she might well have been the only black getting off the train in this neighborhood. I wondered but I didn't know, and that made me wonder about myself, about how little I knew about how somebody different from myself might have felt: a poor black girl from the Lower East Side immersed suddenly in the rarefied opposite world. From the beginning of New York, there's been a major difference between the Uppers and the Lowers of the East and West Sides of the city, a difference defined and explained, then and now, by money. I knew how I'd felt, as a brown-skinned male, in some Upper East Side neighborhoods, and I'd been wearing the uniform of the New York City Police Department. It wasn't always welcoming.

But when I exited the train station at 68th Street, I could

have been almost anywhere in Manhattan. Kids and bums and purveyors of everything from incense to hot dogs to bootleg videotapes, CDs, and books, crowded the mouth of the station. Even as familiar as this corner was to me—this was my stop back when I walked the beat—I was surprised by the noise and the congestion and the dirt. But it didn't take long for the scenery to change. I walked north on Lexington Avenue for five blocks and hung a left at 73rd Street. By the time I walked the block to Park Avenue, I was in a different world. The world of the Upper East Side. The world of Mr. and Mrs. Elliot Payton, who had lived for more than fifteen years in a top-floor, twelve-room apartment.

William Vargas was the doorman, had been the doorman for more than eight years. He was perhaps ten years older than me and about forty pounds heavier, though we were the same height. But he looked like a tank, not a sausage, in the black uniform with its gold braid and buttons. He wore gold wire-rimmed glasses and a gold wedding band, which made him look like the husband, father, and peewee league coach that he was. Yeah, Ernie Sanchez had told him I wanted a word and he didn't mind, as long as I didn't get in the way of his door. I promised not to get in the way.

Yes, he knew Mrs. Payton . . . Dr. Mason. He called her Mrs. Payton when she was with her husband or children, Dr. Mason when she was alone. She was "the nicest lady in the building. That is the truth," William Vargas said, laying his right hand on the middle of his chest, across a swath of gold braid. What made Mrs. Payton/Dr. Mason so nice, and so memorably so, was the fact that she spoke to him— the doorman! Always. Good morning, good afternoon, good evening. And she called him Mr. Vargas! Him, the doorman! Merry Christmas, Mr. Vargas. Happy Easter, Mr.

Vargas. And Mr. Payton and the children, as polite as she was. Always. "And it wasn't no act, either! You know how some people do things just to say it's what they're doing, or to be that, whatsittheycallit? Politically correct?"

I tried to convey to William Vargas that yes, indeed, I did know what how some people's behavior is dictated by others' reaction to that behavior, but William didn't need to hear from me. He was on a verbal roll, recalling and telling how Jill Mason Payton gave a gift certificate "for special underwear" to the wife of the night doorman, who had had a mastectomy. "Can you imagine? Who would think to do something like that? Doctor Mason, that's who! She knew that special-made underwear cost a shitload of dough!"

I had to ask: "Special underwear?"

"You know! When a lady, she loses a breast 'cause she's got cancer, she gotta have some special-made underwear."

I nodded. I knew. What I didn't know was how Jill Mason would know to make such a gift to the night doorman for his wife.

William Vargas looked at me strangely. "From her maid," he said to me in a tone borrowed directly from Yolanda. Of course. From her maid, whose name I wrote down, along with the fact that she lived in Parkchester, in the Bronx.

During our conversation, William Vargas had tipped his black-trimmed-in-gold cap and opened the door to admit and release at least two dozen men and women, addressing most, if not all, of them by name, and not one of them had acknowledged his presence or his actions with a word or a glance, to say nothing of calling him "Mr. Vargas." He had tipped his hat and assisted mink-and-diamond-wearing women into taxis and not one of them had even looked at him, to say nothing of thanking him. No wonder he could remember every word Jill Mason Payton had ever spoken to him.

"What about the husband?"

"I told ya already, stand-up guy. Just like her."

"But how did he feel about her? You ever notice any tension between the two of them? See any problems?"

Vargas bristled as if I were questioning the sanctity of his own marriage. "They were solid," he said, raising his right hand and crossing the middle finger over the index finger in a sign of inseparability. "You shoulda seen how he looked at her. You know how a man looks at his woman: pride, lust, and the rest of you sonsabitches keep away? That's how he looked at her. Always. And always had his hands on her. Around her shoulder or holding her hand or around her waist. And if the kids were with 'em, they were holding their hands. He always held the little girl's hand and she held the bigger girl's hand."

Vargas left me standing alone for a moment while he stepped into the street to meet an approaching limousine. He opened the back door of the stretch, then hustled back to the front door of the building just in time to open it for two women who'd make Jill Mason look like a pauper. Wearing half a million dollars in fur and jewels between the two of them, they followed Vargas to the limo and into it. Neither one of them looked his way. He saluted and closed the door and big bus eased silently into the traffic that seemed to part for it.

And Jill Mason was back downtown riding taxis and the subway? That's what I was thinking when Vargas told me I'd have to come back later, after the lunch rush. "Lunch is big business around here. Everybody either goes out to it, or invites people in to it." And, on cue, another limo eased up the curb. Vargas opened both doors and from the car emerged four richly-clad women whom the doorman greeted and addressed by name. None returned the greeting. I watched and listened, and one of them looked at me, the up-and-down, head-to-toe perusal, wrinkled her nose like at a bad smell, shoved past me, literally. Vargas was right, I needed to come back later. After the lunch rush.

The porter at the building where Jill Mason practiced the art of psychiatry also was William—Robinson—a sixty-year-old black man who told a similar tale to that of William Vargas. "Mr. Robinson," she called the porter, and always had the time to chat with him for a few seconds. How were his wife, his children, his grandchildren? Did he have a good holiday? Was he enjoying the lovely weather? She'd given him tickets to the fiftieth anniversary celebration of Jackie Robinson's integration of major league baseball, because she knew he loved baseball. She gave all the cleaning ladies in the building fifty-dollar Macy's gift certificates for Christmas. Every year. Yes, the beat cop had told him Phil wanted a word and why, and Mr. Robinson couldn't think why anybody would make trouble for Doctor Mason.

"I was the porter in this building the first day she came to work here, and I was on duty her last day here. In that whole time, I never heard anybody say a word against her, even the old school fellas."

And who, I asked, were these old school fellas?

"Old men who don't think women should be doctors, and definitely not black women. But every one of 'em, to a man, spoke politely to her, even if they did try to vote to have her removed from the building when she first came."

"How did she take that?"

He shrugged, and his shoulders lifted almost to his ears. "Same way she took everything. Couldn't tell if it bothered her or not. Always calm, always polite; never saw her mad, and saw her upset only twice."

The first time, he said, was when a young patient of one of her colleagues committed suicide in the office bathroom. " 'I told you she was suicidal.' That's what she said to that other doctor. They were in the hallway and I was in the trash room, and I heard 'em. 'You were over-medicating her instead of believing her, and now she's dead. I hope you burn in hell!' That's what she said to him. 'I hope you burn in hell.' She was cryin' and she went into the back stairwell. I went in after her. Gave her my handkerchief. You know what she did? The next week gave me a dozen pure linen handkerchiefs with my initials on 'em." He pulled a per-fectly laundered and starched linen hankie from his pocket. "Still got 'em. Use one of 'em every day."

"And the second time?" I prodded him.

He shook his head sadly. "After Mr. Payton and the little girls were killed. She tried to work and just couldn't. I never seen anybody so tore up." He shook his head again, and I thought he was finished. "And, come to think of it, she was put out about how her partners acted when she said she was leaving. Tried to sue her, they did."

"Sue her for what?" I asked.

"To keep her from leaving," William Robinson said with alacrity. "She's one of the best child psychiatrists in town. They say she knows more about child abuse than almost anybody. She testifies in court all the time. No sir, they didn't want her to leave and said they'd sue if she did. She told 'em to go ahead, she didn't care, and off she went. Will you tell her I said hello?"

Listening to the Williams, Vargas and Robinson, it felt like they were talking about some mythological creature, and yet I'd sat face to face with a very real human being that very morning. Was taking her a barbecue sparerib dinner and a bottle of wine in a few hours. I knew this woman! Did I think she was a saint? I'd never met anybody that good in my life.

I walked the ten blocks back to Jill Mason's former residence, keenly aware of my surroundings. I'd just left a building comprised totally of practitioners of the medical profession: psychiatrists, plastic surgeons, urologists, cardiologists, oncologists. Not a GP or a dentist or a clinical social worker in sight. Up here, it was the limousines causing the traffic jams instead of the taxis, and fur coats were as commonplace as leather jackets downtown. The population was whiter, older, maler, and definitely wealthier. I wondered if Jill Mason had ever felt really and truly at home here? I wondered if I'd ever have the nerve to ask her.

What I wanted to ask William Vargas was whether Jill Mason had enemies where she lived. Hard feelings with any of her neighbors? I was surprised to hear that Elliot Payton had almost come to blows with one of the residents who had tried to make Jill's parents enter the building through the servants' door. Surprised but pleased. Now they were acting like the kind of human beings I was familiar with. Somebody does you wrong, you deck 'em and worry about the good-conduct medal later.

". . . but since it was before my time, maybe you better ask him," Vargas was saying.

Damn. "I'm sorry, my mind was imagining Payton laying some rich guy out on the sidewalk, messing up his Brooks Brothers. Ask who what?"

Vargas grinned. "He coulda done it, too. Dude worked out two hours every day and boxed at the Y twice a week. The night man. Ask him about the time Mrs. Payton smacked some old broad who spit on her. Like I said, it was before my time."

I egged him on. "I don't care if it's second-hand info right now. I'm just building a profile." I raised my eyebrows and my hands to the sky.

"Well, the way I heard it, this old broad was on the elevator and Mrs. Payton was getting on, or the other way 'round. Anyway, the old broad takes a look at who's comin' to dinner and starts screamin' about how she ain't ridin' with no nigger. Tells the operator—old man, he's dead now—to close the door and don't let her in! He don't know what to do, he's just standin' there, and this old broad is callin' both of 'em niggers. Then she turns and spits right on Doctor Mason, who draws back and slaps her silly and tells the operator to close the door and take her up to her floor, tells the old broad she can walk if she don't wanna ride."

I tried to ask a question and couldn't, tried to make myself remember that this wasn't *Gone With the Wind* Vargas was talking about, but real life that had happened right here, inside the building behind me, less than twenty years ago, because that's how long Jill Mason had been married to Elliot Payton. This stuff sounded like something out of some dusty old history book, or on a public television documentary. Like stories *mi abuelitos* would tell. Or Itchy Johnson, or Mrs. Gillespie, Sandra's close-to eighty-year-old Grandma whom I'd met a few times. But Jill Mason was only fifty years old, and in her lifetime—and mine—somebody had spit on her and called her a nigger in the elevator in the building where she lived.

!Madre de Dios!

I must've said it aloud because Vargas said, *"Ave Maria Madre de Dios."* Then the phone rang and we both jumped.

I reached inside my coat and grabbed the thing. My heart was pounding when I flipped it open. Yolanda had never called me on the cell phone before, and it had to be her because she's the only one with the number.

"Digame," I said, willing my voice to be steady. It didn't work, and by the time Yolanda's hissed words were out of her mouth and roaring in my brain, my hand was shaking. I closed the phone and dropped it in my pocket. I gave William Vargas my card. "I owe you, *Hermano*," I said to him, "anything, anytime," and shook his hand. Then I ran the six blocks to the subway, ignoring the looks of displeasure and worse that I elicited from those who didn't move quickly enough out of my path.

Come back right now! There's been another one. Another little girl raped. This is the seventh one, Phil! Bert Calle overheard the cops talking. His daughter wasn't the only one killed. And Phil, Carmine's daughter is one of them.

Chapter Four

There must have been thirty people in the office when I arrived, men and women, most of them sitting on the floor and clustered in groups of varying sizes, and they were eerily quiet and still. Almost as a unit, they looked at me when I entered, and I could feel their anticipation. It frightened me. I sought comfort and saw Carmine. I kept searching until I spotted Yolanda and, nodding greetings as I traversed the crowd, I kept moving until I reached her at the rear of the office, near the kitchen.

"What are these people doing here?"

"Didn't you understand what I said?"

"Yo, what the hell are all these people doing here?"

"Trying to hire you, goddammit!"

I don't think Yolanda had ever been truly angry with me and she certainly had never cursed me. I stepped back from her and turned to look at the people in my office. They all were standing now, looking back at me, all that anticipation crowding in on me, pushing on my chest.

"Mr. Rodriquez." One of the men emerged from the group and walked toward me. I didn't know him. He was older than me by a few years and shorter by a couple of inches and he looked like men I'd known all my life, men who worked hard at physical labor jobs, never making enough money, who ate too much of the wrong food and drank too much beer and never seemed to figure out where babies came from. Good men. Nice guys . . . most of the time. Would have a stroke or a heart attack and die too

60

early, leaving equally-tired widows and barely-grown children.

I extended my hand and he took it, and I could feel the calluses that confirmed that he earned his living with his hands. His name was Daniel Esposito and his youngest daughter had been raped on her way home from school eight months ago. The shame with which he told me this—head and eyes lowered, feet shuffling, words low and hesitant—made me angry. Some piece of shit had destroyed his child and he was ashamed! Then he looked up at me and I saw anger in his eyes.

"There have been seven and the police knew and they never told us. Fuckin' bastards never told us!"

Esposito's fury became the crowd's fury. They surged toward me and I had to will myself to stand my ground. I sought out Carmine and fixed him in a stare that dared him to flinch.

"Yeah," he snarled, "all right, my kid, too. I guess that makes us the lucky ones. Ours are still alive. Fucked up in the head forever, but still alive."

A woman moaned and, snake-like, the crowd inched closer to me.

"What do you want from me?" I asked.

A woman I did know, a Jamaican who owned a standing-room-only café called El Caraibe on Rivington Street, stepped forward and opened the handles to a Starbuck's Coffee shopping bag. She upended it and deposited a pile of money and checks on the desk. "We want you to fix this mess," she said through clenched teeth. "This is to hire you to work for us and talk to us like we deserve and to tell us the truth."

"Mrs. Edwards," I said. Her name was Arlene Edwards, and I knew her because I ate at her place a couple of times a month. I looked from her to the pile of money, to the crowd of people who'd backed me up against the wall in my own office, to Yolanda. "There's nothing . . . I can't . . . it's the job of the police to investigate assaults . . ."

Daniel Esposito was on top of me before I could stop him. "Rape, goddamn you! Rape! Not assault! Seven little girls have been raped and two of them are dead and the fuckin' police ain't done shit!"

I was a changed man and I knew it. Esposito had me by the coat lapels and I hadn't knocked him down yet. My fists were knotted at my sides and my teeth were grinding but Esposito was still standing, still in my face. I uncurled my fists and took hold of his wrists and waited for him to release me. Which he did, with an apology, which I accepted. Then I tried to explain the limitations the law placed on private investigators, the primary one being that the cops would jack my ass up to the sky for messing around in their business. And a serial rapist was definitely their business.

"Then why haven't they caught him yet?"

"Why didn't they tell us about it?"

"I wouldn't let my kids walk to school if I knew that bastard was out there!"

"What the hell are we supposed to do? Wait until the fucker gets tired of raping little girls? Maybe switches to little boys?"

"Or moves on to another neighborhood?"

"I thought you cared about this neighborhood, Rodriquez. At least that's what you always claimed."

First a series of body blows, then the low, sneaky one below the belt, to the nuts. Works every time. I caught my breath and straightened up. "Here's what I can do," I said, and laid out a plan that would allow me to nose around and ask a few questions. The fact that the victims all lived in the same neighborhood was useful, as was the fact that they all were in the seven- to nine-year-old age range. Selective serial rapist, and a pedophile to boot. I could talk to family and friends of the victims without getting into too much trouble with the cops. I hoped.

"And I'm gonna have to talk to your children," I said as gently as I could, knowing that was the last thing I wanted to do and they wanted me to do. And even as I felt that dread, I thought of Jill Mason. That's why she was treating Carmine Aiello's daughter! Then I realized that even if I could direct all those little victims to the good doctor, she couldn't and wouldn't tell me shit about whatever they told her.

I realized that I had a headache, the dull, thudding kind, the kind aspirin didn't help. I waded into the crowd to get to my desk and got a notepad out of the drawer. "I need every one of you to write your name, address, and telephone number on this pad. If you're here with your husband or wife, I need both names. If your spouse is not here with you, I still need his or her name. And if your child— your daughter—has been a victim, like Mr. Esposito here, I need for you to speak with Miss Aguierre."

Yo and I spent the next couple of hours interviewing our new clients and getting contracts signed. I'd counted the money and been overwhelmed to find more than five thousand dollars in cash and checks. I wrote out a receipt for each of the checks and tried, in vain, to account for the cash: of those who'd contributed in cash, none could recall exactly how much. In true "baby boy" form, I decided to let Yolanda worry about how to account for a couple of thousand dollars in cash. Teach her to get angry and curse at me.

By the time everyone left and we were alone in the office,

neither of us had the energy to do anything but sit in numb silence. I wanted a beer but couldn't will myself to get up and go get it. Yolanda kept flipping through the pages of names and addresses and signed contracts, just turning the pages, one after another. *"Pobrecitas,"* she whispered to herself. *"Siete ninas. Pobrecitas,"* she said.

I stood up. I didn't want them to be poor little things, and I couldn't think of them as victims. They already were more than that to me. I knew Carmine and I knew Jill Mason, links to one little girl who now was more than a victim. And I knew Arlene Edwards, which made her granddaughter more than a victim. And Daniel Esposito had grabbed me in my chest and screamed in my face and I'd let him. That made him personal to me, and, therefore, his daughter more than a victim. *Pobrecitas*, my ass! I began to pace back and forth for no reason other than I could no longer sit still. I wasn't thinking so much as I was feeling. And feelings always got me in trouble.

"This is a good thing you're doing, Phil," Yolanda said quietly, sadness weighing down her voice. "A right thing."

I didn't know about all that. "It'll probably get me in trouble with the cops, so maybe keep the door locked when I'm out. We wouldn't want any unexpected searches and seizures of files or records." I was being flip when I said it; then the thought scared me. I really was tap dancing on the high wire, and a slip could maim me for life.

"I'll do a search for all assaults on juveniles for, what do you think, the past year? Eighteen months? Two years?"

I stopped pacing and looked at her.

She looked back at me. "What?"

I couldn't answer her, didn't know how. Didn't know how to understand her interest in this case from the beginning. I knew she could work magic with the damn computers, but why couldn't she care about everything we did with this same intensity?

"The time is less important than the location. These are cluster crimes. That's what to look for. Any more rapes of little girls in this area. Any cluster serial rapes of young girls anywhere in the city."

She looked at me for a long, hard minute, then turned and faded away behind the Shoji screen. I realized I still wore my overcoat, so I took it off and threw it across one of the desks. Then I sat down at my own desk, removed my spiral notebook, and began writing. It had been a long, tough day, and it wasn't over yet.

Jill Mason greeted me wearing a pair of gold-rimmed reading glasses low on her nose and a harried, rushed expression on the rest of her face. She apologized for the latter, waved me in, relocked the door behind me, and told me to make myself comfortable while she finished at her desk. She said it wouldn't take long. I told her to take as long as necessary. I could do with a few minutes of calm and quiet.

A cloth-covered folding table sat in the middle of the office. On it were two plates, two wine glasses, knives, forks, and a pile of napkins. I busied myself unloading the bags of food and uncorking the wine and arranging it all on the table. It was an impressive-looking spread—a slab of ribs, a whole chicken, sweet potato soufflé, lettuce-and-tomato salad, and a decent Sauvignon Blanc, which I uncorked and let breathe. I was beginning to have some appetite. I looked up to see how Doctor Mason was progressing, and she was walking toward the table.

"I must admit, Mr. Rodriquez, that I've looked forward to this all day." She smiled and looked much less harried.

"Hope you like sweet potatoes."

"Love them! My grandparents were Southerners—my mother's parents—and my mother's Sunday dinners are still the stuff of the South. Best food in the world!"

I was thinking that Itchy had gotten it right about her grandparents being from the South. No lie there. Then I thought, why would he remember such a thing? After so many years, why would he remember something like that? Why did he care? Was he best friends with them? Or maybe that's just the kind of thing old people remembered . . . where somebody was born . . . when somebody died.

I noticed that Doctor Mason had a healthy appetite, and, considering that Yolanda could out-eat the entire defensive line of the Giants, wondered if that was a trait of small women. They must have more in common than appetite, small women, because Doctor Mason stopped eating long enough to ask me why I was watching her eat. Something Yo would do. I told her and she smiled a smile which almost reached her eyes. She said she hadn't eaten all day and was ravenous. She also said, in her quiet way, that she was just regaining her appetite. She hadn't eaten very much or very often after the deaths of her husband and children. I told her I could imagine that was the kind of thing that could take away an appetite, and we ate in silence for another few minutes.

She spoke first. "I installed the security system after the break-in. I thought they were looking for drugs. I don't keep any here, but patient records are here, though they are well protected."

"In the computer?"

She shook her head and pointed to what looked like an end table. "In the safe. It would take dynamite to open it."

I went over to the table, knelt down beside it, ran my

hands along its edges, pushing and prodding, and a door opened to reveal the steel casing within. "Clever," I said.

"The computer is downloaded every day and the discs go in there. The dictation goes in there. All my notes and files go in there." She exhaled deeply and shook her head. "I wasn't worried about the files, and I don't keep any drugs, but I didn't like feeling vulnerable." She shivered a little and drank a sip of wine. I noticed that her hand shook slightly when she put the glass back on the table.

"So then the phone calls started," I said.

She nodded. "Nasty, horrible things. Calling me a murderer for killing my husband and children. Calling me a drunk driver. I wasn't drunk at the time of that accident, Mr. Rodriquez. I hadn't been drinking . . ."

I raised my hand to stop her. "You don't need to explain or justify yourself to me, Doctor Mason. I'm here to stop whoever is doing this to you, not to help them."

"I just wanted you to know." She squeezed her eyes shut for a moment, collected herself, and continued. "I thought I'd been as devastated as it was possible to be and still live. Until I heard that voice accuse me . . ."

I stood and walked away from her while she pulled herself together again and marveled at her strength. I wondered who her shrink was, and wondered how she had anything left to give to her patients. How she had the strength to listen to other people's shit all day, as Yo had described it.

"What can you tell me about your assailant, Doctor Mason?"

"Not as tall as you, or as muscular, but he was strong. He grabbed me from behind, so I didn't see his face. I saw his hands—light complexioned. He could have been Caucasian or light Hispanic. No marks that I could see, but he did have chewed, ugly nails, and his hands were dirty. And he smelled dirty, as if he hadn't bathed in a while, or washed his clothes."

I watched her remember the attack with all her senses. I could see her nose wrinkle as it recalled the smell, and her eyes narrowed slightly. Then she shook herself, shook off the memory, and I was struck again at how small she was.

"He could have hurt you if he wanted to," I said.

She nodded. "He told me as much—"

I cut her off. "He spoke to you? What did he say?"

"That he could kill me if he wanted to, but he didn't, not then. He was just warning me . . ."

"Verbatim. Tell me exactly what he said, verbatim." And I knew she could.

She closed her eyes and cocked her head a little to the left. "He said, 'I could kill you right now. We don't want you here. Go back uptown, where you belong.' Then he shook me hard and slammed me into the wall and he ran away."

She had just left her parents' building when she was attacked. Her assailant had been waiting in the narrow space between two buildings and grabbed her as she walked past, pulling her in toward him, backwards. Mean bastard, and a smart one.

"I'm going to have somebody pick you up every morning and take you home every night, starting Monday. It will be one man in the morning and a different one at night, but the same two men every day. They will always come inside to get you and they will always take you inside and check the location before leaving you." I raised my hand. She'd tried to interrupt me several times and I wouldn't let her. "This is crucial, Doctor Mason. You live by a daily routine and whoever is trying to hurt you knows what it is. I don't want you to change it—I understand that you can't let other people mess with your life like that. Please don't argue with me about this."

She sighed deeply and closed her eyes. She walked away from the table, over to her desk, and stood there, arms wrapped around herself, looking down at the photographs of her family. Then she came back to the table where I was seated and drank some of her wine.

"Perhaps it would be better if I let him kill me."

"Better for whom, Doctor Mason? Certainly not the seven little girls from this neighborhood who've been raped in the last eight or nine months. They need you alive and well, so you can help them become alive and well again."

Her eyes opened wide but she didn't say anything.

"Several of their parents were in my office earlier this evening, including Carmine. His daughter is just one of the victims. I'm not sure if it's correct to call her lucky; two of the other victims were murdered after they were raped."

Tears filled her eyes but they didn't spill out. "Will you find him? Whoever is hurting the children?"

God. There was that question again, and my answer had to be the same. "I don't know. I don't think so. I don't think I can. But what I can do is try to keep you safe, so you can help those little girls. Carmine said you saved his daughter's life."

It was her turn. She raised her hand and stopped my words before they left my mouth. "Don't say anything patronizing or platitudinous, Mr. Rodriquez. I don't need to hear it and I don't want to hear it."

I shrugged and poured some more wine in her glass and she drank it.

"There's something I didn't tell you."

I sat still, waiting to hear it.

"The voices were different. The one on the telephone was different from the one in the alley. They weren't the same person."

I heard Yolanda's voice. *Shrinks know secrets.* The words did back-flips in my brain and made me shiver. Suppose that's why Jill Mason was under attack. The rapist knew she was counseling one of the victims . . . one who could identify him.

I heard William Robinson's voice. *She testifies in court all the time.* Suppose she was about to testify against a perp . . . or suppose somebody she'd testified against and put away was out now . . . All the suppositions could be true and it wouldn't matter one damn bit, because Doctor Mason wouldn't tell me. Couldn't tell me.

I sat on my couch, looking out at my magnificent view of traffic crossing the Manhattan and Brooklyn Bridges. Another Yolanda idea: I'd bought two units in a shit building in a shit neighborhood a few years back. The neighborhood now was being called the new SoHo, my building was a yuppie paradise, and the rent I charged for the smaller unit paid the mortgage on itself and on my top-floor digs. Because the building was in a part of the East Village that juts out into the East River, I have this spectacular view to the south, which usually soothes and smoothes out the rough edges of any day. Tonight, it depressed me. The happy crackling of the wood fire made it worse. A bad case of the Friday night blues.

I was tired of being alone and didn't know what to do about it. I wanted a Susan like Spenser had, but had spent too many years behaving like Hawk when it came to women. Yolanda's advice was to stop worrying about it and when I least expected it, the woman of my dreams would stumble into my life. Well, she hadn't yet and I needed somebody to talk to about today. About what I was feeling. But the best I could do was consume the remainder of the barbecue, which Jill Mason had insisted I bring with me, wash it down with Samuel Adams, listen to Carlos Santana talk about his Black Magic Woman, and worry about what the hell I'd gotten myself into.

I knew I had no business stepping into anything as messy as a serial rapist case but the whole thing made me angry. Either the cops knew they had a serial rapist on their hands and for whatever reason didn't alert the neighborhood, or they didn't know, which in a way was worse, because that meant seven- and eight-year-old girls were being raped and murdered and nobody cared enough to notice a pattern; meant that every little girl in the neighborhood was in danger. And winter had arrived early.

Chapter Five

Mike Smith and Eddie Ortiz welcomed the responsibility for keeping Jill Mason alive and well. No matter how long and loudly they proclaimed their joy at being retired, the truth is that they were cops and always would be cops, and that meant they bored very easily when confronted with normal, daily life. I'd approached them a bit hesitantly, not wanting to appear ungrateful for the timely fashion with which they dispatched the skip-trace job, and not wanting to seem too demanding of their time. They jumped all over the opportunity, refining it beyond my original vision, which had been to have one of them pick Doctor Mason up in the morning and deliver her safely to work and the other do the same at the end of the day.

"Jeez, Rodriquez, ain't you got no imagination?" This from Mike Smith, a dead-ringer for Lieutenant Fancy on "NYPD Blue": heavier, more muscular, but with that same dark, intense dignity. Mike had walked a beat in Harlem for twenty years, learning a lot about imagination along the way.

"Yeah," chimed in Eddie Ortiz, something looking like disgust written all over his hairy face. "You get nothin' for your money, you do it that way." And he laid out a plan for me that made so much better sense than my own idea that I didn't bother with embarrassment. I went directly to shame. Even hung my head.

The way Eddie and Mike arranged it, Mike would be Jill Mason's escort on both ends of her day, and Eddie would lounge in the shadows, looking for somebody who might be looking for a way to get to her. The good doctor would be safe and I could worry about other things. Like what exactly it was I thought I was going to do for a room full of frightened parents, some of whose daughters were rape victims and worse. I was in over my head, but I knew that when I accepted their money. An angry Yo on one side of me and angry parents on the other side. I did the only logical thing: I capitulated. But because it was logical doesn't mean it was smart. Lots of dumb things happen for good reasons. The question was whether I could salvage the situation without further manifestations of dumb.

I knew that my clients wanted—expected—me to catch a serial rapist, but I had no intention of doing any such thing, not to mention no authority, which was a fact that bore mentioning, except nobody wanted to hear it. I also, truth be told, had no real experience in that area. I hadn't been an investigator when I was a cop. What I *could* do was get information for them. Maybe not enough to ease their pain, but more than they had, which was that seven little girls had been raped and two of them murdered, probably by the same lowlife piece of shit, and nobody in the police department had cared enough to just sit down and talk to them, even if there was nothing substantive to say.

What I couldn't do was stroll over to the station house and wander upstairs to the squad room and casually ask the detective in charge why he was handling this case in such a fucked-up manner. For all I knew, he had a plan and was working it. That I thought he should share that plan with the victims wasn't worth the buck-fifty it cost to ride the subway. Which, strangely, I didn't feel like doing this morning, even though I was on the West Side.

I'd missed my ritual morning walk because I was busy

introducing Jill Mason to Mike Smith, while Eddie Ortiz watched from some hidey-hole and was so good at his job that I never saw him, and I was looking. Now I was trying to decide whether to stop by the office and see what information Yolanda had elicited from her computers, or pay a visit to Carmine and get a sense of what was happening in the 'hood . . . Holy shit! The realization smacked me in the face like a sucker punch: Carmine didn't live in the same neighborhood as the other victims. Lower East Side, yes, but closer to Little Italy than Alphabet City, west of Allen Street. For some reason, that fact hadn't registered with me on Friday night, when all those parents were crowding around me. They shared a common problem, so I'd ascribed certain common denominators to them, like living in the same neighborhood. But they didn't live in the same neighborhood.

I was running before I could stop myself, weaving in and out of pedestrian traffic on the sidewalk and vehicular traffic in the street, running like I was dodging bullets instead of the hostile glares of walkers and drivers. And though I was headed toward the office, it felt very much like I was running away from something . . . or trying to outrun something.

There were two people in the office, seated at the desks and talking with Yolanda, when I burst into the room, and all three looked up at me with that look that demands an explanation.

"It's important, Yo," I said to her, and, "good morning, folks," I said to her visitors. Our visitors, since I supposed they were clients or prospective clients, two women in their mid to late forties with their Bruno Maglis firmly planted on the rungs of the upwardly mobile ladder from the looks of them.

"Have you found out something about who's hurting the little girls?" asked the one with the platinum hair—expensive salon job, not the do-it-yourself variety.

I looked hard at her, certain that she hadn't been in my office on Friday night, and I was about to say as much, when the other one—who, on closer inspection, most definitely was the sister or other close relative of the first one, though her hair was darker and she was shorter by three or four inches—spoke up.

"We all know about what you're doing. That's why we're here."

I felt nauseous. "You have a vic . . . ah, a daughter who's been . . . ah . . ." I couldn't finish and it took them a second to understand why.

"Oh no!" exclaimed platinum. "God forbid, no!" She was shaking her head back and forth so forcefully that I could see the diamonds winking on her earlobes when her hair moved.

"We want to help," said the look-alike. "We grew up in this neighborhood and moved out when it got so bad."

"If we'd known it was gonna clean up like it has, maybe we'd a stayed," said platinum with a shrug.

"As I was saying," said look-alike, "we keep in touch and we heard about what . . . about these terrible things, all weekend the phone rang. And we heard how you were helping and we know your kind of work is expensive."

Yolanda raised a piece of paper that I recognized as a check. "Miss Golson and her sister, Mrs. Stein, have retained us to protect their property."

I was beginning to feel like Alice down the hole. I knew better than speak, so I waited. I could tell by the look on Yo's face that I should prepare myself for what was coming, but since I didn't know what I was preparing for, I forced a half-smile from tight lips and nodded politely, if stupidly, toward Miss Golson and Mrs. Stein.

"They own the building the little Cummerbatch girl was thrown from."

The little Cummerbatch girl. Arlene Edwards' grand-daughter. My nausea turned to anger. Yolanda must have been watching me, because she quickly continued her explanation.

"I told them that because they weren't connected directly to this case, they couldn't retain us, but they wanted to contribute financially. So, when I learned that they did, in fact, have a connection, we worked out an agreement whereby they hire us to secure their building—check the doors and elevators, the laundry room, and the roof access. Make sure no outsiders can get in, make sure the residents are safe . . ."

Yo's words trailed off into what sounded like a warning wrapped in a question. Didn't I understand what she was saying? Was I that stupid? Smile and thank the ladies and take their money, you fool! I heard Yo's eyes saying those things to me, so I shook hands with Miss Golson, whose name was Shirley, and her sister Eileen—Mrs. Stein—and as I was accepting the ring of keys that would give me access to every door in the building they owned, I understood that I now had legal and legitimate access to a crime scene. My smile became genuine, my handshake firmer, my gratitude for their business expressed heartily.

"Hell of a good job, Yo," I said after they'd gone.

Yolanda gave me one of those looks, but her heart wasn't in it. "The cops aren't gonna give you an engraved invitation to their party, and you can't help anybody standing on the outside looking in." Then she shrugged as if what she'd done was as normal as breathing. And for her, it was.

"You know a lot about this business, Yo, more than you let on."

"The issue has never been that I don't know the business, Phil," she snapped at me. "The issue is that I don't like the business, but no way I could run this office and not know what we can and can't do, and ways to get around the can't-dos."

She was angry and I didn't know why, and it didn't look like she was going to tell me. So I told her what had brought me there in such a hurry. She began frowning as I was talking and when I was finished, she vanished behind the Shoji screens and reappeared as quickly as she'd departed. She was waving a sheaf of papers at me, proceeds, I knew, from her various computer searches. She'd also stuck her computer glasses on her nose, which confirmed a suspicion I'd harbored for a while about the status of her eyesight. One of these days, I'd gather up enough nerve to mention it.

"None of those little girls really lived in the same neighborhood," she said, pointing to a sheet of paper that listed the names and addresses of all the victims, "though they all attended the same two schools," she said, pointing to the names and addresses of the schools on her list.

I studied the list. "Time to play stick the pins on the map," I said, more to myself than to Yolanda. She had the kind of brain that contained its own map. Not only could she visualize the addresses, she could see how they connected to each other—or didn't. I needed to see it all laid out before me in neatly ordered grids. "So if they don't have location in common, it's something else. I'll double-check the schools, to be certain we haven't missed anything there. And clubs and organizations. The Girl Scouts—"

"Brownies," Yo said, and shook her head at me when I

looked confused. She wasn't talking about food?

"The little ones belong to Brownies. Girl Scouts is for big girls. You know, like Cub Scouts and Boy Scouts?" She was talking to me in that "speech for the mentally deficient" voice and I was about to get annoyed when she said, "And don't forget church."

"Church?"

"Church, Phil, find out what churches they attended."

"You're joking, right?"

She raised her eyebrows at me but didn't say anything. I was about to defend myself but realized even before the words left my mouth that they were stupid. I was prepared to say that kind of thing happened elsewhere, not in my neighborhood, but it was no joke what was happening to these little girls right here in my neighborhood, and certainly no joke that churches weren't the safe havens we'd once been lulled into thinking they were.

One of our first major expenses in the early days was for maps: four-foot-by-four-foot sections of the city, enhanced so that every street and alleyway was visible. We hung up the Lower East Side section and spent the next couple of hours going over everything we knew, point by point, me marking the relevant locations with colored flags that suctioned onto the map surface, rather than literally punching holes into it. The girls were all eight or nine years old and attended one of two schools. There were no other common threads. They were different races—black, white, Latina; they were from different economic circumstances, ranging from quite comfortable (Anna Cummerbatch and Terry Aiello) to bean sandwich poor (most of the others); and Yo was right—they all lived in different neighborhoods. All in the East Village and the Lower East Side, but every neighborhood down here had its own identity, not to mention that the word "neighborhood" carried a different definition and connotation in the five boroughs of New York City than in some other parts of the world. A "neighborhood" in, say, a city like Los Angeles or Atlanta could encompass a few miles. Here it was more like a few blocks. Chinatown was a neighborhood. Little Italy was a neighborhood. The Bowery was a neighborhood. The Lower East Side was both a neighborhood *and* a designated part of town, and within that was a neighborhood the real estate moguls and gentrifiers dubbed LoEsida.

I looked at the map and at where the little flags of different colors hung on the map's surface, and superimposed faces of little girls on the flags. There also was nothing similar about their names, their sizes, their hair color. Yet there had to be a common denominator. Unless there were seven different rapists . . .

The super at the apartment building owned by the Golson sisters was relieved to see me. The way a rat is relieved to see a cat instead of a cobra. He was sick and tired of the cops, he let me know, but he was sick and tired generally of people asking him questions to which he had no answers, and interfering with his performance of his duties. Which, he informed me, were many and varied.

"It ain't easy keepin' a buildin' this size in good workin' order, sir, I can tell you that." His name was Basil Griffin and yes, he was a native of Trinidad and how did I come to know that? He softened only slightly when I explained how my best friend in the police academy was Trinidadian and how we're still friends though we don't see each other as often as we'd like. I didn't explain why a black man rising up through the ranks of the New York City police department has time for nothing but keeping the people trying to prevent his rise off-guard and at a safe distance.

"I know you're busy, Mr. Griffin, and I'm sorry to take you away from your duties, but I need your help." And I also need to rule you out as a suspect, I thought to myself, as I scrutinized the man. Who had better access to a building and its tenants than the super who just happened to live in the front apartment on the first floor?

"Come on then," he said gruffly, and turned away from me and toward the elevators at the end of the lobby.

"Where to?" I asked.

"To the roof, man." He said "mon." "Isn't that what you want to see? Where the little girl was t'rowed from?"

I shook my head. "Not just now, Mr. Griffin. What I need to do is understand how this building works. When people come and go. How many of them come and go, and how many remain home during the day. Who works nights? Is this a friendly building—do people talk to each other and visit back and forth between apartments—or do they keep to themselves? Are there any problems? Like some kid makes too much noise—playing his music or riding his skateboard in the hallway—or some kid deals drugs, or somebody doesn't like somebody because they're black or they're gay? That's the kind of thing I need to know, Mr. Griffin, because whoever killed Arlene Edwards' grand-daughter and threw her off this building knew her, and he knew this building."

Basil Griffin had been listening to me, his eyes locked on my face, shifting from my eyes to my mouth, as if he could see the words coming out, and until I mentioned Arlene Edwards, his eyes had been cold and flinty and practically unblinking. He blinked when I said her name.

"You know Arlene?"

"I consider her a friend," I said.

He nodded his head up and down a few times and hooked the fat key ring back onto his belt. "These things you want to know, they're better things than what the police wanted to know."

"And what did they want to know, Mr. Griffin?"

"Stupid things!" He spat the words like ridding his mouth of rancid meat. "Did I see anybody strange in the building or with the little girl! I watch for that child to come home every day, except when she goes to her Grandma at the restaurant. How stupid! If I see somebody strange with that child—with any child—he don't get the chance to t'row them from 'top the buildin' ', I can tell you dat!" All the Caribbean returned to his speech with the anger, and he took two deep breaths to calm himself. Unless he was a hell of an actor, Basil Griffin just removed himself as a suspect in my book, for certainly had he seen the perp, we'd have a dead rapist instead of a dead child.

I followed Griffin onto the elevator and he inserted a small key into the control panel and we rode down a floor to the basement. The door slid open and deposited us into the other world of the New York City apartment dweller: the world of mesh and metal storage cages and of laundry rooms, of recycling bins and garbage collection bins, of generators and compressors and conductors of steam and heat and air and water. These basement labyrinths—the size of a closet or encompassing a square block, depending on the building served—reflect the condition of the buildings they support. This was one healthy building.

Every corner of the basement was illuminated, revealing a new, high-gloss paint job. There was no hint of garbage odor, though the trash collection cage was in full view to the left of the elevator. The whir and rumble of washing machines and dryers were comforting background sounds, as were the heat and the clean smell they generated. Even the locked storage bins reflected a sense of cleanliness and order. I remarked on the fact, thinking of the state of the storage bins in my own building, and in buildings in which I'd lived. Clearly having Basil Griffin as the superintendent would have made a difference, for, as he told me succinctly, he didn't allow disorder in the storage bins. Dirt and disorder breed "vermin," he noted, and he didn't allow vermin in his building. And I couldn't picture a rat or roach attempting to scurry across this floor, in search of garbage that had no odor. Couldn't picture any of the two-legged variety, either.

Basil Griffin's forty-square-foot office was a further reflection of the building and of himself. Two walls of floor-to-ceiling metal shelves held neatly-arranged boxes of everything he could possibly need to maintain his sense of order. My visual scan spotted light bulbs and garbage bags; nuts and bolts and screws and nails and hooks; an array of hand and power tools; tins and tubs of cleaning and disinfecting powders and solutions; mop and broom heads and handles; five-gallon buckets of paint; fifty-pound bags of rock salt. Home Depot had nothing on Basil Griffin's storeroom.

Along one wall was a desk-cum-worktable and affixed to its surface were laminated schematics of the building. Basil Griffin pointed to each apartment and told me who lived there. Told me in great detail who lived in each unit and how long they'd lived there and where they worked and how long they'd worked there. He knew who was home when; he knew who was ill; he knew which marriages were in trouble. He knew that nobody who lived in "his" building had raped and murdered the daughter of Errol and Sylvia Cummerbatch and tossed their child's body from the roof.

"How do you do all this alone, Mr. Griffin? This basement is cleaner than most people's apartments."

He looked at me hard, then gave me a slight, sly grin. "You wanna know who else works here in this buildin'? Then ask me who else works here in this buildin'."

Nothing slight or sly about the grin I gave him. I'd probably never have enough experience to put one over on this guy. "Who else works here with you, Mr. Griffin?"

He told me: Alvin Boggs, from six in the morning until two-thirty in the afternoon, Monday through Friday, for the last eighteen years; Javier Lopez from two-thirty in the afternoon until eleven at night, Monday through Friday, for the last eleven years. On Saturdays and Sundays, he said, Gregory Jenkins, the newest employee, works from noon until four. "Three years and he hasn't missed a weekend," Griffin said, adding that the man was so grateful to be off the midnight shift he wouldn't dare miss a day. He hesitated only slightly when I asked for their addresses, phone numbers, and Social Security numbers, and he readily supplied a physical description of each man.

We left his office and I followed him around his domain as he showed me the new locks he'd installed on the laundry room door and on all the doors leading into and out of the basement. The door to the garbage cage was equipped with a spring lock, so that the gate automatically shut—and shut quickly—behind anyone entering or exiting that space. No way to get trapped inside there. No way or place for anybody to hide in this basement, I noted, as I followed him back into the elevator for the twelve-story, nonstop ride to the roof.

It was immediately apparent that the plate and lock on this door were new. "People liked using the roof," he said quietly. "For sunnin' theirselves, and growing their gardens. We had real pretty gardens on this roof. Flowers and plants and fruit trees. Even a palm tree. Lady in Six-G is from California and she missed her palm trees. Grew it on the roof in the spring and summer, took it back down to her apartment in the cold months."

He opened the door and we stepped out to the roof. The bedraggled vestiges of the garden were silent witness to the ugly horror that had occurred here. The plants seemed turned away, their boughs and branches drooped and dangling like heads held down in shame. Two weathered Adirondack chairs sat hunched together in one corner of the roof, faced away from where the sun would be if there were sun. Our feet crunched on the gravel carpet that covered the roof. I looked at Griffin, the question asked silently.

"Over there," he said, gesturing with his head toward the northeast corner of the building, and as I walked toward the edge of the roof, the wind suddenly picked up and smacked me in the face with a hard, frigid hand. My eyes watered and I wasn't certain it was because of the force of the cold air.

"Did the police check for footprints, scuff marks, that kind of thing?"

"Yeah," Griffin said, nodding. "They did all that. Took pictures, picked up pieces of gravel, took measurements." He shrugged. "I don't think they found anything."

I didn't think so, either. The girl was dead before she was thrown from the roof, so there'd have been no need for a struggle. But in the interest of thoroughness, I stepped to the edge of the roof and looked out, then down. I tried to imagine a little girl's brown and broken body on the pavement below and found that the imagining made me dizzy. I stepped quickly back and turned to catch Basil Griffin watching me.

"Why you say you won't find who did this?"

"I'm not a cop, Mr. Griffin. If I do anything that gets in the way of an official police investigation, I could lose my license. And I can't risk that."

"So what can you do?"

"I can try to find out what the police know that they haven't told the families. I know that the police believe that divulging too much information too soon can jeopardize an investigation. But I also believe that victims deserve as much information and truth as possible."

Basil Griffin harrumphed. Really and truly harrumphed, like some fat British guy in one of those highbrow BBC or PBS programs. I was impressed with the sound he made, if not with its intent. "They deserve more than that," he said, not attempting to conceal his contempt.

"I agree," I said. "I just don't know how I can give them more than that."

"You can find the evil bastard who's hurting little girls," Griffin said, and turned and walked away, leaving me to follow him down from the roof.

I called out to him. He stopped and turned back to face me. "I'd like to talk to the other guys—Boggs and Lopez and Jenkins. Is that all right with you?"

He gave me a look I couldn't read. "I can't stop you, can I?"

"Probably not," I said. "But this your building and it's not right to enter another man's house without first knocking on the door."

He gave me another look, and this is one I read loudly and clearly. It nailed me to the wall, and not with gentle, pain-free suction cups. I knew what he was going to say before he opened his mouth. "You think you got no right to find this . . . this monster. I think, Mr. Rodriquez, you got no right not to try."

★ ★ ★ ★ ★

"Can't you find out things without the police having to know what you're doing?" Yolanda clearly was on the side of the victims and Mr. Griffin, leaving me standing alone in the defense and protection of our mutual livelihood. "After all, you were one of them. You know how they operate. You should know how to operate around them."

"I didn't say I couldn't operate around them, I said I couldn't get in their way." And to demonstrate my intentions, I brandished the piece of paper on which Basil Griffin had written the names, addresses, and Social Security numbers of his three assistants, and I added his name to the list before passing it on to Yolanda. "As soon as you get a chance," I said.

She was edgy and tense and I kept asking her what was bothering her. After the third time, when she almost bit my head off, I stopped asking. I also stopped talking to her. I went to my desk, retrieved my notebook, and began logging all my impressions of Basil Griffin, of the building, and all the things he told me. Then I read the pile of information Yolanda had collected for me from her computers. Some of it chronicled local cases, but a good bit of it detailed serial assaults and murders of young girls in other parts of the country. That this should be so common an occurrence as to produce so much information was frightening and sickening. That's what I was thinking and feeling when I realized that Yo was standing at the corner of the desk. I looked up at her and almost reached out to grab her. She looked sick and weak. What the hell was *wrong* with her?

"They knew him," she said quietly. "Those little girls. Whoever is doing this is someone they knew."

I nodded. Either that or they thought they had reason to trust him. I'd skimmed an FBI profile in the material

Yolanda had prepared and it suggested the same thing.

"And he's still around, Phil. He'll do it again." Something in her voice, some sad and ugly thing that I'd never heard before, raised me to my feet. I reached for her but, instead of allowing the embrace, she gave me a piece of paper. My itinerary for the next three days: all day tomorrow at NYU doing the security audit; three appointments the following day for a new client—a big East Side limousine service instituting a policy of background checks on all its employees, following the robbery of several customers by drivers; and appointments the day after that with the principals of the schools attended by the five rape victims.

I opened my mouth to thank Yolanda, to tell her how much I appreciated what a masterful job she was doing working this case, but she wrapped her arms around herself, shivered, and walked away, returned to her world behind the Shoji screens. So much for partnership. And so much for sitting around feeling like a useless piece of shit.

I was out the door and headed toward Arlene Edwards' restaurant without a well-formed idea or a concrete plan. I was fueled by mad. And hunger. I was so pissed off at Yolanda that I'd gotten all the way inside the El Caribe, had straddled a stool at the counter, and was being stared at by Arlene's youngest son, Bradley, before I knew what I was doing.

"What's up, mon? You look knackered."

"Well, good, Bradley, 'cause that's how I feel. I'm also hungry."

"That part I can fix. The other part, you're on your own, mon," he said with a wide grin, the resemblance to his mother startling in that moment. He also, in that moment, looked markedly younger than eighteen.

"I'd like to talk to your mother, too, if she's free," I said, looking around and realizing that it wasn't often that Arlene Edwards wasn't visible in her establishment. She no longer did the cooking, though she supervised it; and she no longer ran the day-to-day operations—that was a job that Bradley shared with his two-years-older sister Sarah, until they both completed their studies at Hunter College.

He nodded and a mantle of sadness settled around him like a shawl. "She's in the office. She just sits there, staring at her menus and recipes and at photographs of home." He sighed deeply, like an old, weary person. "Come on. I know she'll want to see you."

I slid off the stool and followed him through what I now noticed was a crowded dining room. Every table was occupied, as were most of the stools at the counter. Two waitresses were delivering trays of food-laden plates to the tables and, when I passed close by one of them, my stomach rumbled at the scent. I followed Bradley through the kitchen and thought I'd faint at the sensory overload.

He knocked on the door marked OFFICE and though I didn't hear anything from within, he turned the knob and opened the door. "Phil Rodriquez is here to see you, Ma. And he's stayin' for lunch. Why don't you eat somethin' with him?" His voice was gentle and persuasive and, as I followed him into the office where she was seated at an old roll-top desk, I saw her look up and smile gently at him.

"I'm not so hungry, son," she said to him. And to me, "Hello, Phillip. I'm glad you came. I was going to call you later."

I walked over to her and did something I'd never done before: I took her hands, leaned down, and kissed her cheek. She gripped my hands and held them tightly for several seconds before releasing them.

"Maybe I'll eat some peas and rice, Bradley," she said to her son. "And you know how Phillip eats; put everything on the stove on his plate."

We all smiled real smiles, brief though they were, and Bradley left, closing the door. I sat down in an old-fashioned wooden swivel chair that was the mate to the one occupied by Arlene. I leaned back too far and felt as if I would tip over backwards. I quickly righted and composed myself, but she hadn't noticed my tilt. She was shuffling a thick pile of papers—menus and recipes, Bradley had said.

I watched her and waited for her to be ready to talk. I wanted her to hurry, because she was in so much pain I felt its weight. Her dead granddaughter . . . her murdered granddaughter . . . her only grandchild . . . was the child of Arlene's oldest daughter, Sylvia, who was a physician's assistant with a private practice in Brooklyn Heights. Looking at Arlene, I couldn't imagine what condition Sylvia was in. I'd met her once, when Yolanda and I were having dinner at El Caribe. It was when Sarah'd had her appendix out, two years ago, and Sylvia was pulling her shift at the restaurant. Present too that day was Norman, Arlene's eldest son, and a bright little sprite named Anna who seemed to be everywhere at once. Two boys, two girls, and all of them so devoted to their mother—and to each other and to the first and, so far, only next-generation child in the family—that he couldn't imagine being in the same room with all of them present. The grief would be paralyzing.

"Arlene."

She raised her eyes to mine and I thought, as I did every time I saw her, what a magnificent woman she was. She always reminded me of the actress who had played James Earl Jones' love interest in a short-lived television series a few years back. Gabriel something-or-other was the name of it and, like most of the really good stuff on television, it didn't last. What was the name of that actress . . . she'd died a few years back . . . Madge Sinclair!

"Basil Griffin told me you were at the building. You could have talked to Sylvia and Errol."

I shook my head. The last thing I wanted to do was talk to the parents of another murdered child. I had no choice but to talk to Bert and Angie Calle—there was no buffer. But I could and would avoid talking to Sylvia and Errol Cummerbatch by talking to Arlene Edwards. "Tell me about her," I said, and settled back into the chair, though not too far back, to wait for her to talk. I figured she'd need a while. She surprised me.

"She was an absolute delight, that child," she said, a delightful smile lighting her face. "Happy, playful, bright, funny. She was named for me. Did you know that? Anna Arlene. And she never caused a moment's trouble. Came home from school on time every day and went right to her desk to do her homework. That's why Sylvia knew immediately that something was wrong that day. She didn't run to meet her at the door. She hadn't been home at all, you see." She ran out of breath, words, and energy at the same time.

"When and where was the last time she was seen, Arlene, and was she behaving according to her routine?"

She nodded her head vigorously. "Yes! She left the school with the same friends she walks home with every day."

I wrote down their names and streets where they lived. I also wrote down the name of the woman who met her own daughter at the corner every day and who'd seen Anna Arlene that day, had watched her turn the corner and head home, her door key in her hand. The child had gotten to the corner of the block where she lived, safe and sound.

Then what happened? Did somebody follow her in? Was somebody already inside, waiting? Who else was on the sidewalk in front of that building who might have seen, who might remember? Before I could ask, a knock on the door heralded the arrival of food. Bradley, the tray hoisted over his shoulder and balanced on one hand like a pro, entered cautiously, then relaxed when he saw that his mother was composed and that our conversation was calm. He lowered the tray and rested one side of it on his mother's desk and balanced it on his raised knee. He placed a plate of steaming pigeon peas and rice before his mother and another before me. Before me, he also placed a plate heaped with curried chicken and curried goat, and side dishes of fried plantain, meat pies, and spicy greens. From his back pocket, he removed napkin-wrapped utensils for both of us.

"I'll bring you something to drink in a little while. It's really packed, Ma. And people want to know how you are," he said almost shyly.

"Tell them I'm grateful for their concern, Bradley, and that I'll be out to the dining room shortly."

I'd already unwrapped my silverware and laid my napkin in my lap before Bradley got the door closed, and I had a fork full of curried chicken aimed for my mouth when Arlene stopped me with a look. I waited, food suspended mid-air, to understand the reason for her expression. Then she bowed her head. Grace. I listened, said "amen" at the appropriate time, and began inhaling food.

"This is the best island food in New York," I said between chews and swallows, and it was. I'd been eating it for more than ten years. "But I can tell you didn't cook it." I knew that would elicit a reaction from her.

She stopped chewing and raised an eyebrow. "And how can you tell that, sir?" Her tone was polite, but she'd left plenty of room for annoyance if she didn't like the answer.

"This is cooked by recipe. And it's wonderful. Don't get me wrong. But when you were doing the cooking, Arlene, it was cooked by instinct. The spices varied, the cooking times varied, and you always experimented. I remember the time you sautéed some beef jerky in coconut milk and ginger, just to see how it would turn out. And it wasn't too bad!"

She laughed a real laugh and let it ring out for a while. It was a beautiful sound, but it hurt my heart and made my eyes sting and I had to fake choking to get my napkin up to my face.

"I'm glad you came to see me, Phillip," she said when she'd stopped laughing. "You're a good man, but your memory is not so good. It was coconut milk and coriander and it was terrible!"

Yolanda remained edgy and distant over the next several days, but she was very pleased with my work for NYU and for the limousine service, the owner of which had written a healthy retainer check and promised enough steady business to keep Eddie Ortiz and Mike Smith busy at least a couple of days a week, right through until the first of the year. I felt pretty good about things, too, which was, as Yo would say, a growth step for me, since both those jobs had taken me away from my morning routine for more than a week.

I was back on it this morning, however, walking my route despite the steady, cold downpour that had stalled vehicular traffic and created an umbrella traffic jam on the sidewalks. Neither snow nor sleet nor rain . . . Mrs. Campos and Willie One Eye were their usual cordial selves. They'd missed my daily visits, they said, but not only understood the call of duty, were happy for me that it was business that had kept me away. These people, too, were proprietors of their own businesses. So was Itchy Johnson, but his reception was a different matter.

He was flat-out rude and inhospitable to me when I walked in. "Leave that raincoat and umbrella up there at the front," he yelled at me. "Don't want water drippin' all over the damn floor."

I stopped unbuttoning my slicker and turned around, ready to head back out into the rain. The young barber in the chair closest to the door said, barely audibly, "Don't mind him. He's had his ass on his back the past few days. Been askin' 'bout you." His lips had barely moved while he spoke and he had continued cutting zigzag patterns into the hair of a kid young enough to have been in school that time of the morning. He motioned toward the back with his head and I turned back toward Itchy and he was watching me. I finally unbuttoned the coat and hung it on the rack and stuck the dripping umbrella into the stand and made my way back to the back of the shop. Itchy was seated at his table and he thumped it with his fist when I reached him. An invitation to sit.

"How are you, Itchy?" I asked, pulling out a chair.

He grunted but didn't utter words of greeting. Instead he said, "Seems like you been keeping busy."

I nodded. "I have. We've got a full plate. A few new clients added to the old ones and all of them getting busy at the same time."

"Still taking that fat wop's ill-gotten money?"

I almost stopped breathing. I'd never before heard Itchy use a racial epithet, but that's not what surprised me. Most people, no matter their color or ethnicity, will stoop to maligning another group given the right circumstances; I'd known that all my life. What concerned me was that he seemed to be watching for a reaction from me. "Carmine is a client, yeah, Itchy," I said carefully. Maybe too carefully.

"So that means you've seen that Mason broad?"

My scalp tingled and little bumps raised up all over my body. This was different from the "wop" comment. This was more sinister than mean-spirited. "You mean Doctor Jill Mason?"

"Yeah, I mean Doctor Jill Mason." He spit the words out of his mouth in a not-so-charitable imitation of my tone.

"No, as a matter of fact, I haven't seen her lately," I said, my antennae up and searching for—I didn't know what. I found out soon enough.

"Well, good." Itchy's fist hit table a couple of times and he seemed relieved. "Didn't make sense to me you jumpin' in that girl's business on that fat wop's say-so. He oughta stay in his own damn neighborhood and mind his own damn business and you can do the smart thing: take the fool's money and run!" Itchy laughed and slapped his thigh, not realizing how widely he'd missed the mark. "Anyway," he said, no trace of mirth remaining. "Everybody knows she's been a few bricks shy of a full load since that accident. Come to think of it, she always was a little strange. Even when she was a little girl."

"I need to go, Itchy," I said, hoping I was keeping my voice calm and my tone neutral. *He* was calling somebody strange? I passed the young barber and gave him a look. He rolled his eyes toward the ceiling but kept on cutting. I put on my wet coat and retrieved my wet umbrella and stepped out into the rain. I hoped it would wash away the ugly feeling I'd gotten from Itchy.

★ ★ ★ ★ ★

I should have expected Yolanda's "I told you so" look when I related the encounter with Itchy. She thought he was scum, and not just because of the Bumpy Johnson lie, but even she was shocked by his denigration of Jill Mason. We speculated back and forth for a few minutes about potential reasons for the old man's obvious dislike for a woman everyone else, including me, adored. In the end, Yo concluded that it was Itchy who wasn't playing with a full deck. Then we got busy discussing the meetings with the principals of the schools attended by the rape victims.

"First thing you do, Phil, I'm telling you, is you let those principals know you don't blame them for what happened, that it's not their fault."

"Well of course it's not, Yo! You think I'm gonna walk in the door and start accusing people of what? Being accomplices to rape? I'm not that dumb."

"I didn't say you were. And I certainly know you're not gonna walk in laying blame. What I'm saying is, walk in absolving them. Walk in letting them know *you* know what a tough job they have and how well they do it. 'Cause believe me, those two women feel guilty. They feel like one of their own children was murdered."

"Okay, okay, I hear you. But my bottom line is I've got to find out from them what those little girls had in common. Because they did have some common bond, and whatever it was got them raped and murdered." And I wanted to find those answers from somebody—anybody— but the victims themselves. I'd been putting off talking to the little rape victims and would continue to put it off, forever if possible.

But I didn't learn anything from the principals. Both had been ordered not to talk to me. When I asked why they hadn't called to cancel the appointments, two hours and twenty blocks apart, both had shrugged with the same casual weariness, as if it were something I should have expected. And perhaps I should have. We live in a society that loves to place blame, and especially in the face of tragedy. It was the schools system's job to make sure that it didn't take the blame. Therefore, the official school system position was that it talked only to the police, and then only under a court order.

Okay, so this was proving to be a bust, but I couldn't do nothing. I'd planned to walk the neighborhood later in the week, to walk the routes to and from home and school that all of the little girls took every day. No time like the present. I took out my notebook, turned a few pages, read a few more, and started to walk. As I walked, I tried to remember what I felt and thought when I was eight years old on those walks to and from school. Not this school and not these blocks, but a similar school and similar blocks not too far away. I also tried to put myself—my eight-year-old self—in the space of having to "be careful" because there was a nutcase around who was hurting little kids. Then I realized that the kids walking back and forth on these blocks, to and from these schools, hadn't been warned to be careful, at least not publicly and not recently, about what had happened to their classmates.

I was standing in front of Bert Calle's building, trying to rationalize the police department's failure to issue a blanket warning, when I heard a voice behind me.

"You lookin' for Bert 'n Angie, they ain't around."

I turned to face Daniel Esposito, looking weary and ragged. Looking like hell, actually. He hadn't shaved in several days. Or bathed. Or changed clothes. But he had been drinking. His eyes were ugly and red-rimmed, and he stank.

I refused to allow myself to back away from the man. His grief smelled as strongly as he did.

"You're not doing so well, Dan," I said, extending my hand.

He saw me see him struggle to focus his eyes and dropped his head in shame, but he took my hand, briefly, then dropped it, too. "Fuckin' shitty, man." And all the shame in his voice wasn't due to being seen drunk and dirty in the light of day.

"Where are they, then?" I asked, to have something to say.

"Bert took Angie and the kids up to Connecticut, just to get outta here for a while. Her parents live up there somewhere. He'll be back tonight, I think."

"Probably a good idea, a change of scenery," I said, to have something else to say to this weary shell of a man, a man who, despite his obvious distress, I had difficulty liking and feeling sympathy for.

"Angie's a real mess. Kinda like me. I oughta be at work but I just can't seem to get myself together, you know what I'm sayin'?"

"Can't be an easy thing to handle," I said. And in truth, I couldn't imagine my daughter a rape victim. I cringed inside when I thought of Arlene's little granddaughter, whom I'd seen once in the restaurant. And I'd seen the body of Bert and Angie Calle's daughter. No. I couldn't imagine how I'd deal, if the raped daughter were mine. But something told me I wouldn't have Daniel Esposito's shame. Anger, rage: that I could understand. Pain and sorrow and hatred I could understand. But how the hell did he get the nerve to feel ashamed, when his little girl was broken and maybe never would be mended? He couldn't get himself together? Carmine could. Bert could. Why couldn't he?

97

"Did your daughter like to go anyplace special after school, Dan? With her friends, maybe?"

He shrugged and struggled to focus his eyes. "I don't know. My wife, she the one knows those kinds of things."

"Maybe before, Dan." I was engaged in my struggle, trying to sound and be gentle. "But haven't you asked, haven't you tried to find out what she did every day, where she went?"

"What the hell difference does it make now, Rodriquez?" He slurred his words a bit, and wobbled a bit, the unsteadiness caused as much by his anger as his drunkenness.

"The difference it makes now, Dan, is that whoever hurt your little girl is still out there, maybe hanging out in the same place, watching and waiting."

I left Daniel Esposito standing where he was and went to find myself a drink. Not as many as Esposito had had, but enough to help take the edge off everything I was feeling.

Chapter Six

I spent the next couple of weeks feeling a lot like Daniel Esposito had looked that day in front of Bert Calle's place. I felt ragged and out of sorts and nothing made sense. Which *really* didn't make sense because in reality, life was good and prosperous. It was *me* that had the problem. I didn't feel good that nothing bad had happened to Jill Mason because I knew, somewhere deep inside, that something bad was waiting to happen to her and that it would happen as soon as she no longer was protected, which would be soon because Carmine didn't have an endless supply of cash, as he'd informed me as recently as last week. And I had nothing new to tell the parents of the two dead girls and the five whose bodies were alive but whose spirits were dead. So I felt guilty and incompetent and worthless.

About the only feel-good aspect of my life I could point to was that Yolanda—the real Yo that I know and love—had returned. That snappish, edgy, remote sister had beat a retreat and was, I hoped, long gone and far away. I could tell that there still was something beneath the surface bothering her, and I continued to hope she'd tell me about it, but I knew I wouldn't ask again. Knew I couldn't. So in addition to guilty, incompetent, and worthless, I also felt a little bit sad and lonely. Yolanda was my best friend and I'd thought I was hers, yet there was something inside her capable of altering her personality and I didn't know what it was and she wouldn't tell me. Or couldn't.

"Carmine wants you to call," she said as we exchanged

coffee for juice and the greeting that was our ritual. She gave my shoulder a gentle squeeze, letting me know that whatever had been troubling her had not been me. "And he sounded more tired than irritated, you know?"

I nodded. I knew. That's how he'd sounded last week, when he'd told me he was running out of money, and it had worried me then and it worried me now; for Carmine to relinquish, even for a moment, sounding like the baddest bad-ass on the block was a serious matter. I picked up the phone and dialed his number—I'd called it so often lately that I knew it—and, after two rings, got Theresa's voice on the answering machine. Since I didn't have a message to leave, I hung up and opened the cover of my notebook where I'd written the phone number of the pastry shop the fat man liked, the one I'd come to frequent on my own. I dialed and said my name when the owner answered. No, Carmine hadn't been in yet, which was unusual. Yes, she'd tell him I called. Maybe he was sick, she offered; so many people had succumbed to an early-season flu that had arrived with the early winter.

"When did Carmine leave the message to call?" I asked Yo.

"The phone was ringing when I walked in the door. He didn't say where he was, just for you to call. But I told you he sounded weird. Something's wrong with him."

"Yeah, something's wrong with him, and it ain't the flu," I muttered, more to myself than to Yolanda, whom I didn't think could hear me anyway because I thought she was behind the screens working at her computer.

"Something's wrong with everybody," she muttered from right behind me, and laughed softly when I jumped.

I frowned, ignoring her humor at my expense. "What do you mean by that, something's wrong with everybody?"

She frowned, too, and shook her head, running her hands through her massive tangle of black hair. "I'm not sure I can put my finger on any one thing. It's just that everybody seems out of whack. Carmine. Arlene Edwards. Bert Calle. Those sisters who own that building, they came by yesterday saying Basil Griffin was ready to quit because people blamed him for what happened to the little Cummerbatch girl. Even Doctor Mason—"

"Doctor Mason!" I know I shouted because this time it was Yo who jumped, and because I heard the sound of my own voice. But I couldn't help it. "You've talked to Doctor Mason? When? Why?"

"Yes, I've talked to Doctor Mason. When? Every two or three days. Why? Because she's a client. I make it a habit to talk to our clients, Phil. Surely you know that. I call Arlene Edwards. I call Bert and Angie Calle. I call Carmine and Theresa. It's my job, Phil, to talk to our clients."

The words hung between us on the chilly air for a few very long seconds, and I used the time to wonder at my reaction.

"Is there a reason I shouldn't talk to Doctor Mason?" she asked carefully.

"No, of course not, Yo. It just surprised me to hear you say you'd talked to her. And I guess to hear it in the same breath as you saying that something's wrong with everybody. I suppose because I feel the same thing and I don't know what it means. I do know that I'm afraid to pull her protection but I don't have any choice. I think Carmine, in his way, knows it, too. He's not a rich man, no matter what he wants people to think, and he can't afford to have us watch her forever. And I think he's afraid of what will happen if we stop watching."

"She is, too. But she almost wants it to happen, so it will

101

be over with, whatever it is."

Yo had spoken quietly, almost more to herself than to me; and since I was still wary of her mood, I hesitated before responding. "She said that?"

"Not exactly that, no. But that's what she meant, Phil. She's tired of being afraid. Honest people don't like living in fear. They'd rather face their troubles than keep looking over their shoulders, waiting for the trouble to catch up to them, especially if it's trouble they don't deserve."

I thought about that for a moment; thought about the truth of it and about the fact that this wisdom came from some place in Yolanda that was new. New to me anyway. Whatever was moving through her was changing her and it was interesting to watch and to experience, if not easy. I drained my coffee cup and stood up. I didn't know where I was going or what, exactly, I was going to do. But I knew that I couldn't spend another moment sitting and waiting for something to happen. I needed to make something happen. I needed to be out and about in the event that something happened that was not of my making.

Without Yolanda having to prod and prompt, I armed myself with a phone and a weapon, something I realized I'd been doing quite regularly. I pulled a knit cap low enough on my head to cover my ears and wrapped a scarf around my neck before putting on and buttoning my coat. The gloves remained in my pocket. I always put them on last, and only when I was so cold there was no recourse. The opening of the door almost gave me all the recourse I needed. A gust of wind off the East River all but ripped the door off its hinges and I had to struggle to get it closed. When I did, I turned left, hunched down into my coat, hands deep in my pockets, and hoped that Carmine had decided to put in an appearance at the pastry shop, since that's the direction in which I was headed. Because that's the direction in which the wind was at my back.

Nobody at the pastry shop had seen Carmine. I had a cafe con leche and a discussion of the history of early winters in New York with the owner's mother, a short, round woman with sad eyes who missed her native Southern Italy despite having spent enough winters in New York to talk like a climatologist about them. I left a note for Carmine and, keeping the wind at my back, I walked the four blocks to the elementary school Carmine's daughter attended. Different school, different principal, I could hope for a different result. I got as far as the secretary in the front office.

No, I was told in no uncertain terms, I could not see the principal without an appointment; and no, I could not make an appointment to see the principal without permission from the deputy superintendent's office. And given what I wanted to discuss, that permission, we both knew, would not be forthcoming. I hadn't been in the building long enough to get warm, and so I didn't see any harm in continuing to allow the wind to direct my path. I began walking north on 1st Avenue, head down and shoulders hunched up to meet my ears.

"Hey, Buddy! Watch yourself!"

The jab to my shoulder snatched me out of my reverie and drop-kicked me immediately onto the defensive. I was prepared either to apologize, if necessary, or to punch back, if required. A glance around me brought a quick apology to my lips and my hands raised, palms up and out, to the guy whose foot I'd just trampled. He grumbled something and brushed past me on the crowded sidewalk, jostling a couple of other people in his haste. As I was wondering why there were so many people around, I realized that I was outside the Beth Israel Medical Center and that it was lunchtime. I was a civilian island in a sea of hospital personnel: stethoscopes were visible around necks even beneath coats and scarves, and hospital greens, blues, and pinks peeked from beneath overcoats.

Beth Israel. All of the rape victims had been treated here. I knew that. I also knew that no doctor in his or her right mind would discuss such a case with me but I went inside anyway, partly to get out of the cold. And partly to follow a hunch. I'd been too long around Yolanda. Here I was being moved and motivated by forces I didn't understand and I didn't see anything wrong with that!

I entered the lobby through the revolving door and swam against the sea of humanity trying to exit the building. I made my way to the information desk where three women worked three sides of a square kiosk. A surly-looking male guard perched like Jabba the Hut on a stool at the fourth side. I waited in line long enough to get hot, and had removed my hat and was working on the coat when my turn came and I asked who I could talk to about the hospital's rape counseling program. The woman's face remained immobile, but her eyes changed behind the half-glasses she wore low on her nose. They narrowed, then widened, then softened. She told me to wait just a moment and she picked up the phone and punched in five numbers.

"Connie? This is Ellen. There's a gentleman here in the lobby. He wants to talk to somebody in your office. Can you see him?"

Connie must have agreed because Ellen the Information Lady hung up the phone and smiled at me. "Take those elevators over there," she said pointing behind me, "and go to the third floor. Turn right and go to the end of the hall. Social Services is on the left. Connie can help you."

I thanked her and wished I had a longer ride than just to

the third floor because I needed more time to think of something to say to Connie. The Information Lady obviously thought that I, personally, was in need of assistance . . . thought that somebody close to me had been raped . . . and somebody had. Dammit! Arlene Edwards was my friend and her granddaughter had been raped. Carmine Aiello was my client and his daughter had been raped. Bert Calle was my client and his daughter had been raped. Damn right I personally was in need of assistance! And by the time I walked down the third-floor hallway to Social Services, I knew exactly what I would say to Connie.

"How do you do? I'm Consuela deLeon. Please come in."

She met me at the office door and robbed me of whatever it was I'd planned to say. She was, next to Yolanda, the most beautiful woman I'd ever seen. And though I wouldn't want Yo to hear me say so, Consuela deLeon might even have a point or two on Yolanda Maria. I followed her through a maze of cubicles to the rear of the huge room and into an office of grace and warmth that reminded me of Jill Mason's office. It was smaller, certainly, and less elegant, but it was a caring place. I could feel that; and Consuela deLeon was not somebody I could—or would want to—bullshit. I could feel that, too.

I took the seat that she indicated and waited for her to decide where to sit: behind her desk or in the chair adjacent to me. She chose the latter, which made my decision about how to approach her a lot easier.

"My name is Phillip Rodriquez, Miss deLeon, and I'm a private investigator. I represent more than a dozen families in this community, about half of them parents of little girls who have been raped, and two of them parents of murdered girls. They hired me to help them because they're not satis-

fied with what the police are doing. But I'm not doing anything, either, and it's making me crazy, Miss deLeon.
Those people are in pain. Their little girls are in pain. And I
don't know how to help them. I honestly don't know why I
came here or what I think you can do, but I was tired of
doing nothing and coming here is at least better than that."

She didn't say anything for a long time. She sat very still.
First she looked intently at me, then she looked away.
Stared at the wall . . . or at nothing. I wasn't sure. Maybe
she was looking at something inside herself. But she didn't
move or speak for quite a few minutes. And because she
didn't, I didn't. Which gave me an opportunity to stare at
her.

And maybe that made her uncomfortable, because she
got up and went over to a low, wooden file cabinet behind
her desk, opened a drawer, and removed a file and placed it
in the center of the desk. Then she came back and sat near
me.

"Not many men come to see us, Mr. Rodriquez. That's
why Ellen called me directly and that's why I agreed to see
you. The women come: the victims themselves and their
mothers or grandmothers or sisters or best friends or
cousins. But their husbands, brothers, lovers, fathers—they
almost never come. I was hoping you were a husband or a
lover, so we could tell you how to help your woman."

The thought made me colder than the wind outside. "If I
had a wife or a lover and she was raped, I would come here,
Miss deLeon, because I would want to know how to help
her. But all I have are these clients. Can you tell me how to
help them?"

She gave me a small, sad smile that made her even more
beautiful, and for the first time I realized that she wore
glasses. Gold rimmed glasses and gold hoop earrings. And

no gold band. "Without naming names, I think we probably already help some of your clients. But I don't know how we can help you, Mr. Rodriquez."

"It's Phil and you can help by telling me what kind of man rapes. And rapes little girls. Who is this bastard and where can I find him?"

"He's probably not that different from any other man."

"Bullshit! He's a sick, evil, murdering . . ."

"Yes, he's that. But I meant in his appearance." She leaned toward me and placed a calming hand on my arm. "Of course he's sick. But he may not appear demented and deranged, with long, matted hair and bloodshot eyes, talking to himself. In fact, he may appear quite normal. Everyman. You may even have seen him, Phil. In fact, you probably have, because serial rapists who prey on children often have legal, legitimate access to them. They're not strangers."

I knew that, from the information Yolanda had gathered and from my police department experience, but to hear it from someone who spent her days talking to women and little girls who had been raped made me cringe inside. "Is there anything . . . I don't know, strange or different or worth noting about this case? About these particular rapes?"

She reached across the desk and picked up the file, but she didn't open it. She held it in her lap, both hands on top of it protectively. "You understand that I can't talk specifics to you?" I nodded and she opened the file but still didn't look at it. She looked directly at me. "Something's wrong with the timing. If it's the same guy, the timing for your seven cases is all screwed up."

I must have looked surprised or something, because she laughed. "Yes, I know about your cases, Mr. Rod . . . Phil.

I've been watching and worrying about this situation for a while, and I think it's more than one guy. Don't ask me why, because I can't tell you. I won't do your job for you. But if you come back to me with specific questions, I'll try to give you answers. Fair enough?"

I stood up and offered my hand. "More than fair, Miss deLeon. Greatly appreciated."

She shook my hand—a strong, firm grip with a cool, delicate hand. "Call me Connie. I'll show you out."

I was out on the sidewalk being jostled by the still busy crowd in front of Beth Israel when two thoughts registered in flashing neon in my brain: Connie deLeon had implied that maybe there was more than one rapist, and I'd implied that I would try to find him or them. I didn't feel the cold anymore as I walked west, instead of heading east and back downtown to the office. I kept hearing the words, *if it's the same guy, the timing is screwed up.* What did that mean? And who could tell me? Timing. Rapists and timing. *Serial* rapists and timing. A shrink. A shrink could tell me, but the only one I knew not only couldn't tell me, she wouldn't. But I knew how to find one who would.

"I'm sure there's somebody here who can help you, Phil, I just have to find out who that would be," Jeffrey Dahl said to me, rubbing his bald pate. The administrator in charge of security for New York University was a very pleasant man and he genuinely liked me. When I explained to him what I wanted and why, he didn't pause to take a breath before he said of course he'd help.

I paced up and down Dahl's executive-sized office while he checked his directory and made telephone calls. I looked out of the windows down on the West Village and marveled at the very real difference between my neighborhood—the

East Village—and the historically more well-known Green-wich or West Village. Or just plain "the Village" as the world knew it. As far as I could tell, the only thing West had that East didn't have was NYU and, later, The New School. But as far as I could tell, that had been enough to render the one famous, the stuff of jazz, blues, romance, and movies, and other the infamous haunt of biker gangs.

The office door opened after a quick knock and Dahl's assistant, a former New Jersey Transit cop named Helen something, came in and crossed directly to me and gave me a sheet of paper. I'd asked Yolanda to fax over the exact dates and locations of all the rapes. I thanked Helen and she left and Dahl hung up the phone. "Professor Gertrude Bader in the Med School. Psychiatry Department. She teaches and maintains a practice over there. Check in with whoever is on the security desk. They know you're coming and so does Doctor Bader, but you'd better hurry. She's got a lecture in exactly twenty minutes."

"Thanks, Mr. Dahl, you've really helped me."

"I'm glad I could help, Phil. Anything to help rid society of vermin like that."

I thought of Basil Griffin when he said that word, and I almost smiled. "You're not from Trinidad by any chance, are you Mr. Dahl?" I meant it as my own private joke and was startled that he was startled by the question.

"Nooo," he said slowly. "I was born in Barbados but my parents returned home, to Canada, when I was very young. Why on earth would you ask such a question?"

"Vermin. Americans don't use the term," I said, and left before I needed to try any further explanation.

Professor Gertrude Bader met me at her office door. I was out of breath from running, but at least I wasn't cold any more. "Thank you for your time, Doctor Bader," I managed.

"Don't thank me, young man, because you're not getting very much of my time. And anyway, it's not possible—or advisable—to rush a discussion about serial rapists." She crossed her arms over her breasts and studied me. She was an imposing woman, but because of her aura, not her size. I guessed that she was somewhere in her sixties, but she was nowhere near old, and neither large nor small. What my Grandma would describe as "a healthy specimen of a woman." Her hair was dyed a subdued red and well cut. So was her suit, also a shade of red. Her eyes were green. Clear, cool, unblinking green. Kind, intelligent eyes that saw everything. Eyes that could comfort or kill, depending on the circumstance. "I don't remember your name. I'm sorry."

I told her my name and gave her the list of rapes, murders, and their dates and told her as quickly as possible what I was doing and why. "I just was told that this list suggests more than one rapist. Is that possible, Doctor?"

She raised the green eyes from the paper and penetrated me with them. "Of course it's possible. Likely, even." Then she shrugged and I wished the world could take shrugging lessons from this woman, because I swear I heard her shoulders say, "But so what?"

"Tell me what I need to do to make it possible for you to have a rational discussion with me about this list. Please, Doctor."

She smiled at me then, but only with her mouth, a slight lifting of her lips. Her eyes had changed; they had darkened, like the sea does when a storm is brewing. "Find out the level and type of violence in each of these cases, especially where death occurred. That's a different crime, separate from the rape—" She stopped talking suddenly and looked closely at me. "You do understand about the different kinds of violence associated with rape, don't you, Mr. Rodriquez?"

I shook my head. I was feeling a little queasy. I didn't know that, and I didn't want to know that there were different kinds of rape. "I know that rape is about violence and not about sex."

"You've got a lot of homework to do, young man, and I suggest that you take your time about it. Don't try to rush through this. I said I'd help you and I will, but you waste my time and yours by being unprepared."

I felt that if I opened my mouth I'd throw up, but I had questions to ask. "The murders are different? They mean something different than the other five rapes?"

She nodded her head. "I think so."

"Would the cops know this?" I asked.

Her entire demeanor altered and she looked at me as if I were in need of her counseling services. "Of course. This is New York City, after all."

Of course. This is New York City, after all. Of course. This is New York City, after all. Of course. This is New York City, after all. The words rang in my brain, bounced off the cell walls, swirled through the gray matter. The words and their unspoken meaning, for I knew full well that Doctor Bader's implication was that this was one of the most sophisticated police departments in the world, with not only access to every imaginable investigative technique and tool, but which had pioneered quite a few of them. Of course, the cops knew they were looking for more than one rapist. They just hadn't felt the need to tell the parents of the victims . . . or the parents of the potential victims. But why? WHY?

Doctor Bader had said take my time, but I didn't have

time to take. I'd already wasted too much time relying on the cops to do what I thought was their job. And maybe that's exactly what they were doing, and I was the one not doing his job. I'd gotten myself so caught in not getting in the way of official police business and thereby jeopardizing my license that I had, instead, neglected the needs and interests of my clients. Maybe it wasn't my job to find rapists and murderers, but it was my job to tell the people who paid me how they could help protect themselves and their children from the walking nightmares that had invaded their worlds.

Arlene Edwards first looked horrified, then frightened, and then, finally, angry. That's when she reached into her desk drawer and got out the notebook and pen and began writing down everything I told her. She made me sit down opposite her and speak slowly and I had to repeat everything twice. Her lips had compressed into a thin, tight line and her eyes flashed something I'd never seen in her before, and I had known from the first moment I saw her that she was made of the kind of stuff that didn't bend or break. But now, on this cold, soon-to-be-December night, I was looking at a stranger. And listening to one, for the Island-accented English she spoke this night was so thick I could barely understand her words. The more she exhorted me to speak slowly and carefully, the faster and more idiomatic became her speech. It took me a moment to understand what was happening, but I finally realized that the woman finally had reached her breaking point and only through sheer force of will was she keeping herself from splintering apart.

Bert and Angie Calle were shattered, completely and totally, and didn't do a thing to try and control or conceal the fact. And because of that, it took me several lengthy attempts at an explanation, before they understood what I was telling them and what I was asking them to do. Angie kept crying, which, in turn, prompted wailing from the three-year-old twins, which prompted Bert to yell at everybody to shut up. Then he would bury his face in his hands and sob, which would start Angie again, until I finally walked him outside, thinking the cold would help him get control of himself. It worked. He listened to me, heard what I said, and promised to get on it first thing in the morning, after leaving his overnight shift at the Fulton Street Market. I made him promise that he would, and then I made the mistake of going back inside with him, to tell Angie good night. She grabbed me with one hand and Bert with the other and begged us not to leave her. Begged Bert not to go to work and leave her alone to be raped and murdered; begged me not to leave them unprotected.

I took a taxi back to the office because I didn't have the strength to walk. I was so emotionally spent that I'd planned to do nothing more than leave a note for Yolanda, lock up, and go home. The only reason I went back at all is because I'd never ended the day without returning to the office, no matter how late, and I wouldn't start now. I was surprised to find both Yolanda and Sandra there and told them so, barely disguising what I realized was displeasure at having to interact with any more human beings that day. Even human beings I loved, like Yolanda and Sandra.

"It's not really that late, Phil," Sandra said, looking carefully at me from the tail end of a warm, loving hug.

"I guess not," I said, in no real hurry to leave her embrace. Maybe some human interaction was okay. "I still get screwed around when the time changes and it gets dark at four o'clock in the afternoon. And I feel like shit, which isn't helping anything. I guess it feels like nine or ten o'clock, because I wish it were. That way, I could eat and go home and go to bed and obliterate this day."

Sandra laughed, kissed me on the head again, and pushed me away from her, feigning annoyance with me. She was not normally a demonstrative person. In fact, quite a few people found her downright inhospitable, but I knew better. I hadn't known right away, of course. When I first met Sandra, eight years ago now, I loved her because Yolanda loved her and I loved Yolanda. Now we had our own relationship and I loved her because she was warm and funny and generous and smart. And because she tolerated no bullshit. Ever. From anybody, for any reason.

"What's so bad about this day that needs obliterating?" She and Yolanda were readying themselves to go out into the cold.

I told them about my conversations with Connie deLeon and Doctor Bader and how there probably were two rapists and how much it pissed me off that the cops hadn't let people know; and then I launched into what I realized, in that moment, was what I really wanted to obliterate from my day and that was the knowledge of there being different kinds of rape. Rape based on how much and what kind of violence was used. The understanding that, armed with that knowledge, I now had to find out from the parents of each of the victims exactly *how* their daughter was raped. That I now had to find out exactly what was done to Anna Arlene Cummerbatch and Lisa Calle before they were murdered.

I'd been pacing and periodically pounding the walls with my fists while I ranted, and I hadn't been watching Yolanda or Sandra. But now I turned to Yo, to tell her that it would be a good idea if she was with me while I talked to the parents. She was shaking all over. Shaking her head at me, back and forth that no, she wouldn't do that. Shaking and shivering from head to toe, like she already was outside. She wrapped her arms around herself and made a sound that scared me. I reached for her and Sandra yelled at me.

"Goddammit, Phil, what the fuck is wrong with you! Are you crazy, you son of a bitch? What did you do that for?"

I looked at Sandra, stunned, wanting to reply. Then Yo ran out of the door and Sandra started after her. I found my voice. "What the fuck, Sandra! WHAT? WHAT?"

She stopped at the door, holding it open, the wild, cold wind blowing in at us. "You don't know, Phil? Aw, shit. Fuck. You don't know, goddammit." And she was gone, out into the night to catch Yolanda. And I was left to wonder what it was I didn't know. And the wondering hurt as much as the anger Sandra had thrown at me. Hurt almost as much as watching Yolanda in whatever pain she was in. I'd never seen her close up and shut down before; had never seen her light flicker and fade. But I had just watched Yolanda die—there's no other way to define what I'd seen happen—and the pain and fear in my gut and higher . . . up around my heart . . . made me physically sick.

I went into the bathroom and threw up. I'd wanted to do that since my visit to Doctor Bader. When I came back out into the office, Carmine was sitting at one of the desks.

"Carmine," I said.

"Rodriquez," he said, and kept sitting there huddled in his overcoat, holding his fedora in his hands between his knees.

"We need to talk, Carmine," I said.

He nodded but still hadn't looked up at me. "Yeah. I got your note you left at the café. About Doc Mason."

"Yeah. And about your daughter."

Now he did look at me and I wished he hadn't. To use

Jill Mason's term, all the bombast had gone from him. He was as hurt and sad as Bert Calle and Arlene Edwards and Daniel Esposito and all the other parents of all the other little girls. But looking at Carmine was different because he was somebody I'd actively disliked. And I'd disliked him because I hadn't thought him capable of the kind of human emotion I saw etched in his face. I was looking at a man being destroyed by the pain of another person. "What about my daughter, Rodriquez? You found out somethin'?"

I nodded. "Maybe. Looks like there are two different perps, Carmine. Two rapists, not one. And they . . . they do it . . . the crimes are different. The one who kills is different from the one who . . . from the other one."

"Lousy fuckin' cops. About time they finally got somethin' figured out." His eyes slid away from mine and roamed the room, settling on the back wall. "Where's Miss Aguierre this evening? Lookin' at her would sure as hell make me feel a lot better."

"She's gone. Carmine, listen. What I've got I didn't get from the cops, but they've got something I need and I need you and the other parents to get it for me. *Capiche?*"

"This shit about two perps, the cops didn't tell you that?"

I shook my head. "I got it from somebody at Beth Israel, Carmine. Somebody who is not supposed to be talking to me. That's why I need to come by the same information another way. Then I can have this expert over at NYU analyze and confirm it for me."

"Shut the fuck up wit' alla this confirm and analyze shit, Rodriquez! You're tellin' me that not one but two fuckin' scumbags are loose on our kids and the cops are what? WHAT? Talk to me, Rodriquez! Tell me the cops at least know as much as you know!" He had crushed his hat between his meaty hands and his eyes were wide and wild and spittle had formed at the corners of his mouth.

I raised my palms and shrugged. "I don't know what the cops know or don't know, Carmine. Not for certain. My guess is that yeah, they know they're looking for two different guys." I thought about what Doctor Bader had said: *This is New York City, after all.* "I can't explain why they're working it like they're working it, but I guess they've got their reasons. I can tell you that as the parent of a victim, you're entitled to certain information. Like the police report. Like the hospital report. I need that stuff, Carmine, from you and from all the other parents. I already talked to Arlene Edwards and Bert and Angie Calle and I'm going to talk to the other parents."

"Whatta you want with the police report and the hospital report? That's about my little girl, Rodriquez. Whatta you gonna do wit' that?"

"Doctor Gertrude Bader, at NYU, is the specialist I told you about. She studies the brains of these psychos. She knows what makes them tick. She can do what's called a profile. Can tell me who to look for. She can tell me for certain, once she reads all those reports, that there are two different perps."

"What kinda doctor is this Bader broad?"

I winced. I could envision Doctor Bader hearing herself being called a broad. "She's a psychiatrist and she teaches in the med school."

"Same kind as Doc Mason, right?"

I nodded. "Yeah, that's right."

"Which means she's gotta keep confidential anything she reads in those reports, right? Just like Doc Mason?"

I wanted to smack myself. My heart was breaking for fat, mean Carmine Aiello. "That's right, Carmine. Your daughter's privacy is totally and completely protected."

He nodded. "I'll get the fuckin' reports. First thing t'morra mornin' I'll get 'em, you can count on that." He opened and unfolded his crushed fedora, as if it were a natural act, and attempted to smooth out the wrinkles. "By the way, Rodriquez," he said on his way to the door. "What made you change your mind?"

"About what, Carmine?" I asked.

"About findin' these fuckin' rapists, that's what. You weren't gonna do that, remember?" His snarl was back in full force. This was the Carmine I knew and hated.

I remembered and I didn't know what changed my mind and I told that to Carmine. Then something like the truth sprang from my mouth. "Maybe it's my turn to shit or get off the pot. Which reminds me. I'm pulling Jill Mason's surveillance. Nobody will try anything with her covered like that, and it's time to get out of your pocket."

He nodded and scratched his balding head. "Yeah, my pocket's feelin' the pinch, no question about it. But I gotta tell you what a piece of shit I'll feel like if somethin' happens to that lady—"

"Not a goddamn thing is going to happen to that lady, Carmine, I promise you that! Not a goddamn thing is gonna happen to anybody, especially to any more little girls!"

He gave me a weird look, shook my hand, of all things, and exited into the bitter cold. Almost as if I'd stepped outside my body—like in those descriptions of near-death experiences—and hovered above, I watched and listened to myself explode and was surprised, amazed, and even a little bit impressed. I didn't get angry and emote—it wasn't my style; and I certainly didn't make a habit of pretending to be a knight in shining armor, ready to gird up and ride to the rescue of damsels in distress. So what the hell was I doing?

How the hell did I think I could prevent harm from coming to Jill Mason? How did I imagine that I could prevent another rape or murder of a little girl on the Lower East Side? I could not. But with every cell in my body I wanted to be able to protect them.

And then I crashed back down to reality and returned to myself and understood that the cause of my reaction was Yolanda and whatever was tormenting her. And tormenting me. Because for the first time since we'd met, I was not tethered to her. She'd broken away from me and I was drifting.

I somehow had failed to protect Yolanda, to keep her safe, so perhaps I could save and protect the others. And if not that, then I could find the piece of shit who was doing the harm.

Chapter Seven

I woke up to ringing and pounding. Everywhere. In my head and at the door and from wherever the telephones were. After incredible effort, I managed to sit up and open my eyes. I was in my bedroom, on the bed, on top of the covers, fully clothed. Including shoes. The phone was ringing, the doorbell was buzzing, and somebody was pounding on my door which, being steel, sounded like a warm-up for the end of the world. And all of it was happening, simultaneously, inside my head.

I held it in my hands and squeezed, praying that all sound would cease, but God doesn't answer the prayers of drunks. I'd learned that from my favorite aunt in response to the behavior of my favorite uncle. Now I knew how Tio Enrique felt when he held his head and prayed for deliverance. What I didn't understand was why he subjected himself to this experience on a weekly basis. I groaned loudly, which was a mistake, and inched myself toward the edge of the bed, far enough so I could dangle my legs over the side. I released my head and placed my hands on the bed and pushed myself to my feet. I prayed some more: that if I passed out, I'd fall back onto the bed instead of onto the floor. But I only swayed, and wondered whether that meant my prayer was answered. I didn't see the phone that lived in the bedroom.

I answered the door first, since I didn't know where to look for the phone that lived in the living room if it wasn't on the table or on top of the television. I've never liked phones that didn't hang on walls or sit on tables and I was promising myself to be truer to my personal likes, when Mike Smith barreled into my living room.

"Man, answer the damn phone!"

"Can't find it, Mike," I mumbled and leaned into the wall as he brushed past me toward the sofa. He tossed about the pillows and some newspapers and picked up the handset.

"What!" he shouted into the instrument. "Who is this?" He looked meanly at me. "He's here but he's in no shape to talk." He gave me another look. " 'Cause he's sick, that's why. Got some kind of virus. Or maybe food poisoning. Puking his guts up. But I'll tell him you called." And with that he disconnected the call and tossed the phone back onto the sofa. "Will you push the buzzer and let Eddie in the building, please?"

He grimaced but I understood that it was supposed to be a crocodile smile and I pushed the door-release button. "How'd you get in, if Eddie couldn't?"

"None of yours," he growled, sounding mean enough to make me think he meant it. "I've been calling you for two hours! You stink! What the hell are you doing drunk?"

"None of yours," I growled back, sounding considerably less ominous. "I'll be back," I said, feeling a lot like I really and truly had either a virus or food poisoning. "You could make some coffee," I added, and headed toward the bathroom as I heard Eddie's feet pounding up the stairs. I stood under the shower, alternating hot and cold for as long as I could stand it, and by the time I dried and dressed, my head was beginning to clear and my stomach to settle. That's when I began trying to remember when, how, and where I'd gotten drunk enough to sleep in my clothes on top of the covers. I remembered three round-trips between

Sandra's place in Brooklyn and Yolanda's, and a dozen phone calls to both places from several bars. I didn't remember much else and didn't think I wanted to. I smelled coffee.

"What are you two doing here?" I stumbled through the living room and into the kitchen, where Eddie and Mike were sitting at the table, each with a mug of coffee and a third waiting for me. I sat down.

"Are you okay, *Hermano?*" Eddie asked, concern and worry darkening the deep furrows of his face.

My hands shook slightly as I lifted my coffee cup and they both noticed. I drank a few beers or a few glasses of wine on a semi-regular basis. I almost never drank to excess, and so rarely got drunk that I could remember—and count on very few fingers—each time. Anybody who knew me for longer than a month knew this about me. Mike Smith and Eddie Ortiz had known me for many years. "I don't feel so wonderful this minute, but I'm not out of control. What are you guys doing here?" I asked again.

They exchanged a visual signal before Mike answered. "We don't think it's such a good idea to cut Doctor Mason loose. We think there's a squirrel watching her, looking for a chance to make a move."

I squeezed my eyes shut, hoping to put enough pressure on my brain to remember fully what message I'd left for them regarding Jill Mason, because obviously I had, at some point before I'd begun drinking, left them a message. "Why am I just hearing about this squirrel?"

" 'Cause we really didn't have anything to tell you," Eddie said dryly. "We notice this guy almost every day, in a different spot, always working real hard not to seem like he's there and not to seem like he's watching Mason. He hasn't made a move, so there was nothing to tell. But he's there and he's watching. We don't want to cut her loose, Phil."

"No choice. No more money," I said, and chugged the rest of the coffee, hoping to jump-start my heart muscle. "Anyway, this limo service job has kicked into high gear, and there may even be a second company interested. I need you there." I got up from the table, got the coffee pot, re-filled all the cups, and sat back down.

They looked at each other again, like some old married couple who no longer need words to communicate, but I couldn't read the message. "Who's Sandra?" Mike asked.

I jumped and sloshed coffee out of the cup onto my hand, and felt the burn. "Why?" I asked, licking the coffee off my hand.

"That was her on the phone," Mike said, an odd note in his voice. "She said for you to call her as soon as possible at her grandmother's place."

Sandra's grandmother was sacred to her, and her Sugar Hill home was sanctuary. My hands began shaking again as I considered the gravity of her asking me to call her there. I'd met Mrs. Gillespie, had visited her home on the occa-sion of her seventy-fifth birthday party a few years back, but I'd never received the slightest indication that to call there would be acceptable. Sandra was one of those people who had definite boundaries, and her grandmother definitely was off-limits to everybody except immediate family, Yolanda, and God.

"Is there something we ought to know?" Mike asked.

"Anything we can help you with?" Eddie added.

"I don't know," I answered with more honesty than I'd expected or wanted to share. "Something's wrong with Yolanda and I don't know what it is." I knew there was no love lost between the two of them and Yo, but they understood and accepted her importance to me. "But when I find out, if I need your help, I'll ask."

"You want us to stop by the office and check on her?"

I shook my head. "She's not there," I said, perhaps a little too quickly.

Eddie shifted in his seat. He heard everything I hadn't said. "Where is she?" he asked in a deceptively calm voice.

"I don't know for sure," I said, more slowly, "but when I get a fix on what's going on, I promise I'll fill you in."

They stood up in unison and each man offered me his hand. I shook their hands and thanked them and still was drunk enough that I could have said something about valuing their friendship, but they both were too macho for that kind of talk. So, instead I told Mike he made a damn decent cup of coffee.

"Have to," he growled. "It's a necessary condition for a long and happy marriage."

So much for macho, I thought, as they slammed the door behind them, leaving me with a solid reminder that I'd be days ridding myself of this hangover. I looked around for the phone and spied it nestled neatly in its base on the coffee table. I picked it up to dial and realized that I had no idea what Sandra's grandmother's phone number was. Shit!

My hands shook again as I hauled the hundred-pound Manhattan phone directory from the bottom of the kitchen cabinet and lugged it into the living room. They steadied a bit as I leafed through the G's until I reached GILLESPIE. I wouldn't have thought it was a common-enough name for there to be so many of them. I ran my finger down a couple of columns until I found the one on Edgecombe Avenue that I was looking for. And my hand shook again as I punched the numbers. Sandra answered.

"It's me," I said.

"Are you all right?" she asked, in kind of a whisper.

"No, goddammit, I am not all right!" I didn't whisper, and paid the price. Hammers pounded in my head and caused lights to flash behind my eyeballs.

"I teach all day today. I won't be finished until three. I can meet you at your place by four, if that's convenient."

"What the hell is convenient, Sandra? Convenient would have been for somebody to tell me last night what the hell is going on, so I wouldn't have died of worry and fear. Convenient would be for you to tell me right now what the hell is going on, instead of talking to me about your goddamn classes!"

"Phil, please. I know and I'm sorry." She still was speaking in the kind of low voice that indicated she either didn't want to be overheard, or she was trying not to disturb or wake someone. Her grandmother? Or Yolanda? "Will you meet me?"

"Whatever, Sandra," I snarled and hung up the telephone. Now that I knew that Yolanda was safe, if not necessarily sound, I allowed my anger full rein. They were treating me like some miscellaneous acquaintance, instead of like a person of crucial importance in Yolanda's life. Hell, in both their lives!

I replayed last night in my mind and didn't gain any more insight into what had triggered Yolanda's escape—there was no other word for it—from the office, but I did recall that after Carmine left I called the other parents and asked them to do what I'd asked of Arlene Edwards and of Bert and Angie Calle and of Carmine: get the police and hospital reports regarding the rapes of their daughters. That knowledge calmed and pleased me. I hadn't been so out of touch that I'd lost all sense of self and of responsibility. That had occurred later in the evening, when I began drinking and riding the goddamn train back and forth to Brooklyn and generally behaving like an idiot.

I shook my head, hoping to clear it of idiot-related memories, and readied myself to go out into the world. Mike and Eddie had straightened up the living room, so all I had to do was turn off the coffee pot and put the cups into the sink. I'd wash up later, since I had to be home at four o'clock. I'd bring in dinner and make it an early evening. Exactly what was called for to eradicate a monster hangover. Then, as I was thinking of Mike and Eddie, I remembered their message: some "squirrel" was keeping watch on Jill Mason. A weirdo. A nut case of some kind. But what kind? A real genuine, bona fide, craze-o, or one of the neighborhood freaks allergic to gainful employment and looking to pick up a few bucks by scaring a rich woman? If they had thought for a second that the guy was professional and dangerous, they'd have alerted me the first time they spied him, and they'd have done more than suggest that we keep watch on Doctor Mason. But whatever or whoever "squirrel" was, he worried them enough to mention it.

I grabbed up the remote and switched on the television to New York 1 for the weather report: cold, cloudy, windy. New York in December. I switched it off and bundled up and spent the two-story descent to the street trying to decide whether to skip my morning rounds when the first snowflake nailed me right between the eyes. *Cold, cloudy, windy.* I wasn't so hung over that I'd missed hearing the word "snow" in the weather forecast. I looked up into the truly cloudy sky and was smacked by a truly windy flurry of stinging flakes. Decision made: no morning rounds for me. So I walked slower than usual, letting the cold work on the hangover while I worked on sorting out my feelings.

The first thing I felt still was anger. I couldn't help it. I was mad as hell at Yolanda . . . and at Sandra. And I was hurt that they had some secret they were keeping from me. And the wound cut even deeper because they felt it necessary to keep a secret from me. Then mad took over again: how dare they mistrust me! Shit. This was getting me nowhere. I didn't understand why so many people thought it was such a good idea to explore feelings. It felt a lot more productive to assess how good a job the cold was doing on the hangover, and where I was going to stop for coffee and juice, since I was assuming that Yolanda wouldn't be at the office. I knew there was a Starbuck's within a few blocks of the office and I was trying to place the corner in my mind, when the decision to go see Jill Mason presented itself.

Endowed with a sense of purpose, my feet picked up the pace and I resolutely turned the corner, into the wind. I tried, and quickly abandoned, looking for the squirrel Eddie and Mike said was watching the psychiatrist; it was not possible to look for, or see anything or anybody specific, in the driving wind and snow, especially when I didn't know exactly who I was looking for. I tucked my head down and hunched my shoulders up and jogged the four blocks to the building. I pressed the buzzer, said my name when the receptionist asked, and was admitted. The two people in the waiting room were clients: Patricia and Pamela Starrett.

Patty Starrett stood up and crossed the room to meet me, hand extended. She was a large, solid woman, almost as tall as I am, and graceful and fluid as a *dojo*. She had heavy, thick, and copious blond-streaked-with-silver hair which she arranged artfully on top of her head. Her eyes were brilliantly blue and when she greeted me, her smile was warm and her grip firm and dry. She, like Arlene Edwards, seemed to draw strength from the attack on her child. Like Arlene, she displayed no trace of embarrassment or shame, and was totally committed to doing whatever was necessary to halt the rapes and help heal the little victims.

"Your call last night was a true ray of hope, Mr. Rodriquez, and I'll be visiting the hospital and the precinct today."

I nodded at her and looked down at Pamela, a smaller version of her mother. " 'Morning, Pam. You okay today?"

She smiled her mother's smile—a little shyer—and nodded her head, thick blond mane dancing up and down. "Is Doctor Mason your doctor, too?" she asked.

"No," I said, "but she's a really good friend, and I just stopped in on my way to work to say hello to her and make sure she's okay, because I haven't seen her in a while."

"I'm just fine, Phillip, and I'm so glad you took the time to stop by."

I turned to see Jill Mason standing in the doorway between the waiting room and the hallway leading to her office. She had on another of those quietly expensive suits—deep green today—and she was smiling at me and beckoning to the Starretts, both of whom moved toward her. I edged backwards, toward the front door, and, once Patty and Pamela were out of sight, I looked a question at the shrink and her smile faltered a bit but held.

"I'm really quite fine, Phillip," she said, not quite convincingly, and I wondered whether she knew about the squirrel.

"I'll call you later," I said. "What time do you have free?"

She looked at the receptionist through the glass partition, who looked down at her appointment book and turned a few pages. I heard her response and opened the door behind me, promising to call between two forty-five and three thirty. Making the call on time would present no problem because, in the absence of Yolanda, I'd be in the office all day. And that was not a situation I resented. I very much needed to spend several quiet hours reading the information I knew that Yo had been compiling for me, pages and pages of documents that I'd given no more than a cursory reading and, therefore, had not absorbed to the extent necessary. But all that was about to change. Okay, so Yolanda wouldn't be at the office, but I would make good use of the time alone. Between what I'd learned from Connie deLeon and Doctor Bader, and what I understood from their insinuations once I read the police and hospital reports, and what Yo had compiled, I expected to have some concrete knowledge about who was raping and murdering little girls in my neighborhood. And I'd accepted the fact that once I had that knowledge roaming around in my quiet places, I'd have to find him. Them. So that my quiet places could be quiet once again.

I felt every bit as sad and lonely as I knew I would when I entered the empty, dark office. I switched on the lights quickly and opened the blinds and turned on the CD player. Yolanda didn't like music while she worked and I didn't need it when she was present. The wail of Gato Barbieri's sax filled the air as I hung up my coat, the snow melting and dripping onto the floor. My knit cap was almost soaked and I took it into the kitchen and dropped it into the sink, and I opened the bag from Starbucks: two large lattes, and two poppy seed bagels with cream cheese from B&H. Funny thing, but I'd lost my lust for Napoleons. One coffee and bagel went with me to my desk, the others waited in the microwave.

Leaving the kitchen, I turned on the back lights, creating daylight behind the Shoji screens in defiance of the moody ambiance Yolanda preferred. I gathered up every piece of paper from the printers and from near or around the computers, including from the trash cans, which had not been emptied because of the way in which the office had been vacated the previous night. Sitting at my desk, I retrieved all the documents already presented by Yolanda, and began the process of organizing all the material. It took a while, because of the amount of material at hand, and the process was further hampered by the regular ringing of the telephone, which began promptly at nine o'clock and continued unabated until after eleven. Not a single one of the calls was frivolous, and if I didn't have the information the client needed, I took a message for Yolanda to return the call tomorrow.

Suppose Yolanda's not here tomorrow?

The thought scared me silly. Was it really possible that Yolanda would not return tomorrow? Would not ever return? Since I didn't know the reason for her absence, I couldn't realistically predict her return, I told myself. Then I told myself to cut the crap! Whatever was the nature of the immediate problem, it was not the essence of Yolanda Maria Aguierre, I told myself. I knew that person, knew what made her tick, knew what motivated her. And I knew she could not and would not just walk away from me and our business. Yo had never *not* handled anything in her life.

I was finishing up the second latte and bagel, when a handwritten note from Yolanda in the margin of one of the pages caught my attention: *Phil—check this out. Addresses don't match and SS# wrong for this guy.* "This guy" was Gregory Jenkins, the weekend custodian and maintenance man at the building managed by Basil Griffin, the building from which Anna Arlene Cummerbatch was thrown. I grabbed up the notepaper on which I'd written the names, addresses, and Social Security numbers of the three men who worked for Griffin. The first two, according to Yolanda, checked out. So did Griffin himself. Gregory Jenkins did not. The Social Security number that Yolanda checked indeed was for a Gregory Jenkins—Gregory Frank Jenkins—but he was in his mid-sixties and he lived in the Bronx. The Gregory Jenkins who worked for Basil Griffin was supposed to have been almost thirty years younger and a resident of the East Village.

I closed my eyes and called up the conversation with Griffin that afternoon: *You wanna know who else works in the buildin', ask me who else works in the buildin',* he had said; and I had asked and he'd told me. I'd copied the information on the three men directly from Griffin's meticulous files into my notebook, and I'd torn out that page and given it to Yolanda. I now held it in my hand. Could I have made an error?

I opened my desk drawer and took out my daily log, the journal into which I transcribed every event, thought, and action of every day, and opened it to the date I first talked with Basil Griffin. I'd written that I found the man open, honest, and totally believable. And I'd written the names and addresses of his three employees. No errors. I knew I couldn't ask Griffin about the Jenkins discrepancy; he'd fire the man on the spot if he thought he'd lied about his personal information. And he'd kill him if he thought it even possible that he'd harmed the Cummerbatch child. Yet I needed to know . . .

I jumped up and ran to the back of the room and slid into the chair before the client computer. I knew enough—at Yo's insistence—to access client files and I quickly found the Golson/Stein entry. I copied the number and hurried back to my desk. I punched the numbers, knowing that Gregory Jenkins was one of the rapists. Which one?

"This is Phillip Rodriquez. Is this Miss Golson or Mrs. Stein, please?"

It was Miss Golson and I quickly told her what I wanted and she answered my question without asking why I wanted to know. A dream client. Then she shocked me speechless: "It's that Jenkins character, isn't it? He's the only reason you could be asking me whether we'd done background checks on our employees. Basil Griffin and Javier Lopez and Alvin Boggs are three of the most decent human beings I've ever met but Jenkins is scum. Knew it from the first moment I saw him."

I couldn't get any cogent words to come out of my mouth but it didn't matter to Shirley Golson. "I'll get those files for you, Mr. Rodriquez, and have them delivered to your office this afternoon. After all, you should have them. You're the firm that now handles that kind of thing for us. But I will tell you this: if that man . . . if anyone working for the Golson family harmed that child, I personally will castrate the bastard!" And then I was listening to a dial tone.

A sudden influx of calls postponed my ability to have a reaction to the talk with my dream client—if only they all were Shirley Golsons—because the next two hours and forty-five minutes of phone work demonstrated that truly they were not. Damn, but I missed Yo! And so did the clients, especially the male ones who'd had occasion to visit the office. Yolanda could remind them that their payment was late and they'd bring it in person. Yolanda could inform them that the new level and degree of service they requested would cost more money and they'd sign and return the amended contract the same day. Me they gave shit.

My headache was back when I finally got off the phone, but I consoled myself with the fact that for several hours I'd forgotten about my hangover. Now I was hungry and aware of the queasiness of my stomach and the thudding of all those assaulted and insulted brain vessels in my head. I looked at my watch. It was almost two o'clock. I was trying to decide whether to order Chinese, Cuban, or Italian for lunch when the phone rang again. Mike Smith was on the other end, his voice a mixture of excitement and foreboding, and it scared me for a moment. But he calmed me quickly.

He and Eddie were on the job for the limousine company when one of the prospective hires just happened to turn up at the office to check on the status of his application. Mike and Eddie just happened to have in their hands the information that the would-be stretch limo driver was wanted on a felony warrant across the river in Union City, New Jersey. The man had torched his ex-girlfriend's house. With the ex-girlfriend and her two children in it. All three were still in the county hospital burn unit. So Mike and Eddie grabbed the man and called me to tell me to call the cops and that ate up another hour.

I remembered almost too late to call Jill Mason and was hoping she hadn't worried that I hadn't called. Needn't have bothered.

"She's not here, Mr. Rodriquez," the receptionist said.

"Where is she?" I wanted to know, acutely aware how little it took these days to upset and worry myself.

"Oh, don't worry. She's fine. She's at her parents' place. Her mother called."

"Are you sure it was her mother?"

"Oh, yes! I've talked to Mrs. Mason many times on the telephone. Mr. Mason, too. And she even called, Doctor Mason did, to tell you she was sorry. She thought she'd be back sooner but, well, her parents are kinda old, you know?"

I said I understood and asked again whether the woman—what the hell was her name?—was certain that Jill Mason was with her parents.

"She said she'd call you tonight, when she gets home, if you leave a number, Mr. Rodriquez."

I gave the receptionist my home number and the number to the cell phone, which I'd resigned myself to keeping with me, and hung up. Now I was hungry and annoyed, but the annoyed didn't last long. The kid from the messenger service blew into the office covered with snow flakes and resembling a weird kind of ghost: his Gore-Tex riding suit was black with red stripes, his skin was burnished mahogany, and the white snow clung to all the dark places.

"Hey, dude, whattup?" he called out cheerily, the fact that he was covered in snow and riding a bicycle in sub-freezing weather obviously no cause for ill temper.

"*¿Que paso?*" I greeted him, reaching for the package and the slip to sign that he was proffering.

"The weather," he said in the same cheery voice. "Cold as a bitch out there. And you know how stupid they drive in the presence of snow." He shook his head in wonderment, tore off the top sheet of the receipt and gave it to me, and was headed out without another word. I followed him to the door and looked out. Sure as shit: the snow was sticking, and the bike messenger would get where he was going a lot faster than anybody stuck in the traffic jam out there.

I turned my attention to the package from Golson Properties. Shirley meant business. APB Security, based on Long Island, had worked for the Golson family for a dozen years. It was basic, professional work and I experienced a small pang for APB at the loss of regular work, even though it couldn't have amounted to much money. But work was work and money was money.

134

I quickly paged through the documents, searching for the background check on Gregory Jenkins. I found it, along with the report back to the Golsons: no outstanding warrants, no arrests on Gregory Jenkins, SSN 123-45-6789. Same number I had for the guy. But APB had checked no further, and, in truth, there was no reason that they should have. They probably had been asked to make sure that the man wasn't an escapee from some institution. But it wouldn't have been too much of a reach for APB to have noticed that Jenkins had a different address . . . Holy shit! On his employment application, he had listed the same address in the Bronx as the elder Jenkins. And an eerily similar name: Gregory Francis Jenkins. And his most recent place of employment was an address that was all too familiar: Bert and Angie Calle's building. Jenkins had been the night porter there, until he got the job at the building where Anna Cummerbatch lived.

"Gotcha, you son of a bitch!" Or I would have your ass, if Yolanda were here. Goddammit to hell! I ran back to the bank of computers and stared helplessly at them. At the one I knew would cross-check Gregory Frank Jenkins and Gregory Francis Jenkins and tell me what I knew, that G. Frank was the father of G. Francis and that the son was a piece of shit who had to use his father's Social Security number to evade computers like this one. I stood there and swore that when Yo returned, I'd listen to her and learn the basics of each of the machines. Oh, Yolanda, I thought, missing her with an intensity that I wouldn't have wanted to acknowledge out loud. That feeling caused me to wonder what had caused her absence, which, in turn, led me to remember that I was due to meet Sandra at my place in exactly twenty-two minutes.

She was waiting when I arrived, standing in the tiny vestibule looking perplexed but not, thank goodness, annoyed.

"I'm sorry I'm late, Sandra," I said as I charged into the doorway.

"No problem, Phil," she said, looking as I'd never before seen her look: weary, exhausted, worried, and perplexed. "I just got here. And then I wasn't sure whether I'd said four or four-thirty, so I thought maybe I was early." She tried to shrug it off but the weariness prevented so casual a motion.

I opened the door and followed her upstairs, all my anger ebbing away. Whatever was going on with Yolanda had taken its toll on Sandra, too, and no matter that I'd known Yo longer, Sandra was her lover and if she was this beat up by whatever the problem was, I had no right or reason to harbor anger against either of them. Sandra was neither stranger nor guest in my home and therefore knew where to hang her coat and where to leave her boots and find a pair of slippers. While she did all that, I opened a bottle of the red wine she liked and put it on the counter to breathe, along with a glass and brand new cans of cashews and pecans. Sandra liked to say that she had spent the years between seven and thirty on a water-lettuce-and-carrot diet. When she stopped dancing professionally, she finally was able to indulge one of her gastronomic passions, namely, nuts, and specifically cashews and pecans.

I hung up my own coat and unstrapped the gun from my back and shoulders and put it on the closet shelf. I heard water running in the bathroom and tried wondering whether Sandra needed a few moments to gather herself, or whether she thought I did. I used the time wisely. I called the deli up in the next block and ordered two monster burgers with everything, including fries. Then I poured wine for Sandra and a very large glass of seltzer water for me, added three aspirin, and sat down.

She looked better when she came into the living room a few moments later. She'd washed her face—I could see the effects of the cold water—and combed her hair, which had been disarranged by the hat and scarf she'd worn—and touched up her makeup. Not that she needed the stuff. She was as beautiful as Yolanda and, despite having happily abandoned the water-lettuce-and-carrot diet, possessed the kind of body the average woman would kill for. Though she no longer danced professionally, she taught daily and she was the kind of teacher who believed in the hands-on approach, who believed in demonstrating. She never asked a student to do what she could not or would not do.

She sank down next to me and emitted the kind of groan that was pure gratitude. She leaned her head back and closed her eyes for a moment, as if she were praying—which she might have been—then she turned toward me. She raised her wine glass in thanks and toast, and propped her stocking feet up on the coffee table. I recalled Yolanda making a joke once about Sandra's feet, and Sandra had laughed without embarrassment and acknowledged the truth of it: dancers might have great bodies but all of them have ugly feet! I'd never seen Sandra's feet, because they always were covered by socks or stockings, and today was no exception. But I smiled at the memory.

"I am truly sorry about last night, Phil. And so is Yolanda. And she's also sorry that she's not the one having this conversation with you. She should be and she knows it."

My stomach began to churn. This sounded ominous and I didn't like it. "Is there a reason she's not having this conversation with me, Sandra? Is she . . . sick or something? Is she . . . incapacitated?" I pushed away images of Yolanda unable to move or walk or talk but Sandra was shaking her head, dispelling those notions.

"Physically she's fine, Phil. Emotionally she's a real mess." She drank some wine and took a deep breath and turned sideways on the sofa to face me. "Yolanda was molested when she was seven, Phil. Raped. By the man who ran the *bodega* next door. He was a friend of her parents and he convinced her not to tell them. And she didn't, for a long time. This case you all are working on dredged up all that old stuff. She thought she'd worked it out in therapy and group years ago, but apparently she wasn't finished with it. Or it with her. And maybe it's never finished, Phil. I don't know . . ."

There was a sadness and a weariness to those last words that stabbed my heart. I reached over and grabbed Sandra and held her and she let me. "I didn't know you didn't know, Phil," she whispered into my shoulder. "I had no idea she'd never told you, especially knowing how much she loves and trusts you."

Some sharp hurt was stabbing me in the chest and throat. I tried to envision the baby Yolanda, happy and laughing and beautiful. And some inhuman monster destroying all that beauty. "I guess she doesn't love and trust me as much as I thought."

Sandra leaned back and looked me in the eye. She wasn't mad, or anything I'd ever seen in her. "Don't judge her too harshly, Phil. She's being hard enough on herself," Sandra said, and told me what happened last night, how, after Yolanda had run crying from the office, she was determined to "revisit the scene of the crime.

"We rode the train up to the East Harlem and Yolanda couldn't remember where her family had lived. That made her cry even harder. Then she couldn't remember the man's name who raped her, something she'd thought she'd never

forget, but she could see his face and hear his voice. She was practically hysterical by this time. People were looking at us. I didn't know what to do, so I hailed a livery car and took us to my Grandma's. She always knows what to do about everything."

Whatever had been building up in my throat escaped. I tried to push it back down, but it wouldn't go. Sandra must have learned from her Grandma because she grabbed me and held on tight. I was breathing like I'd just run the marathon. I didn't want to cry. Not because I was too macho for such a thing, but because I was afraid that once I started I wouldn't be able to stop. I was saved by the bell.

"You expecting somebody?" Sandra asked.

"Dinner," I said, standing.

"God bless you, Phil," she said, standing, too, and heading for the kitchen. I pressed the buzzer to admit the delivery guy while she was getting plates and napkins and another bottle of seltzer and bringing it all to the table. She was seated and ready when I put the bags down, and sniffing the air appreciatively. The appreciation changed to delighted horror when she opened the bags.

"Phil Rodriquez! Yolanda would kill you if she knew you were feeding me not only a heart-attack burger, but greasy fries as well!"

"You plan on telling her?"

"Hell, no," she said, getting up. "Where's the ketchup? Cabinet or 'fridge?"

" 'Fridge," I answered, stuffing too many fries into my mouth. "And get the hot sauce, too. Cabinet next to the 'fridge."

While we ate, we talked about many things—none of them Yolanda—and we both knew that it wasn't because we were avoiding the subject. There just didn't seem to be much left to say. Not to each other. I needed to talk to Yolanda and I didn't need Sandra as intermediary. And that wasn't a job she wanted, either. We cleaned up the kitchen together, not that there was much to clean. Not a morsel of food was left and the plates practically washed themselves. Sandra had another glass of wine and declared herself exhausted. "I slept maybe two hours last night," she said. I knew the feeling.

While I walked her to the subway, she told me that she and Yolanda were spending the night apart for the first time ever and assured me that it was a good and healthy thing to do. She also told me that Yolanda would be at work tomorrow and that she would talk to me, would tell me everything. It was on the walk back home, when I was alone again, that the sadness filled up my chest again. The sadness and the pain that represented the loss of beauty and innocence for Yolanda Maria Aguierre.

But at least she's still alive, said a voice in my head and I stopped walking, to think about that. Alive, perhaps, but tortured for so many years. Is this what little Pam Starrett has to look forward to? And Carmine's daughter? Those little girls have Jill Mason. Had Yolanda had a Jill Mason when she was a youngster? Knowing what I know about Puerto Rican families of that time period, I didn't think so. Knowing what I know about some Puerto Rican families of *this* time period didn't reassure me as I recalled the shame and embarrassment of Bert Calle and Daniel Esposito. Yes, they were angry, but they mostly were shamed by what had happened to their daughters and it was only through the efforts of the women that the little girls were getting help. So I doubted that Yolanda had seen a therapist twenty-six or twenty-seven years ago.

I was walking back home from the subway stop but I

didn't want to go home. I felt better knowing that Yo was all right and I definitely needed to sleep, but I also was wired and tense and angry. I'd never sleep with all that emotion roaming around inside me. Then I thought of Gregory Francis Jenkins. Tomorrow, you sick fuck. To-morrow, your ass is mine. I suddenly wanted to go straight home and straight to bed, because the sooner I slept, the sooner it would be tomorrow.

Chapter Eight

It beat yesterday morning by a few miles, but I still wasn't ready for the phone ringing before seven o'clock. At six fifty-two.

"*Dígame.*"

"Phil, come over to Doctor Mason's office right away. Right now, Phil, you hear me? *¡Arrive, arrive!*"

Pure stomach-knotting fear got me up and dressed and out onto the street in something less than three minutes, and I was a perfect Buddhist during the eight or nine minutes it took me to run to Jill Mason's: there were no thoughts in my mind, no feelings, no intentions, no awareness of the world around me. I was merely running. As hard and as fast as my body would allow. The fear resumed its position of dominance when I turned the corner and saw the unmarkeds in front of the building. That's when I allowed myself to wonder why Yolanda was calling me from the psychiatrist's office so early in the morning. It wasn't much more than idle speculation—given Yo's state of mind, it made perfect sense for her to see a therapist, and if I had to see one, I'd choose Jill Mason. What I willed my mind not to speculate about was the reason for the panic I'd heard in Yolanda's voice.

My resolve was short-lived. This was a crime scene, no doubt about it. In addition to the squad cars and unmarkeds parked haphazardly at the curb, three uniforms were on guard out front and I knew a few plainclothes detectives would be inside, and one aspect of cop protocol I remembered with certainty was the "nobody out, nobody in" rule: whoever was on the scene when the police arrived would have to remain until officially released, and nobody who wasn't already there would be allowed in, except for official personnel. I was sweaty and out of breath and wearing a jogging outfit. Nobody was going to mistake me for the NYPD commissioner. If I were smart enough to do what Yolanda told me to do, I'd have the cell phone and I could call inside, but I wasn't and, therefore, didn't. So I did the next best thing. I got loud. I started talking right away—identified myself and Jill Mason as my client and the woman inside with Jill Mason as my partner and the person who had placed the call to me and probably to the police as well. The uniform looked at me without ever speaking and pointed me inside, through the small foyer, where I knew I'd encounter a detective who might or might not allow me further, depending on the nature of the crime.

I got as far as the entry to the waiting room before being confronted by the detective and I began my narrative again, in a slightly louder voice. It worked.

"Phil!" Yolanda called out from, I imagined, Jill Mason's office, appearing almost immediately thereafter.

I took a step toward her but the plainclothes guy blocked me with an arm across my chest.

I grabbed him, Yolanda materialized like vapor and grabbed me, and a voice from within called out, "Let Rodriquez in!" All that happened almost simultaneously.

I let Yolanda push me back and away from the plainclothes who clearly wanted a piece of me, and then pull me past him toward Jill Mason's inner sanctum, where another detective—no doubt the one who'd let me in—was guarding the door. I was walking pretty much on my own, though Yo's hand was still tight on my arm, when I saw Jill. She was half-sitting, half-reclining on the Mission sofa covered in the African print fabric. Her lovely face already was purpling and puffy—the perp had known how to work on a face. Her hair was a tangled mess and her blouse was ripped.

I couldn't look at her any longer, so I looked around the office and almost smiled at the sight. It was a mess. The kind of mess that occurs when there's been one hell of a fight. I looked back at Jill Mason, who was looking steadily at me, and gave her the reaction I knew she was waiting for.

"Kicked his ass good, didn't you?" I said.

"Gave almost as good as I got," she said, the words quite slurred through her cut and swollen lips, and she might have smiled, too; I couldn't tell.

Yolanda was still holding my arm and I pulled her close in a two-arm embrace and kissed the top of her head. She leaned into me and totally released for a couple of brief seconds, before collecting herself and leaving my embrace to bestow the same comfort on Jill Mason, who welcomed it. I was thinking how much they resembled close friends in the way they gave and received comfort, and how much I envied women that ability, when the door to the closet opened and a plainclothes detective I hadn't seen before stepped into the office.

"Nothin'," he said in a dry, expressionless tone, his body language as empty as his voice. "Didn't nobody see nothin'. Half a dozen people out there and didn't nobody see nothin'." He looked like a TV detective: ugly coat, ugly hat, ugly shoes, ugly, out-of-shape body. His eyes redeemed him. They were a clear, light gray, striking and unusual, and they conveyed an unexpected warmth.

I looked from his eyes to the door to the closet to Jill Mason and back to that damn door again, remembering the first time I'd been in this office. I'd looked at every inch and corner of this room, and I'd decided that the door was to a closet. It was a wooden door, an interior door, not an exterior door. I took a step toward it and the detective who'd allowed me into the room shook his head at me: don't touch. It hadn't been processed yet.

"That door goes to the outside?" I asked him.

He shook his head again. "To a hallway, which goes to a door to the outside," he said.

I looked back at Jill Mason, whose face was taking on what I recognized as a look of horror, even through the horror already etched on her face. "You didn't know about that door," she said, and it was a statement and not a question. "I didn't tell you about that door. I am so sorry. Only the patients use it. Nobody but the patients knew it was there. Or so I thought, until he left through it. He knew exactly where it was."

Too much. It was all too much. I needed to get out of that office and away from women in pain and go do something that would allow me to feel at least useful. Maybe even productive, because continuing to stand there was making me feel a total idiot. The EMTs were arriving when I got outside and it struck me that I was wondering, while I was standing there watching Jill Mason's face swell and discolor, where they were. They brushed past me, almost shoving me into the plainclothes whose arm I was going to break just a few minutes earlier, and he looked ready to take up where we'd left off. *Just give me a reason,* his eyes and his posture said. Only my desire to get to the back of the building, to see that back door, prevented me from obliging him, because smashing something right now would feel really good. And would be a really Neanderthal or prehistoric thing to do. I didn't care, but Yolanda and Doctor Mason might.

I nodded politely at the man and jogged down the block, turned the corner, and looked for an approach to the back of the building. If the perp had left by that back door, he had to have gone somewhere, and despite what the detective said, somebody had seen something. That somebody may not have shared what was seen with him—and given his warm and winning personality, no wonder. It was barely daylight on a frigid, snow-threatening morning. Who needed his shitty attitude under those conditions? Who needed his shitty attitude under any conditions? I never understood why cops never understood the need to be nice to people. Cops resented it like hell when citizens were hostile or rude or nonresponsive; yet cops gave citizens hostile or rude or nonresponsive behavior a lot of the time.

It took forays into two dead-end alleys before I found the one that put me at the rear of Doctor Mason's building. The alleys of New York City were their own world. Similarly, the rear view of buildings, too, held surprises. The back of this building was above street level, and there were two doors, one at either end of the building, reached by a set of concrete stairs which were linked by a concrete walkway. A uniform was standing guard at the door that provided access to the hallway outside Jill Mason's office and she put her hand on her weapon when I came into view. I raised both of mine and called out a greeting as I approached. I told her who I was and what I was doing.

"Don't touch anything," she said.

I stuffed my hands into the pockets of my warm-up jacket and walked to the other end of the building where a huge green garbage Dumpster was parked. It was almost as clean here as if Basil Griffin were in charge. If the perp had dropped or left anything in his wake during his escape, it would have been visible. I turned back toward the stairs and took in, on the way back up, the fact that there was a steel railing. Had the perp touched it? Wouldn't matter, I told myself. That was TV cop shit. Damn railing outside, in the rain and sleet and snow and funky, dirty New York air, God-knows-who going up and down these stairs, and the prints of Jill Mason's attacker could be lifted right through all the moisture and the grime? Yeah, right.

I walked to the end of the alley where a four-foot wall separated the backs of one block of buildings from the backs of another. I looked up and directly into the eyes of Willie One Eye's nephew. The short-order cook and manager of the diner. He was holding a black and bulging garbage bag in each hand. He wore a knit cap, but no coat. I looked at the man long enough to be certain that he recognized me. I nodded but I didn't speak. He didn't move a muscle, didn't blink, maybe didn't even breathe. I would, I knew, have to wait for this guy to tell his uncle that he had words for me. If, in fact, he did have words for me. That he had information, I was certain. That he'd share it with me, I could only hope.

I turned away from him and was thinking about trying to have a talk with the uniformed officer guarding the door, but two plainclothes detectives had joined her, so I made my way through the alleys, back to the front of the building. A pretty good crowd had gathered and I was wondering whether I could get back inside when I noticed Doctor Mason's receptionist. She noticed me at the same time and let out a shriek that startled several onlookers. I hurried toward her and she toward me, and we met in the middle of the block.

"What's wrong, Mr. Rodriquez? Is Doctor Mason okay? Why are the police here?"

"Doctor Mason is . . . ah . . ." I didn't know what to say

because I didn't know how she was, really.

The woman's hands went to her face. "Oh my God! Oh my God! Oh my God!" Her shrieks reverberated in the frigid air.

I touched her shoulder. "She's alive. She's conscious and talking. But she has been injured," I said. Then I said it again, to make sure she heard me, and I saw it sink in.

"Is it . . . was it the same guy? Whoever has been trying to hurt her?"

"I don't know," I said.

"You've got to stop him, Mr. Rodriquez. Please . . ." She didn't finish because my favorite cop came over to tell her that she could go in. He pointedly didn't look at me, which was a relief. I no longer wanted to smash him. I just wanted to get Yolanda and get to work, and so I followed the receptionist back inside. The paramedics had attended to the patient, who had combed her hair and was wearing a different blouse and sweater, and were packing up their equipment. Yolanda still sat beside Jill Mason, holding an ice pack to her face and another to the splint on her right wrist. She really had put up a hell of a fight.

"Oh Doctor Mason!"

"Margo, everything is just fine," she said, extending her good arm and patting Margo's shoulder, and making comforting noises to the woman. She's beat to a pulp and was comforting Margo and . . . and Yolanda! For she was, as much as Yolanda was comforting and supporting her. Maybe the woman *was* a saint. Or merely the kind of human being we all should be.

Yo left Margo to attend to her boss and came over to me. "You see anything?"

"Maybe," I said, still pissed as shit about that back door and my ignorance of it. "Maybe somebody else saw something and maybe he'll tell me about it. I'll fill you in. Are you coming to the office or staying with Doctor Mason?"

"Definitely to the office as soon as I get her home and comfortable. Margo will stay here and deal with the patients. And with this mess," she said despondently, looking around the trashed office.

I reminded her that we had car services and cleaning services as clients and she gave me a Yolanda Maria Special High Wattage Smile that lit up the room and banished, for a moment, all traces of pain and horror.

"You mean you're actually paying attention to who's paying us?"

"Not only that, but working at learning how to make good and proper use of our computer friends."

She laughed out loud, a sound so beautiful as to almost bring me to tears. "I should nut out and leave your sorry ass to your own devices more often!"

I didn't have to work too hard at feigning a look of dread. "Oh, no! Not that!" I hugged her and then went over to talk to Jill Mason. I knelt in front of her and we locked eyes. Somehow, in our very brief association, it had become apparent that we could communicate volumes without words. I saw in her gaze a steadiness and a calm that convinced me that she was and would be fine. If some asshole didn't succeed in killing her first. And she saw exactly what I was thinking and feeling, because she told me to get over myself.

"Stop being so noble. You are to be blamed for nothing and to be thanked for so much. Mr. Aiello, too."

Oh, shit. Carmine. I'd have to tell him what had happened. I didn't want to think about how that might play out, so I changed the subject, by telling her that we were sending a cleaning service and a car. Margo would, gladly, direct the restoring of the office to its original state and deal with the clients—most of whom would already have heard about what happened before they arrived and would have come solely for information anyway. And Yolanda would go home with her.

"I'll send Mike or Eddie over later today. After you've gotten settled and, ah, cleaned up a bit."

"Only on one condition," she said firmly. "That they're coming to find who's doing this to me and stop him, not to be bodyguards. I want to hire you, Phillip. I want to know why this is happening to me."

I nodded. So did I. "You understand that will mean talking to me to some extent about—"

She stopped my words with her hand again. "I know what it means and I will share with you what I can. But believe me when I tell you, Phillip, that this madness," and she waved her injured hand at the madness surrounding us, "has nothing to do with any current client, and probably not with a past one."

I stood up without comment because not only did I believe her, I knew that the truth of her words would make finding and stopping the madness, as she called it, so difficult as to be virtually impossible. For that meant there was no logical reason for her to be victimized. Which left only illogical reasons, of which there were an infinite number. There also was a squirrel somewhere out there, watching and waiting.

I took a taxi home, stripped out of the sweat clothes I'd thrown myself into for the dash to Jill Mason's, showered, and dressed again, deciding on wool slacks, a silk-and-wool blend shirt, and bucks—not as comfortable as Doc Martens but I could manage a crosstown walk in them if necessary.

My head was too much of a jumble for me to have any clear and definite plan for the day, but I had the feeling that it would not be a jeans and sweatshirt kind of day. And I'd heard it from Yolanda often enough: *Listen to your instincts, Phil.* So I listened. And added a blazer. As much for warmth as for sartorial splendor. No snow was forecast but the temperature wouldn't get out of the twenties.

I took a taxi to Willie One Eye's newsstand. Didn't need to visit Mrs. Campos since Yolanda wouldn't be at the office when I arrived, and I didn't particularly want to talk to Itchy. Willie and I exchanged our normal greetings in the normal fashion and I paid for my papers. His good eye surveyed the area around us.

"My nephew, he don't talk to no cops," Willie said.

"Can't blame him," I said, remembering the jerk from Doctor Mason's office and his shitty demeanor.

"Whatever he tells you, he won't tell no cop. Won't tell nobody but you."

"He won't need to," I replied.

"He's workin' a double shift today. He'll take a break after lunch. 'Bout two o'clock."

"Thanks, Willie. I won't forget."

"I know you won't," he said, and his dead eye smiled at me.

I decided to meet Carmine at the coffee shop and tell him about Jill Mason before he heard it on the vine, and took my second taxi of the day and it wasn't yet nine o'clock. Who—or what—was I becoming that I hopped in and out of taxis like a resident of one of the Upper Sides? *Don't trip this, Rodriquez,* a voice warned me. A voice I knew but had practiced ignoring for a very long time, primarily because I hadn't wanted to hear it. But this time I listened and knew its correctness. I didn't have time to walk twenty blocks. I didn't have time to pay courtesy calls. I had clients who were in real danger and it was my responsibility to act as quickly and effectively as possible to remove that danger. I was, it seemed, functioning like one of those well-dressed, well-paid movie detectives, which made me more than a little bit nervous, since that wasn't really my job. *Bullshit,* the voice said.

Carmine looked surprised when I walked in but waved me over to him with a cannoli and nodded his head toward the counter, and I knew a cafe con leche and a couple of Napoleons would be set before me in a matter of seconds.

"I'm pickin' up the police report later this morning, Rodriquez, if that's what you wanna know," he said by way of greeting.

"Doctor Mason got beat up this morning," I said, without preamble.

He choked on the pastry he was chewing but kept trying to talk anyway, making the choking worse. The owner hurried over and slapped him on the back until he managed to clear his throat. "Is she okay? What the fuck happened? I knew I shouldn't 'a pulled those guys! I knew this fuckin' shit would happen! Son of a bitch!"

I let him rant and rave and noticed that nobody in the place paid any attention to him after the danger of his choking to death was over. Then I assured him that the good doctor would be fine, if sore for a while, and I told him what I knew of what had happened. I even told him of the potential witness who hadn't told the cops anything and wouldn't, but had agreed to meet with me that afternoon. That seemed to soothe him and I secretly appreciated his not even looking like he wanted to ask me who my witness might be. Carmine truly understood the nature of the streets. And he truly blushed when I told him that Doctor

Mason did not blame him and wished him not to blame himself.

"You got any ideas, Rodriquez, who's lookin' to hurt this lady this way?"

"To tell the honest truth, Carmine, no, I don't. It doesn't make any sense, why anyone would want to hurt her. Nothing I've looked at or thought about hangs together or connects to any other piece of the puzzle."

We sat quietly for a moment, drinking our coffee and eating our pastries and pondering how a woman's life could be in such danger for no apparent reason. Then Carmine broke the silence with what I knew instinctively was a true statement.

"Old shit, Rodriquez. Whatever this is about, it's old shit. This ain't about somethin' happened last month or even last year. 'Cause if it was, she'd be dead. New payback is hot and quick. It's the old stuff that's mean and cold and slow. You know what I'm sayin', Rodriquez?"

I did. I knew exactly what he was saying and I knew that his assessment was correct. But exactly how old could this grudge be? And if it was old enough, would she even re-member it? Was it something that would have been impor-tant to her, or only to the person who perceived that he or she was wronged by Jill Mason? How much of her past was she willing to probe? I stood up and dropped some money on the table and pointed my finger at Carmine, daring him to challenge me. He raised his palms in acquiescence, nodded at me what I took to be thanks, and told me he'd see me later, when he had the police and hospital reports.

It wasn't merely cold outside; it was frigid. People were bundled in their layers of scarves and sweaters and bulky overcoats, and then hunched deep down within them, shoulders up around their ears, walking rapidly to whatever

153

inside space would provide respite from the bitter, biting, East River wind. I was as hunched and hurried as the next person, but also enjoying the walk. I'd missed my sidewalk time the last couple of weeks and as I realized how much I was enjoying myself, I slowed my pace. Stepped out into the street to let the others keep theirs. Nothing so annoying on a New York sidewalk as somebody walking like they come from some other part of the country where they never learned how to walk on a sidewalk with other people. I also needed to think, to process the conversation with Carmine. If he was correct in his assessment that the root of Jill Mason's problem was buried somewhere deep in her past—and I thought he was—then the question was why wait until now to dig it up? And I still believed the answer to that was right here, in the present.

Yolanda was at the office when I arrived, and so was a cop, still wearing his overcoat, his gloves and hat on the chair next to him. I knew he was a cop by looking at him—his pants and socks were brown and his shoes black with thick crepe soles—though I didn't know him and couldn't imagine what he wanted. There hadn't been enough time for them to have anything to ask me about Jill Mason; and nobody but me and Mike and Eddie and Willie's nephew knew that I knew anything more than the cops knew about her situation. The lights were on and the blinds were open, the smell of coffee was in the air, and Yolanda was there. It was enough to induce me to say good morning to the cop as I removed my hat, scarf, and coat as I walked past him to the closet in the back.

When I returned, he was standing stiffly at my desk, sans overcoat. His jacket was plaid wool—brown, black, and green. He was a gym rat. His shoulders and neck were so developed that his head was too tiny for the breadth, and his waist and hips were so narrow he looked like a paste-it doll: the kind where unrelated heads and torsos are combined to produce an incongruent whole.

"Mr. Rodriquez," he said, in a barely civil tone.

"That's my name," I replied, my hands in my pockets. Damned if I was going to extend a handshake to this asshole. He was in my space talking down to me?

"We need to talk," he said, adding supercilious to uncivil.

"I doubt it," I said with a shrug. "I don't know you, and I've got too much work to do to waste time talking to someone I don't know."

"This somebody can pull your license, buddy, so you better make the time."

"Not without a reason, *buddy*," I snarled, putting a thick layer of nasty spin on the word, "which you don't have, so instead of you wasting my time and yours with your unfounded and stupid threats, why don't I give you my lawyer's name and you go threaten him? He'd enjoy the encounter so much he'd actually make time for you, even though he doesn't know you, either. But he'd be getting paid to make the effort." I looked in Yolanda's direction, though without making eye contact, as I asked her if she'd mind writing down our attorney's name, address, and telephone number for my "buddy" here. Then I turned my back on him and this time I did make eye contact with Yo. Only hers were closed.

"You've got your nose way deep in police business, Rodriquez," the cop said quietly enough that I knew he was choking on the words. He wanted to jack me up and didn't have a reason to. Yet.

"Not true," I replied, as quietly, determined not to give him a reason. Yet.

"Oh. So that's why all of a sudden half a dozen people are asking for police and hospital reports? Because you're not meddling in police business?"

"Citizens who are victims of crimes are entitled, by law, to official reports from the police and from the hospital. Surely you know that?" I made the question insulting. He got the message. His entire tiny head flushed red.

"Some of these crimes are almost a year old. How come they're just now asking for those reports?"

"Maybe that's why, *buddy*. Because some of these crimes *are* almost a year old and these good citizens have heard nothing from their police department. Nothing but the usual bullshit and run-around, that is."

"You need to mind your own business, Rodriquez."

"I am minding my own business. Those people are my clients and I have every right, every responsibility, to advise them of their legal entitlements and I don't give a good goddamn whether you like that or not."

"You'll give a good goddamn when I lock your ass up."

I extended my arms toward him, hands balled into tight fists but pointed down and not at him. "Oh, please give me another reason to sue the stupid ass police department!" I really was mad now.

"You think you've got the first reason?"

"I think my clients do."

"Name one," he snarled, menace and challenge thick in his voice.

"The lawyer can name them, but I know this: victims have a right to official police records of their investigations, and I know you don't have the right to refuse them. So, if you're stupid enough to arrest me, do it!" I pushed my arms at him and he backed up a step. "Otherwise, get outta my office so I can get back to work."

His tiny pale blue eyes narrowed to slits and the red drained from his face. I knew he was counting to ten or doing whatever he needed to do to keep from losing his cool. And he finally succeeded. "It's not like we haven't been working these cases, Rodriquez. And it's not like they're the only cases we got."

"And how would the parents of those little girls know you were working their cases? When was the last time you had any contact with them? Did you warn all parents of little girls in the area that there was a serial rapist around? Maybe even two of them?" I said that slowly and watched his reaction. It was worth the payoff. He went even paler.

"You really are in police business, Rodriquez," he said slowly, sounding quite threatening and menacing, "and in way deep."

"I'm just paying attention to the obvious. Dates, times, places, degrees of violence visited upon the victims. Shouldn't take a dozen investigators almost a year to draw some very basic conclusions, the most obvious of which is that the MOs differ. A little too much, don't you think? Or aren't you an investigator? Maybe you're just the muscle the real investigators send out to intimidate?"

He was about to blow. I could all but see the steam coming out of his ears. I was wondering what I'd do if he swung on me, when the door flew open and Mike Smith and Eddie Ortiz blew in. I'd left them messages about Jill Mason and their outrage and anger were thick enough to cut. But their words stopped and back-pedaled on their vocal cords when they saw my visitor.

"Temple. What the fuck are you doin' here?" Mike Smith growled at the muscle-bound young cop.

"You know this guy, Phil? I didn't know you knew this guy!" Eddie looked and sounded personally offended and wounded that I would sink so low as to know the cop named Temple.

"I don't know him," I said. "He came to pull my ticket, but he's on his way out. Aren't you, Temple, is it? First name Buddy?" I said, being a real wise ass, and feeling safe enough to be one now that I had Mike and Eddie as back-up.

"First name Aloysius," Mike said with a sneer.

Temple shook his head and, with more grace than I'd have given him credit for, walked over and picked up his coat, hat, and gloves. "My lieutenant would appreciate a call from you, Rodriquez. Bill Delaney. You know him, right?"

"Yeah, I know Delaney. Good man."

"Yeah," Temple said, "he is." He was buttoning his coat and was at the door, putting his hat on. "Funny, now I think about it, he said the same thing about you. Guess he hasn't seen you in a while."

We all watched him leave and I sighed deeply. I'd just taken out on Aloysius Temple the anger and frustration I'd been harboring against all cops for the last couple of months, and especially that which I'd been harboring since this morning.

"I thought he was going to level you, Phil," Yolanda said, coming toward me. "You just scared me green."

"I'm sorry, but he pissed me off. He was in the wrong place at the wrong time with the wrong attitude. Right now, I'm sick of cops with shitty attitudes, especially ones threatening to pull my license. Which reminds me! Yo, you remember the note you made telling me to check on a discrepancy in Gregory Jenkins' file?"

And I told them about Gregory Frank Jenkins and Gregory Francis Jenkins.

"*Gracias a Dios,*" Yolanda said. "Did you leave me your notes?" she asked, and even before I answered she was retreating to her world. Gregory was about to be in big trouble.

Then I told Mike and Eddie about the events of the morning and they alternated between blaming themselves, blaming me, and wanting to go find the squirrel and beat him into pulp.

"We don't know it's the squirrel," I kept saying. I also kept reminding them of my meeting with Willie's nephew. And of the need to find the squirrel—without beating him into jelly—so we could compare him to whoever Willie's nephew saw this morning.

"You don't know for sure that Willie's nephew saw anybody," Mike said.

"He saw somebody." I was sure of it.

"What's this dude's name, anyway? Willie's nephew?" Eddie asked.

I shrugged. I didn't know his name; hadn't asked and hadn't been told, either by Willie or by the nephew.

"Why the hell didn't you know about that back door, Phil?" Eddie whined at me, the accusation hanging there.

"Why the hell didn't you know about it?" I shot back. And we all sat there feeling like guilty, useless pieces of shit.

"What do you want us to do?" Mike asked.

"Go find the squirrel," I said. "Keep an eye on him. Watch where he goes, what he does, who he talks to, where he eats, where he sleeps if you can get that close. Is this guy a bona fide crazy?"

Mike and Eddie exchanged a look and Eddie answered the question. "I don't think so. Not if you mean is he a regular at Bellevue, with papers and a wristband and a padded cell with his name on the door. I think he's probably a little whacko, probably does a little blow, but I think he's mostly just an asshole who likes being mean and hurting people."

"You think he's the one who grabbed her that first time?"

The look again between them, and this time Mike answered. "Yeah, we think probably he's the one. Fits her description. Or as much of one as she had: he's the right size, build, color. And he's sure as hell dirty enough to stink, although I haven't gotten that close to him. Yet."

We were quiet again. Then I asked something I'd been thinking and dismissing and thinking and dismissing for a couple of weeks: "Do you think it's possible that this stuff is related? Jill Mason and these little girl rapes? You know she treats several of them and, as Yolanda pointed out, shrinks know people's secrets. Maybe one those kids knows who raped her and told Mason."

"And she what, called him up and told him?" Eddie asked incredulously. "How would he know to come for her, even if one of the kids did remember something?"

"Maybe he overheard something," I said.

"Like what?" Eddie inquired.

"Like how?" Mike added. "How would anybody, especially a rapist, hear what a patient is telling a shrink?"

I took a deep breath. "Maybe he heard it somewhere else. Remember. Doc Mason and Miss deLeon at Beth Israel and Doctor Bader at NYU and that information that Yo pulls from her computers—all say this guy—and most sick fucks like him—have access to their victims. Take this Jenkins clown. He worked in the buildings where two of the victims lived. How many bits and pieces of people's conversations do you think building porters hear every day? Who pays any attention to them? They're just the janitors, right? But they have full and total access to the buildings."

"But I thought you had this asshole a tight fit for the murders," Mike said. "And the dead girls don't have any connection to the shrink."

"But would you guess that if Jenkins had any drinking buddies, they would be guys he worked with, or guys who did the same kind of work? Like janitors in the buildings where the other girls lived? And would he ever visit those other buildings?"

I could see their brains working as they considered what I'd just said. Between the two of them, they had more than forty years of policing experience, which meant more than forty years of experience with perp behavior. Then they checked their thoughts with each other with that exchange-of-looks thing they did. Eddie answered for them.

"It's possible, Phil, but not likely. I never worked sex crimes but what I hear, dudes like that don't have drinking buddies, you know?"

Yeah I knew.

Something else was bothering me, and I got it off my chest, too, while I was at it. "I might be in over my head," I said. "And if I take Temple's visit seriously, there's no 'might' about it. I didn't start out looking to find rapists and woman-beaters, but I'm looking to find their asses now, and I don't want to put you two in any trouble."

Mike stood up. "We're outta here, Bro. Now that I've warmed up, I can honestly say that I'd rather be out in the cold than in here listening to you lose your mind." And he walked away from me, put on his coat, hat, and scarf, and left.

Eddie looked after him, then at me. "Do I need to say what he just said?"

I grinned at him and shook my head.

"Good. We'll call you when we tree the squirrel."

I sat there for a moment organizing my thoughts. Or, more accurately, slowing them down so that I could organize them. But they were still moving too fast. Too many questions and not enough answers, and the answers that were there did not necessarily correspond to the questions that were there. I was more rattled by Temple's visit than I had let on, and I definitely would pay a visit to Lieutenant Delaney, sooner rather than later. I didn't need the kind of trouble he could make for me if he wanted to. I also was still scared to death by the attack on Jill Mason and took no comfort in the fact that I had known it would happen. Now I had to figure out how to make sure it didn't happen again, because next time maybe we—she—wouldn't be so lucky.

But first . . .

I stood there watching Yolanda. She was dressed in all black today, and her hair was pulled back and tied up with a multi-colored scarf. In the moody light that she preferred—the light from the three computer screens and from a paper-covered Japanese lantern—she seemed much too serene to be looking for a rapist who possibly was a murderer. Her glasses rode low on her nose and her fingers danced across the keyboard as if she were playing a symphony. She stopped typing, hit a key, and the printer began humming. She rolled herself to the right and began typing at the keyboard that I knew operated the client computer.

"Hi."

She looked up at me and smiled, her fingers still working the keyboard. "Hi, Phil," she said, and stopped typing. She met my eyes and I could see the sadness in hers though she continued to smile at me.

"How did you come to be at Doctor Mason's this morning?"

"I had an appointment at six forty-five. I've been seeing

her for a couple of weeks. Late at night or early in the morning."

I didn't know what answer I'd expected; perhaps this one, for nothing else made sense. "Good thing, then," I said, all of a sudden feeling awkward and prying.

"I'm sorry, Phil. I should have told you. About . . . what happened to me when I was a kid."

"I'm sorry you felt you couldn't, Yo. And I promise you that whatever I've done or been to make you feel you couldn't trust me . . ."

She pushed back her chair and stood up so quickly that the chair continued rolling and crashed into the desk, which ordinarily would have gotten her attention; anything potentially harmful to her computers commanded her attention. But she was focused totally on me, her expression a mixture of sorrow and disbelief. "Is that what you think? That I don't trust you?"

"Well . . . yeah, Yo. What else? I mean, when you don't tell me something that important and we tell each other everything . . . what other reason could you have?"

Her eyes filled with tears and she quickly wiped them away with the back of her hand. "Shame. I was ashamed. I've always been ashamed. So has my family. Until Sandra, you were the dearest person in the world to me and I couldn't bear it if you were ashamed of me, too."

I couldn't speak. I thought instantly of Daniel Esposito and the shame he felt. Bert Calle was numb with grief and Carmine Aiello had rage for blood through his veins. I could share the grief and the rage, but not the shame. I felt no shame, just incredible anger, and sorrow deeper than anything I've ever known. How anybody could hurt my Yolanda. I still couldn't speak, so I grabbed her and held on. What words could make a difference after all this time?

I was still searching when the front door opened. "We'll talk later," I said, releasing her and heading out front to see who might be visiting, silently praying that it wasn't a representative from the police department.

It was a client delegation, comprised of Bert Calle, Arlene Edwards, Patty Starrett, and Carmine Aiello. We greeted each other warmly, me exchanging handshakes with the men and hugs with the women. And each of them giving me an envelope.

"The police and hospital reports," said Arlene Edwards with grim satisfaction. "They didn't want us to have them, you know, especially the police."

"But Mr. Aiello's lawyer put a stop to all that," said Patty Starrett.

"I almost let them get away with it," Bert Calle said so quietly I barely heard him, and only slowly understood his meaning because I was watching his face, watching the words leave his mouth through wind-chapped lips. "I was letting them tell me why I couldn't have the papers. Then I heard Mr. Aiello. He was goin' crazy in there and they were putting him out of the office and he saw me and asked me did I have my papers. And I told him they said I couldn't have them and he went crazy again."

Carmine waved him into silence. "Thing is, we got the reports, Rodriquez. Or most of 'em. Calle here brought that other guy's, what's his name?"

"I have Daniel's daughter's," said Bert, again very quietly. "Daniel's working extra shifts, trying to get caught up, you know?" As if to say, *If I can cut this guy some slack, so can you.*

Five out of the seven, including both of the murder victims. Enough for Doctor Bader, I was certain; enough for her to discern a pattern if one existed.

"Are you in trouble with the police, Phillip?" asked Arlene Edwards.

"They told us you had no business requesting these reports," said Patty Starrett, "and they said you could lose your license—"

"Nobody's losin' nothin'," Carmine snarled. " 'Specially not Rodriquez. We don't hear nothin' from the cops for damn near a year, and soon as we start askin' for what's ours they start with the threats? I'll sue their asses myself!"

I held up my hands to restore calm. Theirs and mine. "You had a legal right to these reports, and I had an obligation to tell you your rights since you hired me and paid me money . . . which I took," I said with a grin, which they all returned. "The only thing that matters now is whether there's enough information here for an expert to develop a profile of the rapist. I believe there is and I believe that, when coupled with other information we've developed, we'll have a direction to follow."

"Does that mean you'll know who the murderer is?" asked Arlene Edwards.

I hesitated. "It means specific individuals can be put under the microscope and those individuals' activities and actions can be carefully examined. Now. Before you leave, I'd like for each of you to write down the names of all the people who have access to the buildings where you live, including the mail carrier, if you know his or her name."

"You mean like the porters and the janitors?" asked Patty Starrett.

I nodded, though not too enthusiastically. "Anybody with access. Exterminators, if you know the name of the company. Restaurant delivery people . . ."

"But somebody has to buzz them in," said Bert Calle.

I nodded again, being as noncommittal as possible, and

passed out notebooks and pens. Everybody sat and began writing and I looked up to find Yolanda looking at me. She gave me a thumbs-up and disappeared behind her screens. I resisted the urge to begin reading the hospital and police reports, sensing that most, if not all of them, felt that information too private for general consumption. And I wondered whether any of them had had the stomach to read the reports themselves, if they even knew in real-world terms what those reports contained.

Arlene Edwards finished first, the only one of them whose information was not relevant to the case, for she didn't live in the same building as her granddaughter. The others, one by one, completed their lists and returned the notebooks to me.

"Do you really think whoever is doing this is somebody we know? Somebody who could work in the building?" asked Patty Starrett, clutching the front of her sweater.

"The experts think so," I said. "It happens often enough that it's the kind of thing they look at first: who had access to the victims?"

She sighed and shook her head. "What a world we live in," she said.

"Insanity. Pure insanity," said Arlene Edwards.

"No shit," Carmine intoned, and on that somber note, they all left and I sat down with the police and hospital reports and tried to be as objective and clinical as possible in my perusal. About halfway through, I hoped like hell that none of those good people had read the objective and clinical truth about what had happened to their little girls; by the time I finished reading them, the nausea was sitting high up in my throat. I didn't know how people sloshed through filth like this every day. Maybe that's why some cops had such shitty attitudes: they had to be hard-asses to preserve their own sanity. Maybe, subconsciously, that's why I didn't remain a cop, so I wouldn't have to choose between wallowing in filth or becoming an asshole. Then, like a kid peeking into the living room on Christmas morning, I looked at the lists they'd written for me, and I fully understood what was meant by the term, "grim satisfaction."

"How's it coming?" I yelled to Yolanda.

"You go see Doctor Bader," she yelled back, "and do whatever else you have to do. I'll have this bastard nailed on this end by the time you have him nailed on the other end."

I walked around the screens to stand beside her and waited for her to talk to me. "What?" she said, not looking up from her computer screen.

"I need you to call Doctor Mason for me." Now she looked at me. "I need to talk to her parents."

"Why, Phil?"

"This thing that's happening to her, it's playing out in the here and now, but it didn't start down here, in the East Village, last month. It's old stuff, Yo, I'm sure of it."

Yo thought about what I'd said, and I could watch agreement cross, then cloud her features. "Her parents are old, Phil, and they're both in ill health. And . . . they don't know what's been happening to her. I'm not sure . . . I don't think her father would even understand."

Something else Itchy had been right about. "Ask her anyway, okay?" I said, and I left before I had to further justify a request to question a couple of sick old people about why they thought somebody was trying to kill their only daughter.

Chapter Nine

I was muttering curses and keeping an eye out for an unoc-
cupied taxi but ended up walking the entire way to NYU. I
really hated running late. I didn't like feeling hurried and
rushed, and I didn't like having to apologize to whoever was
waiting when I was late. I'd even buttoned my coat all the
way up and put my gloves on, further proof that it was really and truly cold, if the absence of a single, vacant taxi
weren't sufficient evidence. I was forced to echo the com-
ments and concerns I'd been hearing for the last week or so:
if it was this cold this early, what would January be like?

The young woman in Doctor Bader's outer office—a student judging by her youthful appearance and her ward-
robe—gave a nod of recognition when I told her my name,
accepted the package from me, and told me that Doctor
Bader said to come back at four o'clock. Back outside, I resumed my search for a taxi and succumbed to a narcissistic
pride in my physical condition when I out-sprinted a guy
about my own age to claim a taxi being vacated by an el-
derly woman at West 4th and Lafayette. Not only didn't I
want to make the long crosstown walk into the wind coming
off the East River, I didn't want to risk being even a second
late for my meeting with Willie's nephew. In fact, I wanted
to be a few moments early, so I could sit at the counter and
drink a cup of coffee and eat a doughnut and appear relaxed
and at ease. To relax and put him at ease.

He barely noticed me and didn't acknowledge me at all
when I entered the diner. It was warm inside, like it was the

first time I was in the place, and the patrons were quietly engrossed in their own business . . . the business of eating, of reading books and newspapers . . . of talking to their companions. There were maybe a dozen people here, all of them, like Willie's nephew, familiar with life on the edge; a few of them no doubt still challenging the sharpness of the razor.

I took a stool at the far end of the counter and took off my hat, scarf, and gloves and unbuttoned my coat. He looked at me and I nodded and raised two fingers and then made a circle with my thumb and forefinger. He brought me a cup of coffee and two plain doughnuts. I put a five on the counter and told him thanks. He picked it up and told me thanks and went back to the sink and began washing dishes. I drank my coffee, the only positive thing about which I could say was that it was hot, and ate the doughnuts, which were gooey, quite fresh, and surprisingly good.

My guy, who had eyes or antennae in the back of his head, wiped his hands on the towel at his waist and edged toward the cash register. By the time he reached it, three patrons were in line to pay their checks. That allowed seven people to wrap themselves for warmth and leave the diner. Four remained: two at the opposite end of the counter, and a couple at a booth near the kitchen door. I was wondering what my guy was going to do about them when an Ichabod Crane look-alike emerged from the kitchen and my guy grabbed a pack of cigarettes from the shelf above the sink, grabbed his knit cap and a jacket from somewhere beneath the sink, and walked out the front door. I finished my coffee and my remaining doughnut, wiped my mouth, and followed.

He was seated in the bus shelter half a block away, smoking and hunched against the cold. I joined him. "You need on an overcoat, *Hermano*," I said with a shiver.

"Tell me about it," he said, not even checking to see if I looked as stupid as I felt for making such a remark. "Who knows you're here?" he asked instead.

"You, me, and Willie," I said, not bothering to explain about Yolanda, Mike, and Eddie. I pulled my cap down over my ears, placed my scarf and gloves on the seat between us, and stuffed my hands into my coat pockets.

"I was sneaking some of my garbage into that Dumpster over there," he said, inhaling deeply on the cigarette. "I'm not supposed to do that, you know? But we got this cheap-ass carter company, don't pick up half the time, and we make a lotta garbage in that place. So, I dump over there, okay?"

I let him know that I understood.

"That's what I was doing when this guy comes bustin' outta that door and down the steps. Looks right at me and keeps on goin,' don't slow up none."

"Would you know him if you saw him again?" I asked.

"So would you," he said. "Left side of his face is scratched all to shit. He'll wear those marks for a while. That lady doctor? Must be tough as shit the way she fucked up his face," he said with admiration.

I was thinking about the scratches, wondering whether the paramedics would have taken skin samples from beneath Jill Mason's nails or if the crime scene investigator in charge would have done that. Shit. I knew next to nothing about the conduct of felony investigations; I was foot patrol. I was wondering who I could ask when I realized that my companion had spoken again. "What did you say?"

"I said I also know where the dude works, if he still works in the same place. Got my hair cut there once. Barber shop over on Essex. Too fuckin' much money for a haircut if all you want is a haircut, you know?"

"Lay it out for me, *Hermano*," I said, the bumps raised on my skin and the hair standing up on my neck not a function of the icy wind.

He gave me a look that let me know that my reaction had not been as nonchalant as I'd tried for. "I think you know. And I hope you ain't bullshitting me about keepin' me outta this."

"I don't bullshit. Willie will tell you that."

"Willie already told me that," he said, and lit another cigarette.

"This barber shop," I began.

"I gave you what you came for," he said.

I thanked him and got up, my body stiff and aching from just those few moments sitting in the cold. I offered him my hand and he took it, and what was in it, nodding his thanks without checking the denomination of the bill. I was five feet away when I heard my name called. I turned to see him pulling on the gloves, the scarf already wrapped around his neck. His eyes held mine, then he blew smoke from his mouth and nose and it billowed up around him and he was hidden from view.

I needed to talk to Eddie and Mike, I needed to see Doctor Mason, and I needed to be in Doctor Bader's office in one hour and fifteen minutes. Which meant there was no time for either of the first two needs. I walked toward Doctor Mason's office building. No external sign of the morning's trauma. I stopped and looked at the sign with her name on it. I considered again the possibility that the attacks on her were related to the rapes of the girls, and I recalled Carmine's assertion that the attacks on Jill Mason were spawned by an ancient grudge. I still wanted to believe it was possible that the two cases were connected, but something about what Carmine said still rang true; it had this morning when he said and it did now. Old stuff. An ancient grudge.

There was an empty taxi stopped at the light right before me. I sprinted to it, hopped in, and gave the address of El Caribe. I could have a full meal, the benefit of a private office to make a few phone calls, and still make my four o'clock meeting on time. I also could, as I did as soon as I walked in the door and was greeted by Arlene, order some soup for Jill Mason who, judging from the look of her face, wouldn't be chewing any time soon.

"Some coconut milk soup," Arlene said quickly when I told her what I wanted and why. "And carrot/ginger. And maybe some sweet potato soup."

"She likes sweet potatoes," I said, and wrote down the address. Then I called to let her know the soup was coming and who was bringing it—Bradley would take it, Arlene said—and to have her make certain it was Bradley before she opened the door. Arlene allowed me to eat in her office, at her desk, and allowed me to use her telephone. I talked to Mike and Eddie, to Yolanda, to Lieutenant Delaney. No sign of the squirrel, but there still was daylight left, Mike said. Yo was waiting on her computers to deliver their bundles of joy, but, in the meantime, wanted to know if I'd been getting receipts from all the taxi rides I'd taken lately. I hung up on her. And Bill Delaney said he'd be in his office until at least six o'clock; probably later, given the amount of paperwork he had to clear up.

"You look very handsome today, Phillip," Arlene said, reminding me of Jill Mason. Both called me Phillip and not Phil and I realized that to be a characteristic of certain black women of a certain age: they possessed a formality, an elegance, that was natural and inherent and which had nothing to do with money and which no amount of money could purchase. That characteristic made it possible for Arlene Edwards to seat herself in the visitors' chair adjacent to her desk in her office, to wave me back down in the desk chair, and to be at ease with that choice, feeling no loss of power or control. Indeed, feeling no need for either.

"You look rather smashing yourself, Mrs. Edwards. But then, you always do." Both statements were true. Today she wore a red wool dress that was long enough to cover the tops of the black high-heeled boots she wore. She wore her hair in dreadlocks and had to have done so for a jillion years because, even tied, they hung down her back, well below her narrow hips. She possessed a youthful slimness though I knew her to be in her late fifties. Only recently, since the murder of her granddaughter, had the lines in her face told the truth of her age.

"You know who he is, don't you Phillip?"

"I don't . . . I'm not . . ." I felt foolish. Her question, and the directness of it, had caught me off-guard. Not inclined to lie, I knew also that to tell any portion of the truth was premature at best, and potentially destructive at worst.

"I don't seek revenge, Phillip. That's not why I ask. Did you read the hospital report? Yes? Then you must know that such a thing cannot be allowed to happen again. I won't ever have the love of my first grandchild again, but if I can prevent another parent from living in hell, that I will do. Promise me, Phillip, that you will make sure he won't ever do again what he did to Anna Arlene."

I held my hands out to her. "I can't make that kind of promise, Arlene. You know I can't." I was begging her.

She refused me. "You told us that day in your office, Phillip, that you couldn't . . . wouldn't . . . find him. But you have. Now you can stop him. And you will. You must. And if there are really two of them, you must stop them both."

I all but ran out of Arlene's office. I threw some money on the counter to pay for my meal and Jill's soup, startling Bradley, and was out the door while he was saying goodbye. I was en route to Gertrude Bader's office dizzy with overwhelming dread and something close to fear, for I wasn't certain that I was truly prepared to hear her what she had to say. And I was terrified not to hear it.

I hung my overcoat on the rack in the reception area and experienced a brief moment of anxiety looking for my scarf and gloves, wondering whether I'd left them in the taxi—from which I had remembered to request a receipt—before I remembered that I'd left them on a bus stop bench beside Willie One Eye's nephew—whose name I still did not know—to atone for my embarrassment for the remark about his lack of an overcoat.

Doctor Bader gave me a quick, approving glance when I entered her office and waved me into a chair. She closed the file she'd been reading, removed her glasses, and began talking. There definitely were two rapists: an older man and a younger one. The younger one was the violent one, the one who had done the two murders. Because of the nature and level of his violence, he probably had been institutionalized in the past, though it was impossible to say whether he'd been hospitalized or jailed—that would depend largely on whether he'd been caught when he was a juvenile or an adult.

"Juvenile?" I managed.

"Oh, yes, Mr. Rodriquez. He's been at this for quite some time, and he will continue if he is not stopped." She said the words, unlike Arlene Edwards, without passion, but with no less force. "This other one, however, is a different story, and he's the one who really worries me."

The breath caught in my chest and caused a pain. I was really worried about Gregory Jenkins—I was certain he was the younger one, the violent one. The murderer. And the shrink who was the professor, who understood these people and why they did what they did, was worried about the other one?

"He's probably never been caught, and because he's older, he's been at it for much longer. But he's not violent. In fact, he's probably quite gentle and non-threatening. He's the kind the children won't tell on, unless they've got a very strongly developed sense of self and are surrounded by adults who trust them and whom they trust." She tapped the folders on the desk. "All of these little girls live with adults who pay close attention to them, who notice right away when something is even the slightest bit different."

I thought of the parents: Carmine and Theresa Aiello, Patty Starrett, Daniel and Carla Esposito. Yes. These were people who would notice a difference in their children's behavior and people whose children would mention an out-of-the-ordinary occurrence. "Why are you more worried about him?"

"Because it's quite likely that he'll never be caught." She spoke with such quiet, convincing authority.

"Why not?"

"He's a teacher, a guidance counselor, a priest or a minister, a coach, a candy store owner. He's one of the good guys."

"Then why hasn't one of the victims ID'd him?" I was getting steamed. "If he's the teacher, why didn't one of these kids say, 'Mr. Jones did something bad to me'?" I stood up and began pacing. "One of the 'good guys' my ass!"

"¿Senor Rodriquez?"

"¿Si?"

"Sientese, por favor."

"Sí," I said, and returned to my chair. I listened with growing dread as she explained that this rapist had direct and immediate access to children, but would steer clear of any children who knew him personally. He may teach at a middle school and have daily, direct contact with the elementary school students a block away, none of whom would know him by name or appearance.

"And there's another thing that sets him apart from other kinds of rapists."

I was still wrestling with the concept of there being different "kinds" of rapists. In my mind, a sick fuck was a sick fuck. Period. "What's that, Doctor?"

"The fact that he may actually derive some measure of sexual gratification from his activities."

"What?"

She tapped a folder. "This one? He is motivated purely by violence. Control and violence. Most rapists of adults are driven by violence. But it often happens that pedophiles do seek and receive sexual pleasure from children because of their inability to achieve gratification from adults."

The feeling of wanting to smash something had returned. "So they're still sick fucks, even if they're not violent, sick fucks."

Doctor Bader almost smiled. "Oh, they're very sick fucks, Mr. Rodriquez, and very dangerous ones, don't misunderstand me. They do irreparable harm to their victims. I don't know that any woman—or man, for that matter—ever heals the part of the self that is destroyed by rape. I'm merely trying to explain to you why it is possible that this rapist, and others like him, operate with impunity for years, for decades. Do you understand? This man is smart and crafty and evil. He does not want to be caught and, unlike our other rapist here, he most likely will not make the kind of error that will result in his apprehension."

I stood up, then sat quickly down with a look at Doctor Bader, who waved her hand at me, giving me permission to pace. "If anything could or would trip him up, what would it be?" I asked.

She was nodding her head. "Good. Good. He naturally should not be in the presence of children this young—"

"Hold it! I thought you said he was a teacher or a coach or—"

"He is! That's his job, but not his life. Listen to me: this man is probably fifty, maybe older. He will not have children at all, and certainly not children as young as seven or eight years old. Therefore, for him to be in the presence of a child that young would be a warning signal."

"Would he look like a grandfather?"

"He could," she replied. "But anybody who knew him would know that he was unmarried. That he didn't have children, so he couldn't have grandchildren. He also would be uneasy doing child-like things. He'll look awkward sitting in the sand or making mud pies or riding the merry-go-round. He can't skate or play ball with any grace. This man is not a *lover* of children, Mr. Rodriquez; he is a violator of children."

"A violator of children." Yolanda repeated the words several times. I'd wondered how she would respond to what I had to tell her of my meeting with Doctor Bader, but she was relaxed and calm as she listened, questioned, concluded, with me, that Gregory Jenkins looked good for the rape and murder of the Calle and Cummerbatch children.

He had access to both buildings and he had been arrested as a juvenile and as an adult for sexually-based crimes and had served time in an Ohio jail. He returned to New York, Yolanda thought, a couple of years ago, though it was not possible to be certain. "Computers can only tell what they know," she said often enough for me to believe her. And if Jenkins was smart enough to use his father's Social Security number, he was smart enough to have and use other IDs, so there could be quite a lot the computer didn't know about him.

I read through the thick file that Yo had prepared as she talked me through it. We'd agreed that I'd pay a visit to Lieutenant Delaney, share with him what we knew of Gregory Jenkins, and shift as much weight off ourselves and onto the police as we could, all the while making every effort not only to cooperate, but to demonstrate that we certainly had not interfered in police business. Yo had agreed to the plan, but she didn't like it.

"You're really going to give them everything we've got on this Jenkins creep?"

"Yep. It's enough for them to rattle his cage. Maybe even enough to pull him in. Besides, I'm hoping like hell that they've got some information of their own." They damn well ought to, I thought, as I got ready to leave. And, as I was feeling myself getting steamed again, I took some deep breaths. It would be really dumb to arrive at the precinct for a meeting with a lieutenant who could pull my ticket with an attitude. I reached into my pocket, retrieved the taxi receipts, and gave them to Yolanda.

"Where's the one for lunch?" she asked.

"Lunch?"

"Lunch, Phil. Yours and Doctor Mason's," she said wearily.

I walked out, the equivalent of hanging up the phone on her. The sound of her laughter followed me out into the cold, dark, night air. I walked to the precinct. It was a long walk but I needed both the exercise and the time to order my thoughts, which would take some doing, for these thoughts were the unruly kind. I thought how good it would feel to smash Gregory Jenkins; to smash whoever had beat up Jill Mason; to find and smash the other rapist; to smash some cop threatening my license because I was doing my job. Thoughts of smashing were not good thoughts. I forced myself to think, instead, of where Mike and Eddie might be at this moment. Since I hadn't heard from them in almost four hours, I imagined that they'd found the squirrel and couldn't risk losing him by stopping to call me. I imagined that they'd stay with him until he went to ground for the night and that I'd hear from them then.

I would visit Jill Mason after my Lieutenant Delaney visit. Maybe she remembered something about her attacker. Or about who could be wanting to cause her such pain and harm. Maybe she'd open up enough to tell me whether there was any possibility that the attacks on her were related to the other rapes. Maybe one of those little girls really did know who this second perp was. Maybe, maybe, maybe. Maybe when hell froze the devil would ice-skate. Now where did I hear that the first time?

"You're looking prosperous, Phil," Lieutenant Delaney said when I walked into his office, my overcoat over my arm. Certain government buildings, like precinct houses, always were too hot, no matter the season. I went from freezing to sweating in the minute it took me to get from the front door up to the second floor where Delaney had his office. "Nice threads. You that kinda PI now, you dress from Barney's New York?"

I shook his hand and laughed, not even thinking about explaining to him how women like Gertrude Bader, Arlene Edwards, and Jill Mason made you feel like wanting to look your best. "I knew I had to come see you, L.T., and I remember how you never did much like the sloppy look." Which was true, and I noticed that my remembering that just put me a few points ahead. Bill Delaney was the desk sergeant when I walked a beat uptown those years ago and, for whatever his reason, he had decided to like me, to look out for me, to teach me from the unwritten cop rule book. I had taken everything he had to give because, even though I knew I had no intention of doing twenty years on the job, I wanted to do the best possible job for as long as I was there.

"So you and Temple pissed on each other some today." It wasn't a question, so I didn't try to answer it. "He can be a little intimidating, I suppose, but he did bring you a legitimate concern, Phil. You've got your toes in my pond."

I shook my head. "I'll tell you exactly what I told him, Lieutenant—"

He cut me off. "I heard it once, I don't need to hear it again. I know about your clients and I know about citizens' rights. I also know that when you orchestrate that kind of mass action, you're dancing right on that thin line, and I would be within *my* legal rights to pull your ticket."

"And why would you want to do that, Lieutenant? What would be your motivation?" I'd spoken softly and practically without inflection, but Delaney flinched.

"Because you're endangering an ongoing investigation, that's why." His tone held plenty of inflection.

"And what part of that investigation, Lieutenant, would have been endangered if you'd shared just the slightest bit of information with the parents of those little girls? Don't you understand that those people think you don't give a shit about them or their children? They don't know that you're still investigating diddly. I'm not sure myself that you are."

His face flushed red and his lips turned into a thin, white, mean line. "That's fuckin' uncalled for."

I shrugged. "Prove it. Tell me you've already picked up Gregory Jenkins and got him in the pen downstairs."

"What do you know about Gregory Jenkins?"

"I know he probably killed the Cummerbatch and Calle kids, and it didn't take me a year to figure it out. Christ, Delaney, the guy works in the buildings where those girls lived. Why are you so pissed off at me?"

He nodded at me, his jaw muscles working. "You just screwed yourself, Rodriquez. You just gave me the ammo I needed to nail your ass. Jenkins is purely police business . . ."

I held up my hand to stop him and reached into my jacket pocket and extracted the Golson/Stein contract. "Jenkins is very much my business. I do security for the building he works in. The owners asked me to run background checks on all their employees. Jenkins' address and SSN and age and some other stuff didn't match. I wanted to know why, so I could inform my clients. That's why I'm prosperous, L.T. I do good, thorough work and my clients appreciate it." When I saw that he wasn't going to take the contract from me, I put it back in my pocket.

"Don't push me, Phil. I mean that."

"How long have you known about Jenkins?" I asked, pushing.

He glared at me and for a brief second I saw something in his eyes. Then he broke eye contact when he saw that I saw.

That thing started to happen in my stomach and chest again. "Tell me you didn't know about him before he did the little Calle girl, Delaney. Tell me you didn't sit on this creep and let him kill again when you knew he'd killed the Cummerbatch girl."

"Fuck you, you self-righteous little prick!" He'd pushed his chair back and jumped to his feet. "You couldn't cut it on the job but you think you can slide in here and tell me how to do my job? We didn't *let* Jenkins do a goddamn thing! We didn't *know* for certain that he'd done the Cummerbatch kid—"

"But you thought it, goddammit! You knew about his past! Oh, God. Oh, shit." I collapsed into my chair and held my head in my hands. How would I ever tell Bert and Angie Calle that the cops could have arrested the creep who killed their daughter before he killed her but chose not to? How could I ever look Delaney in the eye again without wanting to kill him?

An ugly sound came from Delaney and I looked up at him. Looked him in the eye and wanted to kill him but knew it would mean going to prison for nothing, because the man would go to his grave not understanding why he'd been killed.

"No wonder you couldn't make it on the job, Rodriquez. You're soft. Look at you, going to pieces. We deal with this shit every day. How far d'you think we'd get if we folded like that? We don't have the time for that bleeding-heart crap."

"You ever talked to the parents of any of these kids, Delaney?" I thought about Pam Starrett. And about Yolanda. "You ever looked into the eyes of a little girl who's been raped? Into the eyes of a grown woman who was raped as a little girl? They have the same look in their eyes and it doesn't ever go away. They don't ever get over it, Delaney. They don't ever heal."

"That's stuff for the head-shrinkers, Rodriquez. I've got a caseload to worry about and I can't close cases if I'm overwhelmed by the touchy-feelies."

"But what about the people part of the job, L.T.? You cared about the people once. I remember that about you." And I did. He was never a touchy-feely kind of guy, but he once had cared about the people he served. Had once believed, in fact, in service.

He shrugged. "What about 'em?"

What about 'em? *You know Carmine Aiello, don't you?* I wanted to scream at him. *Fat, ugly, mean, wop bastard? Only he's not just a fat, ugly, mean, wop bastard, he's a little girl's daddy, and the husband of that little girl's mother. And he takes that little girl to a shrink almost every night and sits there waiting, hoping, maybe even praying, that the shrink can put that little girl's soul back together.* That's what about 'em I wanted to say. But I couldn't. Couldn't violate Carmine's trust that way, or his daughter's privacy, and now knew better than to waste time and breath talking to a man who no longer had a soul. So I got up and grabbed my coat and walked toward the door.

"I don't want to hear this on the street, Rodriquez. I don't want to hear a single word about Gregory Jenkins from any of those families you represent, or I will have your license. Is that clear?"

I didn't trust myself to speak, so I didn't try. I just nodded at him and left. My smashing desire had returned and I ran down the steps and out of the precinct and down the block and far enough away to outrun the inclination to return and indulge the desire to smash Lieutenant Bill Delaney.

I was shivering, so I finally put my coat on and buttoned it. I had an extra scarf and pair of gloves at home, but that didn't help me now. I raised my coat collar and stuck my hands deep in my pockets and walked toward 3rd Avenue where I could get a taxi. I called Jill Mason on the cell phone to tell her I was coming and to remind her not to press the buzzer unless and until she was certain it was me ringing. Then I called Yo to tell her about my Delaney meeting and where I was going next and to ask if she'd heard from Mike and Eddie.

"You're going to need some sensitivity training to aid your interaction with the cops," she said dryly, ignoring the pig-like snort that was my reaction. "Eddie and Mike said they treed the squirrel and that he's in for the night, so they're going in for the night. Eddie said to meet him at Jose Y Miguel's for breakfast at seven thirty. And Phil. Sandra's grandmother wants to see you in the morning, too. At eleven. She wants to tell you something about Itchy Johnson. Only she said 'Malachi' Johnson. She knows him, Phil, from the old days in Harlem."

I tried not to behave like a bumpkin when I got inside Jill Mason's loft. I'd seen this kind of elegance only on screen or in those magazines that try to teach people like me how to decorate their homes. The openness in the loft was breathtaking, and that sensation was enhanced by the view: two walls of glass placed the entire southern tip of Manhattan, including the Statue of Liberty and the Hudson River and New Jersey, right in the living room. And the view would be equally magnificent on a cloudy or foggy night; then it would feel cloaked in gauze and, despite the size of the room, almost cozy. The only thing I could say about the furniture was that I liked it and that it was terribly expensive. Ditto for the artwork—though some of it I did recognize—and the rugs on the floor, which made their own artistic and creative expressions.

"Good evening, Phillip. If you'll leave your shoes at the door, I'll take your coat and hang it up."

I gave her the overcoat and untied and removed my shoes and followed her into the room. When I reached mid-point, I just stopped and stared. From this moment on, Yolanda would have no difficulty convincing me of the need for financial growth. To come home at night to this must soothe a whole herd of savage beasts. I must have said the thought out loud, because she laughed.

"That's a most appropriate way to phrase it, and you're absolutely correct. I am completely at peace here." And she looked it. Her face, of course, was a mess, but her eyes were calm and free of fear, and she moved loosely and easily, as loosely and easily as anyone who'd been in hand-to-hand combat could. She wore sweat clothes. Regular, ordinary sweat clothes, like every other New Yorker: plain black bottoms, a white Columbia University top, and thick white socks. Her hair was combed straight back, accentuating both the beauty of, and the damage to, her face. She waved me toward a couple of love seats and armchairs in front of the fireplace, and I sank gratefully into a chair that could have been a womb. I hadn't noticed the fire from the front door; nor had I noticed the music, which I now heard—Miles Davis? I looked around. Not a speaker in sight. I stood up and conducted a mini-search and couldn't find a likely source for the music.

She returned with an open bottle of wine and two glasses on a tray and a jar of nuts tucked under her arm. I stopped myself from asking for water. I could safely have a couple of glasses of wine, my dismay at my drunken debacle still a clear and fresh and horrible memory. She gave me the nuts and told me to help myself—she couldn't chew them—then

185

sat down and poured the wine. I took one sip and started talking. I told her everything that Gertrude Bader had told me. I hadn't intended that; hadn't known that's what I would say to her; didn't know why I did. She listened carefully and completely. Her eyes never left my face, she never raised her glass to her lips, she never moved an inch.

"I know Gertrude," she said when I was finished. "She taught me in medical school, before she moved downtown to NYU. She's brilliant. And a wonderful teacher." Then she thanked me for the soup. She had never, she said, tasted anything as wonderful. And she had me write down the address of El Caribe. When she could chew again, she said, her first dinner would be there. Since she clearly had no intention of responding or reacting to my description of the rapist that Doctor Bader had profiled, I asked about her health. She'd slept most of the day, she said, having taken a couple of the pain pills. Then her mother had come over and bathed her wounds and held ice packs on her face until the swelling was reduced. In fact, her mother had been here when Bradley Edwards delivered the soups and had shared them. We talked on in that vein for a while and sipped wine and I munched nuts—I'd eaten almost all of them—like we were friends and my presence was a social call. And since we were being sociable, I couldn't go another second without asking.

"Tell me about the sound system."

"What do you want to know?"

"You know what I want to know." What I was *dying* to know. "Where the hell are the speakers?"

"Everywhere," she said. "Literally." And then she explained her love of music, her need for it. "I like to experience it, as if I'm always in a concert hall." So the speakers, she said, were in the ceiling and in the walls and beneath the flooring. "That part was tricky. Drove the architect and his engineer crazy."

"Why speakers beneath you?"

She got up, crossed to the rear of the room, and slid open a cabinet recessed into the wall. There was a moment of silence. Then the music changed. A deep, dark, rich sound rose up and surrounded me. It was everywhere, that sound. I wanted to stand up but felt pinned to my chair. It wasn't loud or vibrating sound. It was just . . . everywhere. I closed my eyes and went with the music. Then it ceased and Miles was back: definitely Miles because I recognized "Sketches of Spain." When I opened my eyes, Doctor Mason was back in the seat opposite me. "That's why. It's not appropriate for all music, but for Wagner . . . ?"

I wasn't sure who Wagner was and was certain I'd probably never again have a reason to listen to him, but if I did, I'd want to listen to it exactly like I'd just heard it. "When my ship finally finds its way to the dock, I'm getting the name of your architect," I said, and then changed the subject. Completely. "We'll have to talk about it sometime," I said, and, I hoped, gently.

She nodded. "I know, Phillip." Then she got up and walked to the far end of the room and disappeared, returning almost immediately with an envelope, which she gave to me. "A signed contract and a retainer. I spoke with Yolanda earlier and asked her how to become a client."

"But you're already a client," I began.

She cut me off. "Mr. Aiello is your client. He was paying you to protect me. Now I'm paying you to protect me. I need to do this, officially and on my own. I may even add a little bombast." She tried a smile but it hurt too much. Then, "Yolanda told me you want to talk to my parents. I can't let you do that. Please believe me when I tell you that

187

they can be of no help to you, Phillip."

I had no choice but to accept that, whether I believed it or not, since the way she'd spoken left no room for discussion or argument. I put the envelope with her signed contract in my pocket, along with the Golson/Stein contract which I'd used against Bill Delaney. I stood up. "I ate all the nuts."

"I ate all the soup. I'd intended to save some for your visit, but I ate it all."

"We're even then," I said, heading for the door. I bent down and put my shoes back on. When I straightened up, she was holding my coat open for me to slip my arms into.

"Day after tomorrow, Doctor Mason," I said. "Three o'clock. Your office or mine, doesn't matter." I'd chosen that day and time because I knew that she would be free at three o'clock on Saturday afternoon.

She nodded and watched me button my coat. "Don't you have a scarf?" she asked with a frown. "And gloves? It's twenty degrees out there, Phillip." She sounded much more like a mother than a shrink and I ached for the children she would never have the chance to nurture into adulthood. Two little girls . . .

I thanked her for the wine and the nuts and told her good night. "Saturday afternoon," I said just before the door closed.

The night was just as clear at ground level as it was in the penthouse, though the view was less dramatic. I turned left and began walking, slowly, because I didn't know where I was going. I should go home and to bed. I was exhausted, but I wasn't sleepy. I knew I'd just toss and turn if I went to bed. I didn't want to go back to the office; that would just depress me. I consoled myself by remembering that Gregory Jenkins was about to be history. One down, one to go. When I was able to sit with Jill Mason for a while, get some decent background, maybe we could close that case, too. Day after tomorrow was Saturday. Saturday . . .

I walked faster. I knew where I was going.

Chapter Ten

"Are you sure his face wasn't scratched?"

"Am I sure his face wasn't scratched." Eddie repeated the words like he was a finalist in the Stupidest Thing I Ever Heard contest. It made me wish Mike were there, so they could exchange the look that suggested that maybe I didn't always play with a full deck; this way, I had to hear what that thought sounded like. But Mike was occupied watching the squirrel's place, a basement room on Avenue D beneath the elevated tracks of the JMZ trains. Talk about shitty neighborhoods. Appropriate, though, for a squirrel.

"If his face wasn't scratched, Eddie, that means there are two of them out for Jill Mason."

"No, Bro, what that means is you're believing Willie's nephew."

I nodded. "Yeah, I believe him."

"You don't even know his name, how do you believe him?"

"Why are you fixated on my knowing this guy's name?"

Eddie looked hard at me. "Fixated." He leaned out of the narrow booth and perused me from toe to head. "You look real good lately, Phil. And you always did talk good, like a college education should."

"I've got a meeting with an eighty-something-year-old woman this morning, Eddie, you know that. And I had meetings with women all day yesterday. You know that, too. And you know how older women don't like . . . why the hell am I explaining myself to you? Why are you busting my chops about what I'm wearing? And why are you fixated on whether or not I know some ex-hype's name?" I'd put some emphasis on "fixated," but it was lost. Eddie was fixated elsewhere.

"You didn't tell me the snitch was an ex-hype," he said accusingly.

"It matters?"

He nodded. "Yeah it matters. Ex-hypes don't tell nobody their names. They had a 'don't ask, don't tell' policy before Clinton knew what his dick was for."

I couldn't help laughing. And remembering that Eddie Ortiz had earned his gold shield working undercover narc in the Bronx long before such activity was glamorized by television detectives. "Eddie, after you eat, go get a haircut at Itchy's, will you? And while you're there, find out what else you can get at Itchy's."

"You can get any damn thing you want at Itchy's," Jose Carbajal said, delivering our breakfasts. "Only it's not exactly *at* Itchy's. You order it, pay for it, then go pick it up. Kinda like the old Sears and Roebuck catalog stores, you know what I mean?"

I had no idea and said so. Jose was a native of Puerto Rico, the city of Mayaguez, the home, also, of my mother's mother. He had lived in New York City for almost fifty years, but he still called Puerto Rico home. He also insisted that he was as American as the next guy, and often proudly displayed his knowledge of things American, like Sears and Roebuck catalog stores.

"You young people got no pride in the past. How you expect to understand your present if you don't understand the past?" He posed the question, expecting an answer.

"You make a good point, Jose," I said, and he did. I just didn't have the time to explore it with him. "But I'm really in a hurry and I'd appreciate anything you can tell me about Itchy. I've got a meeting about him uptown in a little while."

The restaurant was tiny, the five tables on one aisle so close to the five booths on the opposite—and narrow—aisle, that patrons never needed to strain to overhear other people's conversations. Eddie and I had been leaning across the table, almost whispering. Now Jose followed suit. "Anything can be had through Itchy's—TV, CD, computer, cell phone, pager, jewelry, smack, crack, reefer. You tell one of those barbers what you want, he tells you how much, you pay him, and then he tells you when and where to pick up. Usually later that same day, unless it's a special order."

I was speechless. That old bastard had been running a scam right in my face and I'd never seen it. Not even a hint of it. I felt drop-kicked and must have looked it because Jose said, "That's what I mean about understanding the past."

"What?"

"If you knew your history, Phil, you'd know about Itchy."

"I know all about Itchy and his history. It's just the present I seem not to know about," I said. Eddie and Jose did the kind of shifty-eyed thing people do when they're trying not to exchange a knowing look. I looked from Jose to Eddie, who shrugged, and back to Jose. "What would I know, Jose, if I knew my history?"

"You need to talk to somebody from Black Harlem, Phil, somebody who knows about the old days."

"Why can't I talk to you, since you obviously know something?"

"What I know is second-hand stuff," Jose said, straightening up as the pick-up bell sounded. "Find somebody who knows the history firsthand."

Louise Gillespie had lived in the same fourteen-room apartment on the top floor of a building perched on the top of Sugar Hill for fifty-six years. She'd moved in as a newlywed at the beginning of the end of Harlem's glory days, when all the whites finally had run away, and she had refused to abandon her home when the neighborhood hit rock bottom. Her faith had paid off. The late twentieth-century rejuvenation of Harlem sprouted tendrils of hope that, in the early twenty-first century, had blossomed into a full-blown revival. Sugar Hill, which never had deteriorated to the same extent as some of the Valley neighborhoods, once again was a desirable address, and Louise Gillespie could easily pocket a seven-figure fortune should she decide to sell her condo, which she steadfastly refused even to contemplate.

She was a tall, stately woman—I could see Sandra in her face and in her carriage. Her hair was pure white and hugged her head like a cap. She was brown as a pecan shell and wore a russet-colored pantsuit and the kind of shoes referred to in literature as "sensible." She welcomed me warmly and led me down a Persian-carpeted entrance foyer that was as large as some living rooms downtown in my neighborhood, past an elegant living room where I glimpsed a shiny grand piano which made me remember that Sandra's grandfather had been a musician, and into a comfortable sitting room. Floor-to-ceiling bookshelves occupied two walls. The television and music system were relatively new, but the sofa and reading chair and tasseled floor lamp were throwbacks to another era. She told me to make myself at home and offered me food and drink. I told her I'd just left breakfast. She asked me where I'd eaten and I told her and she launched into a vivid remembrance of the Puerto Rican restaurants and night clubs of Spanish Harlem of her youth, places I'd heard my grandparents speak of. Places long gone, like most of Harlem itself—Black Harlem and Spanish Harlem.

"I appreciate your seeing me, Mrs. Gillespie."

"I'm glad to be able to talk to you, Phillip, to tell somebody I trust what I've never told anyone else, not even Sandra."

Another "woman of a certain age" calling me Phillip. How would I ever be just plain "Phil" again? "You know Itchy?"

"Malachi. Yes, I know him. Have known him for more than sixty years. I didn't know the other night that what was troubling Yolanda had anything to do with him."

"Well, it doesn't, not directly."

"Sandra explained it all to me, and I understand the situation. What I want to tell you about is what he did to that Mason girl. I may be speaking out of turn, and if I am, well, then, I'm sorry. But I don't think I am."

I sat still and quiet and waited. I'd had enough experience with Louise Gillespie's generation—including with Itchy Johnson—to know that they did not like being pushed and hurried. Indeed, would not be pushed and hurried.

"He . . . he raped her when she was just a little thing. No more than seven or eight. And then her granddaddy cut off his . . . cut . . . castrated him." She spoke quickly, forcing the words out of her mouth, wanting to get rid of them quickly. Then she wiped her mouth on a white lace handkerchief which materialized from the sleeve of her jacket.

"Mrs. Gillespie, I don't under . . . who raped . . . Itchy . . . Malachi . . . you're saying that he, ah, assaulted Jill

194

Mason when she was a child?" I couldn't say the word "rape." I knew that to call what Itchy Johnson had done an assault was to dignify it, while at the same time minimizing the truth of it, but I just couldn't wrap my mind around it.

The old woman was nodding her head rapidly up and down and still wiping her mouth with the handkerchief and looking like she was sorry she'd told me.

". . . and that Jill Mason's grandfather . . . ?"

The head with its cap of white hair still moved up and down; then it shifted direction. Back and forth now. "Back then, you couldn't go to the police with that kind of thing. And Colored couldn't—wouldn't—go to the police for *anything*. So, a situation such as that had to be settled personally. You know? For example, if a boy did something to a girl, a teenager, if that girl had brothers, then her brothers took care of that boy. You understand my meaning? Jill was a baby. A grown man had hurt her. So it was a grown man who had to make it right, you see?" And she wiped her mouth again.

I told her everything Itchy had told me about the Graves and Mason families and she nodded. "All that's correct. Only Malachi didn't move downtown 'til way later. He left Harlem for a while, after Jill's granddaddy . . . afterwards. He went back down South somewhere, Loo'siana or South Car'lina. Used to have conjure folks and root doctors in Loo'siana and South Car'lina. 'Cause just like we couldn't go to the police back then? No way in the world he could go to the doctor or the hospital with that kind of problem, you understand my meaning?"

I told her I did, and was about to ask a question when she answered it. "He came back in the nineteen seventies sometime, maybe seventy-one or seventy-two. A few years after the riots. Came back up here to Harlem, but enough people still remembered him and what he'd done to that baby, so he moved on downtown. He didn't move back up here until three or four years ago."

"Itchy . . . Malachi . . . he lives up here? In Harlem?"

Louise Gillespie nodded her head and pursed her lips in what I knew to be a disapproving gesture. "On 139th Street. He finally made it to Strivers Row. Sixty years too late, but he finally made it."

I was calculating, matching her words with the dates she was attaching to events, and trying to match it all to what I'd thought I knew; trying to match what she was telling me with what Itchy had been telling me for years. "So he didn't own that barber shop he has now, the one on Essex Avenue, he didn't have that in nineteen fifty-five?"

She made a rude noise with her mouth and shook her head sharply. "Certainly not! Is that what he's telling people? No wonder he slinks back up here in the dead of night. I'm telling you he didn't move downtown until the nineteen seventies. But more importantly and in the second place, there weren't enough Negroes in that part of down-town to support their own barber shop."

"Not enough Negroes . . ." The words stopped on my tongue as the thought froze up in my brain. I understood her words but not what they meant. I must have looked as dumb as I felt because she bailed me out, gently and hu-morously, but not without some small sigh of exasperation.

"You young people really should know more about your history. But maybe that's our fault for not teaching you better. Anyway." She took in some breath and let it out in a string of words that told me more than I'd ever before known about the part of New York City in which I'd grown up. Black people who lived on the Lower East Side of New York by and large lived in the housing projects along the

East River: the Jacob Riis, the Alfred E. Smith, or the Lillian Wald projects. "And not projects like we see today. These were beautiful places, where families lived, where parents raised their children and taught them things and sent them to school to learn more. Two parents in the home, and both of them working. Green grass and trees outside, and a view of the river from inside. A black man owning a barber shop back then, it would have been along FDR Drive somewhere, not over where you're talking about."

I forced my brain to slow down. There were too many thoughts to process, too much information to make sense of. I thought about what Jose had said. "Back when he lived here before, Mrs. Gillespie, up here in Harlem, what did Itch . . . Malachi do for work, and where did he live?"

"He worked in his uncle's barber shop on 148th Street and St. Nicholas Avenue when he worked, which wasn't often," she said.

"Is that because of his, ah, racketeering activities?" I asked in what I hoped was an inoffensive tone. Wasted effort. The woman was looking at me the way Eddie and Mike and Yolanda did when I said something they thought was really dumb. She didn't know what the hell I was talking about. "He was involved in numbers and book-making," I said by way of explanation. "He was part of one of the big Harlem numbers operations."

Louise Gillespie gave a most unladylike snort. "Is that what he told you?" Then she laughed out loud. "Malachi Johnson was no big-time gangster. He was a petty thief, a robber. He broke into people's homes and businesses, he stole cars or bicycles or rubber bands—if it wasn't nailed down and he thought somebody would buy it, he'd steal it."

"He didn't work for Bumpy Johnson?"

"Who?" Mrs. Gillespie wrinkled her brow again in that concentrated effort to recall the past. "I don't remember anybody by that . . . Oh! I know who you mean! Stephanie St. Clair's man!" And she gave another great whoop of laughter. "Is he telling people he worked for Madame St. Clair?" Then all traces of humor left her face. "Malachi is a liar. He always was and it seems that he always will be." She shook her head some more, her eyes looking back into a remembered past that so totally excluded me I wished, just for a moment, that I was some other place, and I used that moment to remember what Yolanda had said about Itchy: Nobody tells just one lie.

Then I brought myself back, confused and bewildered. "I don't know about anybody named St. Clair, but yes, Malachi did say he worked for Bumpy Johnson. In fact, he said he was his cousin." I remembered something. That St. Clair name was ringing a bell. "The Queen of Harlem," I said. "Stephanie St. Clair was the Queen of Harlem."

My hostess nodded and a wistful look came into her eyes. "Harlem was an exciting, fascinating place back then. Yes, it was occasionally dangerous, and the extreme poverty that plagued so many Negroes was nothing short of shameful and almost too painful to bear, but what made it so special was the triumph of so many spirits over so much degradation. Harlem, for whatever reason, inspired people."

I was nodding my agreement. "I saw that movie, the one about Bumpy Johnson and the Queen of Harlem . . ."

Mrs. Gillespie changed so fast I almost got up and moved out of the way. In that instant I saw where Sandra got her touchy streak from. "I know what movie you mean and it still makes me mad just to think about it."

"Why?" I asked. "I thought it was a really good movie."

"You ever ask yourself why movies about white gangsters are called things like *Godfather* and *Goodfellas*, but a movie about black gangsters is called *Hoodlum*?"

The thought took the wind out of me.

"Lawrence Fishburne and Cicely Tyson and all those other people, they were every bit as good as those white actors, weren't they? And isn't Harlem's history just as important as the history of Little Italy? So why did their movie have to be called *Hoodlum*? I know a lot of people who wouldn't go see it because of that title. I only went because my grandchildren made me."

I sat in stunned and chastened silence, feeling Louise Gillespie's pain and anger, until the reality of Itchy Johnson's lies took over. I needed to steer the conversation back there and I wasn't certain how to do that. I didn't have to worry about it.

"I'm sorry I went off on that tangent, Phillip. You didn't come here to listen to me be mad at Hollywood. What else can I tell you?"

I could have kissed her. In fact, between Louise and Arlene and Gertrude and Jill, I was beginning to wish I'd been born a couple of generations earlier. These were some women! "How did he get to her? Malachi. How did he know Jill? Was he friends with her grandparents? And how did her parents find out what happened to her?"

"Elijah and Sarah knew Malachi but they weren't friends; Malachi wasn't their kind. Elijah and Sarah were the hardworking, church-going kind. Always two or three jobs, trying to better themselves and make a better way for their children. They wanted Leola to go to City College but she just had to marry that Robert Mason."

Something about the memory disturbed her because she bowed her head and took several deep breaths, and for the first time, she looked like an old woman. I got up and hurried into the kitchen and returned just as quickly with a glass of water, which she took with a trembling hand and drank down.

I was still standing over her, worried. "You don't have to talk about this anymore, Mrs. Gillespie. You've already helped me . . ."

"Just a bit more," she said in a voice decidedly less strong, waving me back to my chair. "It's hard for parents to accept that children have to live their own lives. Anyway. After Jill was born, Elijah and Sarah finally convinced Leola to take some classes at City College, once she got a taste of what real life would be like with a baby and a Colored woman's job. Leola finally saw the light. Elijah had a vegetable wagon by then, and he was making good money. So Sarah quit one of her jobs and took care of little Jill in the afternoons while Leola went uptown to school. Malachi caught her—Jill—coming home from school. She didn't know him but he knew who she was. Everybody did. Wasn't but two blocks and she walked them by herself. Sarah met her at the corner every day and the two of them shared a scoop of ice cream. This day it was raining and Jill was late. Just a few minutes but it was too long for Sarah, so she went looking for her. Hadn't got half a block before she heard her crying, up above. She looks up at an open window above a shoeshine parlor. She runs in the door and up the back stairs before anybody can stop her. Found that dog with her baby girl. And you know the worst thing? All those people in that place saw him go upstairs with that child and nobody said a word. Every one of them knew Malachi Johnson and knew he didn't have any children."

Gertrude Bader's theory come to light. Which means that wasn't the first time for Itchy, though it was the last.

And other things she said ringing bells: Elijah Graves' vegetable wagon and the shoeshine parlor. All of the pieces coming together and colliding in my head, then spinning out of control, each element going its own way.

"Terrible! Just terrible! After everybody heard about what happened, and after Elijah took his justice, there were all these whispers about other little girls. People knew! And not one of them sounded a warning to save a child."

"Mrs. Gillespie, you know that Jill Mason has been attacked?"

She nodded. "Sandra and Yolanda told me. After all she's been through. They say we're not given more than we can bear, but that poor child. Makes you wonder, doesn't it, if all that isn't too much to bear?"

I didn't dare take a stab at the philosophical nature of this thing. I was happy to stick to the mundane. "Do you think Itc . . . Malachi would do something like that?"

She thought for a moment, then shook her head. "He's always been a coward. Mean, but a coward. He always got somebody else to do his dirty work. He always had lots of money and lots of things: cars, jewelry, fancy clothes, whiskey, drugs. And he always had a group of petty hoodlums around, usually younger than him, who would do his bidding in exchange for money or use of a car or a drink. Or drugs."

I pictured the four or five young barbers who cut hair for Itchy while he sat at his table in the back. I thought of what I'd learned from Jose just a few hours ago. I thought of what Willie One Eye's nephew had said. I thought of what Itchy himself had said about Jill Mason and about *how* he'd said it. I wondered if Eddie had gotten that haircut.

"I'm sorry, Mrs. Gillespie, I was thinking about something you said earlier and missed that last part."

201

"I said people always thought that Malachi had Elijah killed. Elijah grew up on a farm and knew more about horses than people. Liked 'em better'n people, too. Nobody ever believed that Elijah Graves got stomped to death by a horse by accident."

"You're saying Malachi killed Jill's grandfather?"

"I'm telling you what people said at the time, and what I knew to be true."

I thought about that for a moment, then remembered something else. "He said, Malachi said, that Doctor Mason didn't want her parents to know what was happening to her. How would he know that?"

"That damn Mildred Miller!" She picked up her glass only to find it empty. I took it, hurried to the kitchen, got her more water from the crock on the sink, and hurried back with it. Like before, she drank it down and wiped her mouth with her hankie.

"Who's Mildred Miller?"

"A fool!" Louise spat out. "An eighty-year-old fool! And she's been one all of her life! Been sweet on Malachi Johnson since before her husband died. She's a friend of Jill's relatives and I'm sure somebody told somebody else and Mildred heard it and told Malachi." Louise shook her head. "No fool like an old fool."

"Would Jill Mason recognize him? Malachi? Know who he was?"

"No," she said emphatically. "Jillie didn't remember a thing about what happened to her. Her Grandma always said that was the only good thing to come out of all that. Little Jill was what the doctors called traumatized." Sadness settled over her like a cloud. "But I'm not so sure about that. I wonder if that's not why she chose to do the kind of work she does: because she *does* remember."

I wondered myself, up on the surface, but deep down inside, I hoped that she didn't remember. I just saw what the remembering still did to Yolanda. I wished every little girl or grown woman who ever had to suffer like that could forget it. I was aware that Mrs. Gillespie was watching me. "Will you tell me a little more about what Harlem was like then? I know this is called Sugar Hill because I've heard Sandra say so, but what did you call where you said Itchy lives now?"

"Strivers Row," she said with a sad smile. "Back then, it was so important for Negroes to feel a sense of accomplishment, and to show it."

"But didn't everybody feel that?" I asked. "Didn't everybody want to show off what they'd accomplished?"

"Not everybody had as much to prove as we did," Louise Gillespie said. "We were the only ones not a hundred years out of slavery. We were the only ones who couldn't get jobs or go to school or live in a decent place because of how we looked, no matter how much money or education we had. So to live up here on Sugar Hill, on Strivers Row, where rich white people had once lived—well, that was a mighty big deal back then." Especially, she said, since people like W. E. B. DuBois and Duke Ellington, Madame C. J. Walker, Joe Louis, and Stephanie St. Clair, all lived uptown, north of 125th Street. "But living well wasn't always the sweet revenge it's reputed to be," the old woman said. "Madame Walker and Madame St. Clair were scorned because they weren't 'quality.' Rich as the Queen of England, both of them, but they weren't educated and they didn't come from so-called good families."

I didn't say what I was thinking, and once again, I didn't need to. Louise Gillespie said it for me. "We tried so hard to emulate whites, to *be* white . . . no, that's not fair. We

203

were just trying to be good enough to be as American as everybody else, to not be hated simply because we were black. But we tried so hard that we lost too much of who *we* were. I think that's why, ultimately, Harlem died." She stood up and motioned for me to follow her down the long hallway and into the living room. She stood before the wall of floor-to-ceiling windows and looked out at the magnificent expanse of New York City, including a bird's-eye view of the Harlem River. "This is why I wouldn't move from here when the neighborhood got so bad. This view, this proximity to heaven, is why I—my husband and I—moved in here, not because we were trying to be like anybody else."

She turned away from the view of heaven to look at me. "Anyway, we weren't rich. We moved here because we could afford it. By the time we got here, the really rich people had moved across the river to Queens. My Ollie was just a musician, he wasn't a band leader like Ellington or Basie, and I was just a school teacher. But like all people everywhere, we wanted to live in a nice place, and to raise our children in a nice place." She turned back to the view. "And it doesn't get much nicer than this." Then she spoke directly to me. "I know you're trying to do some good and to help some people, and I know you like Malachi. But Phillip, son, don't believe everything people tell you. Don't even believe me. Read the history. Or for that matter, go look at the movie again. *Hoodlum.* Look at when those events took place, and how old those people would be today. And one more thing: why would Malachi have a barber shop when he's not a barber?"

"What?" I'd snapped at her and didn't bother to apologize.

"Malachi was the shoeshine boy when he worked for his uncle. He was a shoeshine boy when he got run out of town, even though he was a grown man almost forty years old."

Two Graves Dug

★ ★ ★ ★ ★

Despite all the improvements of recent years, Harlem still looked better from high atop Sugar Hill than it did at ground level, where the ravages of the hard times still were visible in places. And even in the places where restoration had occurred and where the magnificence and opulence of the past were present in a blasted stone façade or a gargoyle or lion or cherub face looking down on the street from atop a four-story townhouse, it wasn't the Harlem Louise Gillespie reminisced about, or the Harlem Malachi Johnson lied about, because Harlem's newest residents were young and white and probably knew less of its history than I did. And despite my mental turmoil, I was enjoying my stroll through Harlem. Following no particular route and having no particular destination, I walked south for a few blocks on Edgecombe Avenue when I left Mrs. Gillespie's, then west for a block or two, then south again, and then east. I wandered in this zigzag fashion, seeing Harlem for the first time, wishing I could have seen it with Louise Gillespie when she was a young woman, wishing that I could keep walking east, into Spanish Harlem, and into the place where my grandparents had been young people.

When I stopped fantasizing and tuned back into the real world and checked my surroundings, I'd made it all the way down to 125th Street and Malcolm X Boulevard, which used to be Lenox Avenue. A street with some stories of its own to tell, I was thinking, when I suddenly turned and headed east. I may have been a stranger to Harlem but I was a native New Yorker and committed subway rider. I knew where all the trains went, and I knew I could catch a Number 4 or 6 Train on 125th Street in East Harlem. I was walking faster now, as the thought that had turned me toward the east took shape. The wind slicing in off the East

205

River almost cut me in half. I ducked my head, burying my chin in my chest, and hunched my shoulders up around my ears. Everybody on the block looked like fast-moving turtles, but I'd lay odds that I was the only one plotting revenge against a friend.

"I don't understand why you like that bastard. I don't know anybody who likes him." Carmine was staring at me with his little beady eyes, daring me to defend Itchy.

I'd asked Carmine to meet me at the coffee shop, telling him I had a favor to ask. "Are you going to help me out or not, Carmine? I need to know." The favor was that I wanted to be put in touch with anybody who'd have known the owner of the Essex Street barber shop before Itchy bought it. His response was to bust my chops for liking Itchy.

He heaved himself up from the table. "I gotta make a call. I ain't had lunch yet and they got food other than pastries here. Good food."

I realized that I hadn't eaten since my early morning breakfast with Eddie and that lunch sounded like a good idea. The waitress materialized beside the table before I could signal her. "Carmine always eats the chicken parmigiana," she said.

"Make it two," I said. "And a couple of beers."

The food was better than good, which really didn't surprise me. What did was the fact that Carmine proved to be a charming mealtime companion. I'd told him about my morning—the part about how two different people had told me if I wanted to know the history of a person or a place, I should ask somebody with firsthand knowledge. Carmine agreed wholeheartedly and proceeded to tell one story after another, many of them hilarious, about people, places, and events, in Little Italy in particular, but throughout the eastern part of lower Manhattan. He mentioned some of the same places that Louise Gillespie had talked about, and embellished the historical facts with tales of gang warfare. "Not gangs like we got today, stupid fucks with automatic weapons shooting up every goddamn thing. We had *civilized* gangs."

I started to laugh. "What, you mean like in *West Side Story*, with singing and dancing and romancing all the pretty girls?"

"Don't make fun, Rodriquez, this was serious business." But he cracked a smile himself as he told me about the some of the black gangs—the Sportsmen and the Chaplains and the Smith Boys—from the housing projects over on the East River. "They drew lines and marked off the sidewalks. If you crossed the line, the fight was on!"

We both were giggling like young hoodlums, recalling the glory days of our youth, when a shadow crossed the table. We looked up, and Carmine got to his feet faster than I'd have thought possible. I followed suit. One look at the old man standing there told the tale: he probably once was five-foot-ten or -eleven, but age had bent his spine. He had more hair in his eyebrows and sticking out of his ears than he had on his head, and it all was white. His eyes were watery and cloudy. I put him at about a hundred and ten, until he opened his mouth. If there really is a God and, unlike Sandra claims, He's a he, this is what He'll sound like when he speaks.

"Carmine says you're making right the harm that was done to his little one."

A chair and a bottle of Chianti, an antipasto, and a loaf of bread, had materialized, and the old man with the deepest, richest, smoothest, most peaceful voice I'd ever heard, sat down and allowed a glass of wine and plate of food be placed before him. I didn't know who he was, but he damn sure was no barber!

"Carmine's being kind. I'm just trying to help is all."

The old man's chuckle sounded like God's would: low and benevolent. His words sounded anything but. "Carmine hasn't been kind a day in his life."

The fat man blushed, then wiped his mouth with his napkin and made the introductions. I was sitting at the same table with Carlo Portello and didn't try to hide my reaction to this news. The old man was gratified at my reaction. Carmine was relieved that not only did I know who Portello was, I had sense enough to be awed, impressed, and scared shitless, all of which I was.

"You want to know something about Mr. Malachi Johnson?"

"Yes, sir. I want to know when he bought that barber shop on Essex Street, whether he lived in that neighborhood when he bought the shop, whether he engaged in any bookmaking activities—"

Just like Louise Gillespie had done, Carlo Portello gave a big hoot of laughter. "I heard that he claimed to be part of one of the big Harlem numbers operations. Is that what you want to know about?"

"In part," I managed to say.

"The answer is no, and I'm surprised he'd float those lies, knowing that I was still around. But then he'd know that I didn't give a damn what he said or did."

I looked straight at Portello and waited. I was afraid to breathe. So was Carmine, I noticed, and despite the nervousness crowding his face, he'd grown in my estimation. He really *was* connected to the top echelon of the wise guys. Portello drained his wine glass, ate a piece of pepperoni, and told me that Itchy had bought the barber shop in 1972, just like Louise Gillespie said, after the original owner "tucked tail and ran." I knew, thanks to Louise, that he was referring to the aftermath of the riots that consumed much of New York in the wake of the murder of Martin Luther King. "He'd been working there for a few years already and the owner knew him. He was the shoeshine boy, but he had a fencing operation on the side that he thought nobody knew anything about."

Portello chuckled to himself. "Punks always think they're the ones invented the scam. Johnson always thought he was smarter than he is." He got quiet and it was clear he was journeying back into the past. When he spoke, his voice was lower, and husky. "Malachi would have to be in his nineties to have done what he said he did up in Harlem. I know because I'm ninety-six and I was a bag man for Luciano up in Harlem. They didn't want us up there, the Negroes didn't, and we shouldn't have gone up there. But we did. If Malachi Johnson was alive and living in Harlem in nineteen thirty-four, he wouldn't have been any more than seven or eight years old, and he wouldn't have been working for the St. Clair organization. They didn't work children, didn't use them as decoys like some of the other outfits did. They were principled people. Ruthless, dangerous, vicious in a fight, but principled."

The old man's eyes cleared and he drank some water and, because Carmine had filled his wine glass, he emptied it again. Then he stood up and we stood up. He was finished talking.

"Thank you, Don Carlo," Carmine said, and dipped his head.

I extended my hand to the old man. "I'm very grateful for your time, Mr. Portello, and for the knowledge you shared. History is my new passion," I said, and meant it.

I spent the remainder of that day and into the evening in pursuit of the past. First I stopped at the video store, checked out *Hoodlum*, bought a pizza, and went home to watch history come to life. I didn't need to watch more than the opening scene, placing the action in 1934. If I'd remembered that, I'd have known that Itchy was lying. That he'd lied about everything he ever told me. And maybe that's what he was counting on—the fact that I belonged to a generation for whom history had little importance. But this was the new me and I watched the entire thing and by the time it was over, I shared Louise Gillespie's anger that the film was degraded by its name. I also was so angry with Malachi Johnson that the strength of the feeling made me ill. I'd never before in my life wished that I hadn't met another human being, but I wished that I'd never met Malachi Johnson. More than that, I sorely regretted ever liking and admiring him, and that I had made me angry with myself. Why had I been so gullible? Then I read every single word of the file on Itchy that Yolanda had provided, and had to get up and go for a walk. Itchy wasn't even as old as he'd implied, nor was he a Harlem native: he was born in 1930 in South Carolina, which made him seventy-five. Which made him thirty-three when he raped the eight-year-old Jill Mason. Which made me totally committed to putting an end of Malachi Johnson and his lying ways.

It was Friday night and the barber shop was a sardine tin of hip young players paying major dollars for haircuts that proclaimed them to be hip young players. And, as I watched the scene through the glass front with high-powered binoculars from across the street, it was apparent that other deals were being made, as well. The third chair barber, the one with the deep, red scratches to the left side of his face, made and received more phone calls than a Hollywood agent. It was to his credit that he ever completed a haircut, but complete them he did, one after the other. As did the other three barbers. But the chairs and benches that held those waiting for service never emptied; the door never stopped opening and closing.

There were five chairs and shoeshine bench, which was empty at the moment. Where was the fifth barber? The white kid? For I now realized, because I needed to, that there were two black barbers, two Puerto Ricans, and the white one. They were all in their early twenties, good-looking, hip-looking young men. Players. Damn smart of Itchy, to sit back there at his table, pretending to read or peruse his photo albums and listen to his old-timey music, while all the time he was orchestrating—what? A fencing ring? Drug dealing? A chop shop operation? Prostitution? All of the above? Damn smart.

"Fuckin' bastard," I muttered and shivered, and not totally from the cold. "Lying piece of shit," I added, just to make certain that my anger didn't fade.

I was deep in the doorway of the closed and gated music instrument store owned by Orthodox Jews, directly across the street from Itchy's Tonsorial Parlor. Every other business in the East Village was just gearing up for Friday night. Thank heaven that sundown now occurred just before five o'clock, and that the owners of the music instrument store were seriously observant. Because the doorway was recessed, nobody could see me watching the activity across the street. And because the doorway was recessed, it afforded some small protection from the whipping wind. But I was freezing. I'd changed clothes earlier—I had on a solid black Gore-Tex winter jogging suit on top of two sets of long underwear—one silk and one thermal. I wore a ski mask that covered everything but my eyes and mouth, and a hooded ski jacket on top of everything. On my feet I wore battery-powered socks and Canadian hunting shoes from one of those expensive outdoor stores. And I was shivering like a leaf on a tree.

"*Hermano,*" Eddie whispered, sliding into the doorway beside me. "The squirrel's on his way. Only he don't look much like a squirrel. Mike almost missed him. He left that dump over on Avenue D and went to a building on East River Drive. Let himself in with a key and came out lookin' like Brad Pitt or some fuckin' body. I'm tellin' you, Mike almost missed him . . . Look! In the green ski jacket."

I raised the binoculars and aimed them toward the green ski jacket approaching Itchy's from the West. It was, I saw, the fifth barber. *This* was the squirrel? He did indeed look like one of those clean-cut but slouchy young actors that young girls—and more than a few grown women—were swooning over. His hair was slightly long and obviously bleached—that was noticeable even beneath the knit cap pulled down low over his ears. He wore thick ski gloves, shoes like mine, and jeans. Everything about him said "cool dude" but his walk. "Is he crippled, Eddie, or have some kind of physical impairment?"

"I think he just walks funny. He might not look like it now, but the dude's a squirrel, I'm tellin' you. He's not one you want to turn your back on."

"Yeah, Eddie, but why does he walk like that?" I was still studying the guy's legs through the binoculars when he opened the door to Itchy's. Then, out of the darkness, a shadow. Mike. And I hadn't even seen him. Because I was watching the squirrel so intently? Or because Mike Smith wrote the manual on working undercover? "Damn, he's good," I whispered.

"The best," Eddie said.

Mike stepped out of the shadows and loped across the street, dodging cars, a bike messenger, and a bus. "Little fuck cleans up pretty good, don't he?" he said with a drawl that made me laugh. "He was halfway down the block, comin' out that high rent building on East River Drive, before I made him. And if it hadn't been for that stupid walk, I'd have missed him."

I asked my question again and Mike laughed out loud. "The stupid fuck's trying to walk black. Like, you know, do a pimp walk or some stupid shit. He thinks he's being cool, doesn't even know it just makes him look stupid."

"Makes him look crippled," I said, watching him as he limped his way into the barber shop. "Think they'll stay this busy until closing?"

Eddie and Mike nodded. "This ain't just about hair, Phil, my man," Mike said.

"Mr. Hollywood is Itchy's right hand. Watch him. He'll take the phone from number three chair . . . see? What'd I tell you?" And as if on cue, scratched face gave the phone to Mr. Hollywood. He clipped it to his belt, walked over to stand behind his chair—the first one on the right side—and waited for a customer to appear. About two seconds.

"The dump on Avenue D," I said. "That's where they stash merchandise." It wasn't a question because I knew the answer. I just needed to hear myself acknowledge out loud that I'd been suckered in a big way, but Mike and Eddie didn't need to hear it so I didn't say it. Instead I told them everything Louise Gillespie had told me, and neither one of them could think of a thing to say for so long my teeth began to chatter, so I told them about my meeting with Carlo Portello.

"We're gonna make a detective out of you yet," Mike said, and the approval in his voice was almost warming. Almost but not quite.

"Let's go eat and warm up," Eddie said, snatching the thought away from me. "Get back about nine forty-five."

The shop closed at ten. "You guys go eat. Remember to get the receipt or Yo will nail my ass to the wall. I've got a run to make. I'll see you back here at nine forty-five."

"You're the boss," Mike said.

"And we always remember the receipt. You're the one who always forgets and therefore always gets his ass nailed to the wall," Eddie said.

"Hey!" Mike called out. I turned back to him. "You think this Itchy dude is going after Doc Mason because he thinks what, that she'll bring charges against him after all this time?" I kept forgetting that Mike and Eddie only knew Itchy through me, through my recounting of his stories of the past.

"I think Itchy's crazy and mean and some more stuff I don't have the right words for," I said, and separated from Mike and Eddie, them headed west, me in the opposite direction.

Bill Delaney listened to everything I said. Then he asked me to tell him again. And again. And a fourth time. That's when I got up to leave. "I don't know if you're losing your memory, Delaney, or you can't get your secret recording device to work, but either way, I've told this story my last time. I'm outta here." I made for the door.

"Why are you telling me all this, Rodriquez?"

"I don't know a lot of cops, L.T. I wasn't on the job long

enough to know a lot of cops. And after last night and to-night, I may just learn how to say that I don't know any cops anymore," and I left, not regretting my decision not to tell him about Itchy's involvement with the attacks on Jill Mason. I'd given him enough freebies. Besides, there are some jobs you take care of yourself.

I still had over an hour to kill but I didn't want to eat. As it was I didn't have much stomach for the night's work; filling it wouldn't be very wise. I walked a while, though it really was too cold for walking. But when I saw where I was headed, I kept going until I reached the subway. I got on the F Train at Delancey Street, a smile growing inside and easing the knot that was there. I hadn't done this in a long time: just get on the subway and ride. I didn't have a lot of time tonight, but, inspired by the impromptu stroll around Harlem, I knew it would be a good trip. It was Friday night. People were out. All kinds of people doing all kinds of things, going all kinds of places, going wherever they could go, and some of them, like me, going noplace in particular. I loved that more than practically anything else about New York City: since the subways went everywhere, so could the people. This wasn't like some cities where access was re-stricted simply because it wasn't possible to get there except by car, and if you were the wrong color or driving the wrong kind of car, somebody noticed. And questioned your pres-ence. Things like that happened in Los Angeles and in Miami, I knew. But not in New York. The subway went ev-erywhere and so, too, could any-damn-body.

The train was crowded, not only because it was a freezing-ass cold Friday night, but also because of where the F Train went: East Village, West Village, 5th Avenue, Times Square, Rockefeller Center, and across the East River into Queens. I didn't have time to ride all the way to

Queens, though it would have been fun. Totally different kind of person on the train in that Borough. No matter how much they wanted to pretend otherwise, residents of Queens looked different from residents of Manhattan. Of course, the reverse was true, as well: residents of Manhattan looked different from residents of Queens. But it was a difference Manhattanites shrugged off; who cared? was their attitude. Queens Borough residents cared.

I got off at 5th Avenue, crossed the platform, and sat on the bench to wait for the downtown train. I hadn't been up here in a long time. In fact, I hadn't just ridden the train for fun in a long time. Maybe tomorrow I'd ride the Number 1 Train all the way down to South Ferry, to the end of Manhattan, to look at the empty space the fuckin' terrorists left in the skyline. Maybe I'd even ride the Staten Island Ferry . . .

I snatched myself out of my reverie. Here I was thinking that by tomorrow, a lot of the mess in my head would be cleared up and I'd be free to enjoy myself, and the hard part of tonight was just getting started. One thing at a time. The downtown train was entering the station. I looked at my watch. I thought I'd get back to Eddie and Mike with maybe a minute to spare.

They were waiting in the music store doorway. I smelled them before I saw them. They smelled like fried onions. "You ate at Julio's," I said.

"How'd you know?" Eddie asked.

"You smell like fried onions," I said, wriggling my nose.

"Oh, he does think he's a real detective now!" Eddie said, fanning at himself, as if he could dispel the onion and grease aroma embedded in his clothes.

We turned our attention to the activity across the street. There were three customers still inside—Mr. Hollywood

216

had one, Scratch Face had one, and one of the black dudes had one. The other two barbers were cleaning up, sweeping and swatting at the counters with a feather duster. I couldn't see Itchy, but I knew he was there, his eye on the clock: closing time in three minutes. Two of the customers got up simultaneously, paid, and left together. That left one customer, in Scratch Face's chair. The three of us waited for the customers to clear the door, then we crossed the street. Traffic was lighter though still steady, and we had to play dodge cars. A taxi tried to hit Mike and he grabbed a folded *New York Post* from his pocket and threw it. The cab slowed and Mike ran toward it, but Eddie grabbed his arm and dragged him back to the business at hand.

"Good shit!" Mike hissed, as two of the barbers opened the door and exited. Mr. Hollywood locked the door behind them. We held back, on edge, waiting for the last customer to leave, praying that we were correct in our assumption that Scratch Face and Mr. Hollywood, because they seemed special to Itchy, would be the last to leave. Three of them, three of us. Righteous odds.

"Here we go," Eddie whispered, as the final customer stood and allowed himself to be brushed off. He took money from his pocket, paid Scratch Face, got his coat from the wall peg, and tried to leave. The door was locked. He stood there for a moment until Mr. Hollywood opened it for him. We heard his thanks and watched him walk west. Mr. Hollywood was still holding the door. We heard him tell "Brian" to hurry his ass; it was cold and Mr. Hollywood was no doorman. Brian stepped out into the cold just as I stepped up to the door.

"We're closed," Mr. Hollywood snapped at me.

" 'Bout time, too," Eddie snapped back, and he and Mike came through the door, taking Mr. Hollywood back into the room at warp speed. Mike locked the door behind us and pulled down the shade.

"What the fuck?" Scratch Face started but stopped when he got a good look at me. Something in his face changed shape, but I wasn't his problem, Mike was, as he soon discovered.

"Where's Itchy?" I asked conversationally, as if it were ten in the morning and I had an appointment for a cut and a shave.

Nobody answered.

"Itchy!" I called out, as I headed toward the back room. "Itchy!" I called again, just as the old man appeared in the doorway. He looked like a peacock tonight in iridescent blue-green pants, matching shirt, and shiny, black pointed-toe shoes. No way he rode the subway in and out of Harlem dressed like that. Then I had a thought . . . more like a recollection as Itchy himself would say. Him getting into a livery car, more than once. Itchy didn't ride the subway at all these days.

"What the fuck do you want?" he snarled at me, sounding so nasty I wouldn't have thought it was Itchy Johnson had I not watched the words leave his mouth. This was the Malachi that Louise Gillespie remembered: mean.

"I want you, you sick, dickless son of a bitch," I said, and enjoyed watching the words travel from his ears to his brain to his eyes. "Let's all go to the back and chat, why don't we?" I said, as I grabbed Itchy's arm and twisted it up behind his back. I still wanted very much to smash something, but angry as I was, I couldn't smash an eighty-year-old man. I desperately wanted to trade Mike for Scratch Face.

The back room was comfortable. Sofa, armchair, hot plate, microwave oven, refrigerator, water cooler.

"This is why we're here," I said, and told them why we were there. Mr. Hollywood looked meaner by the minute. Eddie was right: he was a real squirrel. Scratch Face was a wuss, and started to whimper. Itchy smiled at me, a sneaky, mean grin, so I slapped him, and he stopped that. So much for not smashing old dudes.

"So. You two little fucks like hurting women, do you? Well, your career in that business is over. As of right now. And to show you that we mean business . . ." I paused dramatically, turned, and, in my best Fundamentals of Acting voice, intoned, ". . . if you please, gentlemen." And Mike and Eddie started in on Scratch Face and Mr. Hollywood. It didn't last long. It didn't need to. Like bullies everywhere, the two of them were chumps; even the squirrel, after a couple of expertly-placed jabs to the kidneys, was moaning like a baby and they both were begging for mercy. Eddie and Mike looked at me and I looked like I didn't care what they did, so they each delivered a one-for-good-measure whack, dropped the chumps to the floor, and backed up and away.

When both the chumps were sobbing and writhing on the floor, I asked them to sit up and look at me, which they did, faster than I would have thought possible. I told them what would happen if they ever went near Jill Mason again and made them promise that they never would, which they seemed happy to do. Then I turned my attention to Itchy. "So, Malachi. I hear you've finally arrived."

He had to peel his eyes away from his meek and chastened muscle to glare at me. "What the fuck are you talking about?"

"Strivers Row. About sixty years too late, but as close as you'll ever get to being related to Bumpy Johnson or working for Stephanie St. Clair. But better late than never, is that your motto, Malachi?"

The old man gave me such a look of hatred that I was glad he was old. I'd not have wanted to tangle with anybody that mean looking who was my age and in good health. "Who you been talking to?"

"Somebody other than you, you lying piece of garbage." I walked up close to him, got in his face. "Have you ever told the truth, about anything? Or is the lying such a habit you can't help yourself? Or maybe you even believe that you were a player in Harlem in nineteen thirty-five. Maybe you're really ninety-six, and maybe you're really a barber instead of a shoeshine boy."

I backed up and watched him watch me, watched his eyes change. Most of the mean drained away but what was left wasn't fear. Not yet. It was close, though.

"My life is none of your business."

"You made it my business when you sent these two assholes to hurt a woman who doesn't even remember that you exist."

Now the fear was there. Itchy licked his lips and his eyes darted around the room, flickering from his boys on the floor to me and my boys facing him. "What are you talking about?"

"She doesn't remember what you did to her, Malachi. But others do. Her parents remember. And Louise Gillespie remembers."

"That bitch! I don't give a shit what she remembers."

"How about Carlo Portello. You give a shit what he re-members?"

The fear was back to sharing center stage with mean. "What the fuck do you want, Rodriquez? Spit it out and then get outta my place."

"Drop your drawers, asshole."

He choked and sputtered and called me some dirty names. I reached for his belt but he jumped away from me. "Don't touch me, you spic motherfucker." The mean was back in full force.

I slapped him again, harder this time, splitting his lip and drawing blood, and told him to drop his drawers or I'd do it for him. "I want your little midget dick flunkies here to see what a real midget dick looks like. But then, Itchy, to call you a midget dick is a real compliment, isn't it? And I shouldn't be paying you compliments, the way you like calling other people names: Carmine's a wop, I'm a spic, Doctor Mason's a broad. And you're a midget dick, so why don't you show us?"

He started to speak then, all of a sudden, he sagged. I reached out again and grabbed his belt buckle and pulled it open. I undid the button and pulled down the zipper. The pants fell to the floor. "You gonna do the shorts, Itchy, or you want me to do it?"

His eyes met mine, pleading.

"Do it," I said, trying to imagine Jill Mason as a seven-year-old being raped by a thirty-something-year-old man. "Do it," I said, remembering my broken Yolanda running out into the cold the other night. "Do it, Itchy. Now."

And he did it and his lackeys gasped. So did the three of us, for that matter. No man can imagine life without his identity. To witness such a reality is a truly sobering experience.

"Oh, goddamn," whispered Scratch Face.

"Jesus fuckin' Christ," added Mr. Hollywood.

"That's for Doctor Mason, Itchy. And for Elijah. Just in case you thought you got away with that one, too," I said, and slapped him again. I should have felt better but I didn't. So I kicked Scratch Face in the gut and he threw up all over the floor. Itchy started cursing him like he wasn't human and I knew it was time to get out of there. I still didn't feel any better but I knew I couldn't do anything else here that would benefit another human being.

I was outside, a block away, breathing cold, clean air when Mike and Eddie caught up with me. They stood, one on either side of me. Eddie touched my shoulder and Mike followed suit.

"You okay, *Hermano?*" Eddie asked.

"Yeah," I said. "Sure. Why not?"

"Want to go get a drink?" Mike asked.

"I don't think I drink any more, man," I said.

"If you drink with us, you can. But only if you drink with us," he said.

"And what's so special about drinking with you bums?" I asked, really needing and wanting a drink, and needing and wanting to like his answer so I could have one.

"Wives," Mike said, with that laugh again.

"Yeah," Eddie added. "We got 'em, you don't. That means we could never get as shit-faced as you got the other night and expect to go home."

"And since not going home is NOT an option, we don't get drunk," Mike said happily. "So. About that drink . . ."

"Let's go!" I said. Then, as an afterthought, "Can I have more than one?"

"We'll see," Eddie said with mock seriousness.

We walked a few blocks in silence, letting the cold rid us of the anger and fear and pain that had filled and over-whelmed us those few, short moments ago.

"You need to hurry up and find yourself a good woman," Eddie said, breaking the silence.

I knew that, but I wondered why he thought so. "Why?" I asked him.

"Because," Mike said with real seriousness, "my wife ain't gonna let me stay out drinkin' with you on a regular basis."

"Not even on a Friday night?" I asked.

"Especially on a Friday night," Mike said darkly.

We kept walking, hands deep in our pockets, shoulders hunched against the cold, lost in our own thoughts. The subway was dead ahead, at the corner. I stopped when we got there. "Let's have that drink uptown, in the old neighborhood."

"I know just the place," Mike said with a big, wide grin ridding his face of the earlier darkness. "Best of both worlds: a Puerto Rican Soul Food joint. No point in getting drunk on an empty stomach."

Chapter Eleven

Lieutenant Delaney didn't want to believe that I wasn't responsible for the serious beating bestowed upon Gregory Jenkins sometime on Saturday morning, and didn't believe me when I swore I didn't, but he didn't have much choice. I'd spent that morning, from just after eight until just before noon, at my gym, where I had an intense workout, a full body massage, and a long, relaxing steam. I'd had lunch at twelve thirty with Consuela deLeon, and was having such a good time that I was late for my three o'clock meeting with Doctor Jill Mason at my office, where I remained doing paperwork, with Yolanda, until just after six. Then we left, together, and rode the subway uptown and met Sandra for a light dinner and a performance of the Alvin Ailey Company. Of course I went home alone at midnight, but Delaney didn't care about midnight. Gregory Jenkins had been in the hospital, on life support, for several hours by midnight.

But since he was able to take personal credit for shutting down Itchy Johnson's million-dollar drug and fencing operation, he quit busting my chops about Gregory Jenkins. And maybe he'd finally gotten his secret recording device to work, because he heeded my warning and didn't even try hassling the Calle and Cummerbatch families. I told him that if he tried that, the whole world would know where he got the Itchy Johnson scoop. You bust my chops, I'll bust yours. It felt good to wield power against Goliath. Almost as good as slapping the shit out of Malachi Johnson, then watching him take the big fall. No matter what he's finally charged with, he'll know it's payback for Jill Mason and her grandfather.

It's been almost a month and it still feels good. I've even got the beginning of the Christmas spirit, which it's kind of difficult to avoid since merchants launched their Christmas displays immediately after Halloween. They used to wait until after Thanksgiving, but no matter. Dinner tonight is barbeque chicken and spareribs, cole slaw, sweet potato soufflé, and corn bread. Traversing the narrow sidewalk en route to Jill Mason's office is even more difficult than usual because everybody's a Christmas tree merchant. Ah, but the pine scent mingling with that of roasting nuts makes the journey worthwhile.

"Phillip, come in! I'm starving!"

The table was set and ready and the wine she'd insisted upon buying was open and breathing, ready to be poured. "You finished your paperwork early, then?"

"I rushed through it, I'm *almost* ashamed to say," she said, helping me unwrap the food and serve the plates. "Of course you know how much I appreciate and enjoy this, Phillip, but on a Friday night?"

"You got something against being my Friday night date?"

She laughed—something she was doing more often these days—and poured the wine. "I'm flattered, and eternally grateful that Miss deLeon is the kind of woman she is."

It was my turn to laugh, and to blush, which the good doctor was kind enough not to comment upon. We'd built on the friendship that had developed during the investigation, but we'd never really discussed the outcome. She wasn't ready and I didn't want to. All that was about to change. Our "date" had a purpose beyond good food.

"I see your appetite's back."

"With a vengeance. I'm gaining weight!"

"So, what, you now weigh ninety-nine pounds instead of ninety-eight?"

She tried to shoot me a dirty look but didn't succeed, and changed the subject. "Are you really all right, Phillip? After . . . all that happened?"

"I'm really fine."

"I was worried that you'd done something you might regret in order to help me and while I appreciate not only all you did but—"

I stopped her right there. "The only thing I regret is that you ever had to hurt the way you did. Nothing else. Believe that, please. My conscience is clear." And it was. I had no qualms about what I'd done to Malachi Johnson, and no regrets. Well, maybe one: that I'd ever fallen for his bullshit in the first place.

"I wish that I'd made the connection sooner, so that I could have saved you and Mr. Aiello and Mike and Eddie so much aggravation. I do have that regret," she said, and the heavy sadness that I thought had lifted from her descended again. Then the full impact of her words registered.

"You know. You remember." It wasn't a question.

She'd been about to take a sip of wine but she put the glass down and stood up and walked over to her desk. She didn't speak for a long moment, and I didn't disturb the silence. Then she turned toward me. "One of the requirements for successful completion of a residency in psychiatry is intense psychotherapy, the idea being that med schools don't knowingly send emotionally deficient doctors out to play with people's minds." She smiled slightly. "Good intentions don't always succeed." She was struggling.

"You remembered during your psychotherapy, when you were a resident?"

She nodded. "I had a wonderful doctor."

"Gertrude Bader!" I remembered how still and silent she'd become that night at her place when I told her of my meeting with Doctor Bader.

"I didn't make the connection until . . . well, that doesn't matter."

But I thought I knew what the "until" was: something she'd heard from Yo in their counseling sessions. "Come back and finish your dinner," I said. "I'm not eating all this food by myself. Some of us can afford to gain a few pounds, and some of us can't."

She sat back down and gave me a sly grin. "Surely Miss deLeon isn't complaining?" She arched her left eyebrow, something I'd never seen her do, and then she laughed at me when I blushed again, and choked on my wine. It never ceased to amaze me the things women just seemed to know. I'd never actually discussed Connie with Jill, but she seemed to know how things were progressing on that front anyway. Unless Yolanda told her? But I hadn't discussed Connie with Yolanda, either. Of course, I didn't need to discuss anything, since they'd become like the glue sisters after their first meeting. It also never ceased to amaze me that some men manage to feel superior to women. Talk about ego-tripping.

Jill Mason and Connie deLeon aren't the only good things to come my way as a result of those two investigations. Basil Griffin and I have a bond that exceeds the work I do for the Golson sisters. Yes, they own a lot of real estate and we do all of their security work, but Basil and I eat lunch or dinner at least once a week at Arlene's place. He'll never accept that he's not responsible for Anna Cummerbatch's death, but he'll always be grateful for the chance to avenge it. Basil's an Old Testament kind of guy. Until recently, I'd never thought of myself in a Biblical connotation, but now, well, I suppose I've got more in common with Basil than a serious attachment to Arlene Edward's cooking.

I have breakfast with Carmine once a week—he's part of my morning ritual on Wednesdays and Mrs. Campos and Willie have learned to accept it, if not quite gracefully. Can't do it any more often than that because I really would have a weight problem. Carmine doesn't worry about things like that. He's still too worried about his little girl. She's getting better, but she's not even close to being well. And that's another one of the good things, though Yolanda doesn't totally agree: I accept that I owe Carmine and I owe Dan Esposito and I owe Patty Starrett. But mostly I owe their little girls. No, I can't undo the harm that's been done to them; nobody can, not even Jill Mason. What I can do, what I will do, is find the lowlife piece of shit who hurt them, and when I do, I'll go Biblical on him.

I wonder about these changes in myself. I still shudder when I think how completely I was taken in by Malachi Johnson, and I've promised myself that I'll be more discerning in the future. I also think about the things Bill Delaney said to me. I felt angry and insulted at the time, but I wonder whether he sees something in me that I don't see in myself. Maybe I am too soft, too gullible.

I still walk the routes those little girls took to and from school. I know all the *bodegas* and fruit stands, nail salons and sweet shops and second-hand stores on those routes. I know who's pimping and who's dealing, who belongs and who doesn't. And I know that whenever I see a guy with a kid, especially an older guy with a little girl—or a little boy—I'll check to see if he looks like he knows what he's doing, if he looks like he knows how to play in the sand. And if the kid looks like she's having a good time, and if he looks like her good time is more important than his. And I know that if anything about the situation looks weird to me, that guy is going to have some explaining to do. To me. Because I now finally understand the difference—the true difference—between me and cops: I've got all the time in the world to let my heart bleed, and I don't care who sees me cry.

About the Author

Penny Mickelbury is the author of eight novels in two series: The Carole Ann Gibson Mysteries and the Mimi Patterson/Gianna Maglione Mysteries. *Two Graves Dug* introduces Newyorican PI Phil Rodriquez. In her former life, Mickelbury was a newspaper, radio and television reporter, and she teaches journalism at a Los Angeles middle school. She also is an accomplished playwright whose work was chosen by the California African-American Museum to be part of its Radio Theatre series, and by both the Tribeca Film Center's and the Fountain Theatre's New Works programs. Her short stories have appeared in several anthologies, and she is a frequent contributor to journalistic and literary publications.

She was recipient of the 2003 Audre Lorde Estate Grant and a resident at the Hedgebrook Writers Colony. Mickelbury's work is published in France, where she was the recipient of the prestigious Prix du Roman d'Adventures award for her Carole Ann Gibson series. She lives in Los Angeles, CA.